P9-DNW-761

THE BADDEST GIRL ON THE PLANET

The Baddest Girl on the Planet

Heather Frese

— BLAIR —

Printed in the United States of America
Cover design by Laura Williams
Interior design by April Leidig

Blair is an imprint of Carolina Wren Press.

The mission of Blair/Carolina Wren Press is to seek out, nurture, and promote literary work by new and underrepresented writers.

We gratefully acknowledge the ongoing support of general operations by the Durham Arts Council's United Arts Fund and the North Carolina Arts Council.

This novel is a work of fiction. As in all fiction, the literary perceptions and insights are based on experience; however, all names, characters, places, and incidents are either products of the author's imagination or are used fictitiously. No reference to any real person is intended or should be inferred.

Library of Congress Cataloging-in-Publication Data
Names: Frese, Heather, 1974– author.
Title: The baddest girl on the planet / Heather Frese.
Description: [Durham] : Blair, [2021]
Identifiers: LCCN 2020020219 (print) | LCCN 2020020220 (ebook) |
ISBN 9781949467161 (hardback) | ISBN 9781949467383 (epub)
Subjects: GSAFD: Bildungsromans.
Classification: LCC PS3606.R47 B33 2021 (print) | LCC PS3606.R47 (ebook) |
DDC 813/.6—dc23
LC record available at https://lccn.loc.gov/2020020219
LC ebook record available at https://lccn.loc.gov/2020020220

Contents

One

Kid Dynamite

— 2013 —

My husband is not the first man to disappoint me. That honor goes to Mike Tyson, who I met the summer I was nine, the summer I left Hatteras Island to stay in Ohio for two weeks with my Ohio friend, Charlotte. Charlotte and I became friends while her family was camping on the Outer Banks, and I was allowed to take a sort of reverse vacation to the hills of Ohio. Charlotte's family lived in a pretty, white, two-story house with blue shutters and dollops of woodworking around the front porch. I still think about that house and those green, green hills; about how every day seemed green and blue and gold. But maybe that's just how every day feels when you're a kid.

Charlotte lived next door to Don King, and at that time he promoted Mike Tyson, along with a bunch of other guys, who all trained in tents in his backyard. Every day Charlotte and I would gather up her friends Sarah M. and Sarah N. and make the boxers watch us turn cartwheels. They would stop their jump roping and shadowboxing to look at us and applaud, just like they really cared. When I got home I bragged about Mike Tyson to all my friends. I was the toast of the fourth grade for an entire school year.

Then Mike Tyson raped a girl. Real quick I stopped saying he was my best friend, but kids don't forget things like befriending rapists. This did not help my social standing. Little girls who are best friends with rapists rarely remain popular. Except for Charlotte, who got off the hook because everyone in her town thought Mike Tyson was a good guy. Still, Charlotte and I stayed close, partly because I didn't have many other friends. And then, a few years later, just when I thought my Tyson-induced social pariah status had begun to blow over, he bit Evander Holyfield's ear off. I never mentioned Mike Tyson to anyone again.

My husband is not the second man to disappoint me in my twenty-three years on this planet, not the third or the fourth, so by the time his disappointments start to really roll in, you'd think I'd be braced for them. You'd think his metaphorical ear-biting would not come as a complete and total shock. You'd think I'd be prepared for it when Stephen says, "Evie, we need to sell the house," but I'm not.

"What do you mean, sell the house?" I say. It's morning and the light slices down through my window into my crazy, cozy little kitchen where I spend so much time boiling and baking and basting as a way to breathe. My house is not big and dollopy, and it does not have a front porch, and there's not a bit of gingerbread trim anywhere, but it's white and snug and bright and mine. I think of the morning after we moved in, when Stephen and I sat on the floor and laughed about owning six blenders.

Stephen leans against the counter like he hasn't a care in the world. Casual. He eats a bagel. He's wearing khaki pants, and I wonder if he's going in to work at his father's store today. "I was talking to Royce Burrus at your office when I picked you up the other day, and he said we could get a good sum for the property," he says.

I squeeze out a dishrag and wipe at the kitchen table, looking down and hoping that Stephen doesn't see my face color at Royce's name. I have a tiny crush on Royce. I take a second and listen to the loud commercial blasting from the living room where my son, Austin, is watching TV. "But where would we live?"

"I'm not saying it's a perfect plan," Stephen says. He crosses the kitchen and sits down in front of me at the table. "But we could stay with your folks or mine until the cash clears and then build somewhere."

I sit down. This sounds like an okay plan. This sounds thought-out and maybe even mature. But I know Stephen's teeth are awfully close to my ear.

Stephen links his fingers together and makes them into a steeple. "We could build on the mainland. It'd be a hell of a lot cheaper."

And there it is. He wants to leave the island. *Chomp.* "Maybe if you got an actual job we wouldn't be so strapped that we have to sell our home," I say. I lean forward on the table and my arms get sticky from the damp dishrag.

Stephen's mouth tightens. It's an old argument, and it goes like this—I say, *Get a job.* He says, *I'm staying at home with Austin.* I say, *You're never home with him, and I know this because I drop him off at my parents' every day before I go to work while you fuck around on your Jet Ski.* He says, *I'm above working any jobs on this island.* He doesn't say it in exactly those words, but that's what he means, and that's what he honestly, truly believes. But it's not below me to answer phones and make coffee and peddle beach houses to tourists every day, because I'm just that low. He believes this, too. I know it.

Stephen crosses his arms and the sunlight glints off his watch. "I have a job," he says.

"Part-time stock boy for your father doesn't count," I say. He works in the back where no one can see him and does it out of obligation to his father. His father who basically gave us this house.

Stephen shakes his head. "Goddammit, Evie," he says.

"Austin can hear you," I say.

"He can't hear a fucking thing over that goddamn TV." But Stephen lowers his voice all the same. "I don't know why you let him watch it so much."

I stand up. "You're the stay-at-home father. Why don't you monitor him?" I cross to the living room where Austin sits on his knees, entranced by *Go, Diego, Go!* My son is small and dark-haired, and I'm always a bit thankful that he looks like me. "Come on, kid," I say, reaching down to pull him up from under his armpits. "Time to go to Grandma's."

~

Austin has the charming habit of kicking the passenger seat on our daily rides up the island to drop him off at my parents' inn. I guess if I was strapped down in a car seat, I'd kick too, but it doesn't ease my annoyance. And I am strapped down, come to think of it, with my own seat belt. "How about you cut that out, buddy?" I say. I glance at the rearview mirror, but Austin's looking away.

"I want to hear the Hollaback song," he says, and I die a little inside. Every day he wants to hear "Hollaback Girl." This was cute, at first, until he started singing, "I ain't no harlot snack girl," and I had to correct him over and over so people don't think my kid knows about harlots, even though I know he has no idea what it means. He wants it every day. Every day we drive up the same road and listen to the same song, and I think of Charlotte saying you can't get lost on an island because pretty soon you'll drive off the end, and right now, I want to drive off the end. But I pop in the cassette I've recorded from my dad's old stereo and think about how Stephen goes jogging every morning with his iPod. And then I make myself think about how I want Austin to grow up with a family, with a mom and a dad and a little white house. A little white house that once held six blenders. A little white house that Stephen wants to sell. The morning is bright and sunny for February, and the Pamlico Sound spreads out in shades of blue and gray and green as Highway 12 passes close to the water. Austin kicks the seat in time to the music. I fumble for my sunglasses and sing along with Gwen Stefani.

~

I would not be the first person in my marriage to have an affair. I think about this as Royce Burrus walks in the front door of the office, the little bell jangling his presence. Royce is easily in his fifties. His hair is brown and thin, and he has a small, rounded gut. I find this endearing. I want to rub it like a Buddha belly. I debate whether it would be too forward to tell him so. "Royce," I say. "You are one sexy son-of-a-bitch. Let me rub your belly."

Royce looks startled, yet pleased. This is a notch up from our normal morning routine. Usually, I tell him he's a beast, and he says I look nice in whatever I'm wearing. Royce crosses over to where I sit at the receptionist desk, puts down his briefcase, and shrugs off his jacket. He smells like the outdoors, and his hair is tousled. Royce props an arm on the tall desk. "How's my sunshine today?" he asks.

I feel the familiar zing at his closeness, the stir in my belly and warmth in my face. I think about what it would be like to touch his arm. "I'm mad at you," I say. I pout up my mouth in a way I hope is cute and sexy.

"Are you now?" he says. His eyes crinkle and he doesn't look concerned.

"Why'd you go and tell my husband we should sell our house?"

Royce walks around the back of the desk to stand beside me, and I spin in my chair to look at him.

"I was just bullshitting with him," Royce says. He draws his eyebrows together. I find this endearing, too. "Does he seriously want to sell?"

I cross my arms. "Anyone who got that house would just knock it down and build a monstrosity." And they would, too. A pastel McMansion monstrosity.

"I'm sorry," Royce says. "Didn't mean to put a bug in his ear."

Royce reaches out his hand, and I think he's going to touch my face, and my heart pounds, but then he just smooths his hair and puts his hand back down. I try to breathe. "Get yourself to your office," I say. "The tourists need you."

Royce gathers up his stuff and walks down the hallway. He turns, walks a couple backwards steps, and says, "I'll make it up to you, cupcake."

And I just bet he will.

~

Most of the time my job is kind of fun. I make copies and I make coffee and I answer the phone, and when all the agents are busy, I help clients select beach houses. I have a good memory for which house has what feature, and I'm quick at pulling it all up in the database. So when a Mr. John Bo Cook from Roanoke, Virginia, calls and wants to reserve *Isle Be Back* for two weeks in July, I tell him right away it's not available.

"Mr. Cook," I say, "I'm really sorry, but that house was reserved by someone else three months ago."

Mr. Cook is not pleased. He tells me he wants that house. He says, "If you can't get that house for me, then you're good for nothing." He has a raspy, twangy voice.

I want to tell Mr. John Bo Cook to go fuck himself, but I root through the listings and suggest he try *Mullet Over* or *Nautigull*.

Mr. Cook is insistent. He wants *Isle Be Back.*

I click around on the computer a little more. "It's open for a week in May and a week in September," I say.

But Mr. John Bo Cook says it has to be July. He tells me I'm bad at my job. He says, "Listen, you little whore, I'm the client, and it's your job to make me happy. Right now, you are not making me happy."

This hurts my feelings. I'm good at my job. In four years of working at Outer Banks Realty I've never had anyone speak to me like that. I'm a little bewildered, to be honest, but then I get past that. Then I get mad.

"Listen, John Bo Cook," I say. "You can take your beach house and shove it up your flabby white double-named ass." And I hang up.

I stare at the phone and fight the urge to run down to Royce's office and tell him about it. Luckily, Pansy Friedman comes down the hall at that moment and I tell her about the whore and the hanging up and all of it. I start to worry I might get fired, but Pansy says every once in a while we get one like that, and not to worry, and why don't I take an extra-long lunch. This is fine with me.

Without really thinking about it, I head down the hall, out the back door, and down the steps. I forget my jacket, but it's a nice day, in the high forties and sunny, so I traipse across the scrubby back lawn to my tree. I used to eat lunch here every day when I was pregnant with Austin. It has a low branch that sticks out like a bench, and it's pretty in the summer when the sun shines through the leaves, but of course there are no leaves now. I pull out my phone and check on Austin. He's fine and eating cherry Jell-O. I call Stephen.

"What's up," he says.

"Some guy called me a whore today," I tell him. I kick at the ground and stir up some dead leaves.

"Did he know you in high school?" Stephen asks. He laughs. For the second time today, I hang up the phone on someone.

~

Most of the time my job is kind of fun, but other times it's downright boring, especially in the winter. By afternoon I'm skimming the internet, clicking through the news sites and anything else that hasn't been blocked. I learn about the world's friendliest countries (Canada, Germany, and Australia). I turn the sound down and watch a video of kittens riding a Roomba, then read about how to dress slimmer. The key, it seems, is to not mix tight with shiny and to stay away from high-waisted jeans. I don't know why anyone would wear those in the first place. I start to research the slenderizing properties of Spanx undergarments when I hear a rustle behind me and turn around to see Royce. I switch off the computer monitor quick as I can.

"I promised I'd make it up to you," Royce says. He holds out a little white take-out box. He smells good and it distracts me.

"Did you get me a corsage?" I ask. I take the box and shake it. "Is it a pony? Did you get me a pony?" I open the box and *ooh*. It's a fat square of baklava from a restaurant up in Buxton run by two eastern European guys, and I don't care if their country doesn't make the world's friendliest list because if there was a world's best baklava list, they'd top it. The first time I had their baklava they'd just taken it out of the oven, and the warm, sweet, honey-flaky crustiness was the best thing I'd ever had in my mouth. "Thanks, Royce," I say, standing up to give him a big hug. It starts out as a nice, spontaneous crusher of a thank-you hug, but pretty soon I'm all too aware that my nose is buried against his neck, and his hands are sliding down my back, and I really want to grab his ass, but I let go because it's an open office and anyone could come by.

"I remembered you talking about it last week," Royce says, in an aw-shucks kind of way.

I turn around to my desk and set down the baklava. Then I scribble the words *If you want to share, stay late tonight* on a neon green Post-it and stick it to his left palm. Royce looks down at his hand, and I just about die from the expression on his face, a mix of surprise and pleasure and confusion, like he's not really sure what I mean but is intrigued to find out. After he leaves, I sit down and call my mom to see if she can keep Austin through dinner. I know I've made the right choice when I see that Royce has stuck a little plastic fork into the box of baklava. I lean back and take a bite.

~

Our affair doesn't have a very interesting trajectory. There aren't any longing glances and stolen moments, just pretty regular sex in the office after-hours. After a couple of months I decide I'm falling in love with Royce. It's crazy. It's not like he can bring me flowers or take me out on a date, but he's kind, and he walks me to my car afterward. I still think he's a sexy son-of-a-bitch.

Everyone knows. Of course everyone knows, or suspects. It's a small office in a small town on a small island. I make sure not to take the affair home with me, but it's only a matter of time before Stephen calls me on it. I think the moment has come one night at dinner when Stephen says, "I know what you're doing, by the way." He spears a bite of salmon and watches me as he chews.

I reach over and wipe at Austin's mouth. He's been on a SpaghettiOs kick and has red sauce all over his face. He squirms out of my reach, and I give up. "What do you mean?" I ask Stephen. I'm not even nervous. My heart doesn't pound. I'm resigned, and a little relieved.

"I know you're spending above our limits so there's nothing left for me to go back to school with," he says.

I sag back against my chair. And then a second later I'm pissed. "Austin needed an outfit for karate, and then he had his checkup. I'm not just spending money to spend money."

"Mom," Austin says. He puts down his spoon. "What's bigger? A hippo or a jaguar?"

"This is what I mean, Evie," Stephen says. "We don't need to be spending money on karate lessons."

"Hippo or jaguar?" Austin asks.

Stephen looks at me. "Austin's asking you a question," he says.

"Hippopotamus," I tell Austin. "He needs to be around other kids, and it's good for him," I say to Stephen.

"And what about the bill from the salon?" Stephen asks. He's stopped eating his food.

Okay, that was bad, an unnecessary pedicure, but I'm not admitting it to Stephen. "I needed a haircut," I say. Like Stephen would even notice I hadn't had one.

"Mom," Austin says. "Is a lion or a tiger bigger?"

"I'm not sure," I say.

"Why?" Austin asks. He pushes his finger into what's left of his SpaghettiOs.

"They're about the same," I say. I wonder when I became the poster girl for *National Geographic*.

Stephen stands up and takes his plate over to the sink. "You should have asked me about the karate first," he says.

"A humpback whale or a condor? Mom?" Austin asks. He pushes his finger in rapid circles on his plate.

"Stop playing with your food," Stephen says.

"Whale," I say. "Whales are really big."

"Did you hear me?" Stephen asks me.

"How could I not?" I reach over and hold Austin's arm still. When he looks up at me, his eyes are big and dark. I relax my grip.

"We'll talk about it later," Stephen says. He walks into the living room and turns on the TV.

I take Austin's plate and finish his SpaghettiOs. They're cold and clammy, and the thin sauce tastes like the can.

"Mom," Austin says.

I stand up and pile our plates together. "Yeah, baby?"

"A sloth or a penguin?"

~

I used to have a thing for Sherpas. Actually, I still do. If that doesn't end up working out as a career path, I'd want to be a whirling dervish. I watched a show on the Travel Channel about them once. They spin and spin and spin. That's how my head feels lately when I'm with Royce. It spins and spins and spins. I'm leaning back against him and his office is dark, and the purple lace Victoria's Secret bra I mail-ordered is on the floor.

Royce snuggles me closer. "What are you thinking?" he asks.

Sometimes Royce asks me this question, after. This time I give him an honest answer. "I'm thinking of leaving Stephen," I say. I burrow under his arm a little more. Royce doesn't stiffen, but by his silence I'm afraid I've said something wrong. I nibble on my lower lip. It's sore from kissing. "I didn't mean for you," I say. But this might be a lie. I might want him there to catch me.

Royce turns me around to look at him. "Evie, honey," he says. "There are plenty of fish in the sea, and you just caught yourself a largemouth bass."

I squint up at him. His hair is rumpled, his head silhouetted against the back of the sofa.

A largemouth bass.

I cough. I picture my son asking, "Mom, what's bigger? A large-mouth bass or a carp?" I press my face into Royce's chest and try not to giggle. Stephen, for all his faults, would never say anything that corny. My husband is one sharp cookie. To be honest, I feel bad he had to quit school when I got pregnant. To be honest, I feel bad about a lot of things.

Royce must mistake my silence for me being overcome with emotion because he says, "Don't cry, honey. It'll be okay. I'll take care of you." He rubs his hand up and down over my shoulder. The gesture irritates me. I think of what it would be like to wake up every morning to Royce Burrus rubbing my shoulder up and down like that. I think of having to tell him to smooth down his hair or iron his shirt. And then, inexplicably, I think of Mike Tyson. I think of Mike Tyson, good old Kid Dynamite, grinning at me with that gap-toothed leer, and I want to put my hand over my ear just in case another man who I thought was a good man turns out to be bad.

There are way too many things spinning around in my head, and somehow this has the paradoxical effect of making my head stop spinning for Royce. Royce's hand slides down my arm and rests in the curve of my waist, then moves down again. I look up at him, shifting his hand off. His hair and eyes are the exact same color, and this annoys me. He looks at me big and mopey and pleading. I get up and put on my bra.

~~~

It's a pretty Saturday, so I pack up a picnic and take Austin to the beach. Stephen is off somewhere doing something; I don't even
~~~

bother asking what. I think it'll be good for Austin to get away from the television. Austin holds onto my hand as we walk over the dunes. He holds onto my hand as we stroll down the beach. He holds onto my hand as I try to fix the blanket and spread out lunch.

"Baby, you need to let go," I say. I shake his little hand in mine, then feel guilty as Austin stares up at me. He's got that look on his face like he's about to cry, the one where his upper lip curls into a baby Elvis snarl. I think about the summer I was nine, when Charlotte and I got on an Elvis kick, how we danced around her living room to "Blue Suede Shoes."

"Don't get all shook up," I say, even though I know he won't get the joke. I sit down on the blanket, and Austin curls himself onto my lap. He sticks his index finger in his mouth, a gesture I thought he'd long since outgrown. I pull his hand down. "Let's go look at the water before we eat," I say.

It's barely April, so the water is too cold to get our feet wet, but Austin and I take our shoes off and walk along the shore. It's a gray-green, rolly-crashy sort of a day, with long, lacy breakers and an onshore breeze.

"Look," Austin says, letting go of my hand. The air feels cool on my palm. He runs down the beach and points at something on the sand.

It's a blue jellyfish, and it looks like a cross between a dildo and a conch shell with long, crinkly tentacles spreading over the sand. A Portuguese man-of-war. Austin reaches for it and I swat his hand. He knows better than to touch a jellyfish. He gives me the Elvis curl again and I pull him to me. "The tentacles will sting you," I say. "They're mean."

Austin buries his head in my stomach. He shakes his face back and forth into me. And then the little shit backs up a couple of paces and gives me this *look* and reaches out to touch the jellyfish again.

"Austin!" I say, grabbing his shoulder. "What's your deal, man?"

"I want to touch it," he says. "It looks squishy." He leans closer.

Against my better judgment, I show him how he can carefully touch the ruffly pink top edge without getting stung. "Stay away from the tentacles," I tell him.

"It's pretty," Austin says. He crouches and runs his finger over the safe part of the jellyfish.

It is pretty. The inside of it's filled with clear blue liquid, the color of a summer sky. Or Windex. Or that awful blue Kool-Aid Austin likes. But the man-of-war is tricky, too, the way it pretends to be a harmless seashell, the way the tentacles look like seaweed. I pull Austin away, and we go back up to the blanket, which is blowing away at the edges where the picnic basket doesn't weigh it down.

I smooth things out and sit, then hand Austin a peanut butter and jelly sandwich. Austin looks at it. He pokes at it. He takes a bite and spits it into the sand.

"What are you doing?" I ask. I root around for my own sandwich.

Austin has grape jelly on the side of his mouth. "I hate jelly," he says.

"You don't hate jelly," I say. He loves jelly. Especially grape jelly.

Austin throws the rest of the sandwich down. Grape jelly oozes onto the blanket, and I close my eyes so I don't scream at the thought of the extra laundry.

Austin looks at me, and his I'm-going-to-cry face is gone. He has an I'm-going-to-pick-a-fight face instead, narrowed lips and sparky eyes. "Mother," he says, very formally. "I have always hated jelly."

And this is terrible, but I just want to smack him.

I know he's not a dumb kid. I know he's not the only one who lives in a tense home that's not really a home at all. But when he says, "Mother, I have always hated jelly," and sticks his index finger in his mouth, I want to smack him.

I look out at the crashing waves, the rickety fishing pier. My hair blows back from my face, and the breeze is cool and crisp. I take a deep breath and push it out through my teeth, thinking of the funny *hee-hee-hee* breathing I did while I was in labor.

I hand Austin half of my sandwich. "Then you'll just have to eat bologna."

~~~

You know what I've never understood about soap? Soap scum. Soap is supposed to make you clean, not create scum. And what do you clean it with, because you sure can't use soap, at least not the scummy bar. Do you use a different bar of soap? Doesn't it just get scummy, too, from cleaning the original scummy bar? How can something clean be dirty and something dirty be clean? Has it ever really changed? I bend over the bathtub and scrub at the hard-to-reach back corner and wish we could afford an automatic shower cleaner, the one with the scrubbing bubbles. The front door slams, and Stephen's footsteps clump up the stairs. I lean back on my heels and throw the sponge in the tub. The footsteps stop, and Stephen is in the room with me, his face red and his hair messy.

"Did you think I was stupid?" he asks. He paces around the room and hits his fist against the wall.

I stand up. There's no way to answer this. "Maybe," I say.

"Because you must have thought I was stupid to go and fuck Royce Burrus and think I wouldn't find out."

My first instinct is to tell him to lower his voice, that Austin will hear, but then I remember Austin is with Stephen's parents for the
~~~

afternoon. "How did you find out?" I ask. Curiosity always has gotten the better of me.

Stephen looks at me like I'm a largemouth bass or something equally ridiculous. "If you must know, I went in to the office to ask Royce to take the house off the market, and I saw your little love note on his desk."

Shit. I try a new strategy. "It's not like I did anything you didn't do."

Stephen runs a hand through his hair. "So this is a revenge fuck?" he asks.

"Maybe," I say. I only say this to make Stephen mad, but it occurs to me that it might be the truth. "What does it matter? Besides, I ended it." I did end it. I don't know why Royce still has love notes on his desk.

"And that makes it okay? We can just go back to being happily married?" He huffs a little on the word *happily.*

I turn away from Stephen to wash the shower cleaner off my hands. "Did you think you'd get rid of me that easily?"

Stephen grabs me by the shoulders and turns me around, fast. The water still runs in the sink. "You are suffocating me, Evie. You are suffocating me." And Stephen puts his hands around my neck. He presses for a second, moves my head back and forth once, then releases me. It doesn't hurt. He doesn't press hard. He doesn't shake me hard. But I start to cry all the same. Stephen lets go. "Jesus, why do I even bother? You're not worth it." He steps back with his hands at his sides, breathing so I can see his chest rise and fall.

I slap him.

I slap him and I push past him and I walk out the door.

~~~
~~~

I get Austin. Stephen gets the house. It was never really mine to begin with. It wasn't worth the fight. He sells it, though not through anyone in my office, and I get a little check for the four years I pretended it was my home. And sure enough, a few months later, I drive by and it's not there. It's just gone. Like it was never there at all. It's only a matter of time before some big pink thing is built in its place.

Austin and I move into a room in my parents' inn until I can get back on my feet. I don't tell him Stephen is gone. I tell him Daddy's at work without mentioning that work is in Raleigh. I try to make it a fun summer trip to Grandma and Grandpa's, and whenever he wants to go home to the house that isn't, I let him get in the pool.

It's summer, and I have to leave extra time to get to work because of tourist traffic. Plus Austin throws a fit whenever I go. But at least I only have to drive up and down twice instead of four times now that Austin is already with my parents. I wonder if my son ever thinks of his days as green and blue and gold. Probably not. He probably thinks of his days in terms of Transformers and whichever animal Diego is rescuing. I wonder if he registers the fact that Stephen is gone for good.

One of Mike Tyson's trademark combinations was a right hook to his opponent's body followed by a right uppercut to the chin. I don't know how he moved his hands that fast. People were afraid to fight him; he was that mean. I used to tell myself that maybe he wasn't so bad, that maybe he just liked to fight. There is something about having battles, some kind of adrenaline rush that makes you feel spiky and alive and full of power. Maybe that's what made him move so fast. Maybe he just craved the rush. But I don't really buy it. What I really think is that Mike Tyson was a bastard like all the rest of them.

I drive up the road and it's a lovely end of the day, and I'm sure the sun is doing amazing sparkly things on the beautiful, beautiful water. It's a view people drive thousands of miles to see, but I can't see it anymore. All I can see is the road. I'm twenty-three years old, and for forty more years I'll drive up and down this road to work and back again. I can't quit. I'll never go back to school, or climb Mt. Everest, or meet a Sherpa, or throw a whirling dervish out of whirl. Those days are gone, and now it's just this. This day, these wheels, this road.

Two

Evolution of a Bad Girl

Bad Girls: Are not *good*. They're not good at all. But they are interesting.

They: Cut off their own pigtails. Pull sea oats out of the ground *on purpose*. Make up lies. Bad girls make up lots of lies. Sometimes accidentally. Sometimes *on purpose*.

When they get bigger, Bad Girls: Wear too much eyeliner. Make out in baseball dugouts.

Let boys touch their breasts. (Both breasts. But mostly the left one.)

No one writes songs about being Good. *Good to the Bone. Big Good John. Good Moon Rising.* Michael Jackson would never grab his crotch and sing *You know I'm good.*

Bad Girls don't know they're bad until someone tells them. They just get tired of hair sticking to the backs of their necks. They want to wash away. They want things to be *interesting.*

But once they're told, they realize they've always been B.A.D. Bad.

I just might be the baddest girl you'll ever meet. The baddest girl on the planet.

Three

Part Spell, Part Séance, Part Prayer

— 1999 —

My name is Evie Austin. You say it like it's two letters—E. V. Sometimes that's how I sign my name: E. V. Austin, even though I know it's not true. My middle name is Ann, so it should be E. A. Austin to be true. My whole first name is Evelyn, but I hate that name. It sounds awful, like a little old lady. When my dad dropped off me and my brother to live for the summer at our Aunt Fay's house, which isn't a house at all, but a big old camper van, he took my face in his hands and said, "Evelyn, you be good." I hate being *Evelyn*ed. I crossed my eyes at him and turned my face away. Then he and Aunt Fay started talking. My Aunt Fay said, "No, I do not want to keep them at your house. What if she comes back?" And my dad said, "She's not coming back." They were talking about my mom, who moved to Buxton for the summer for an important job. If it wasn't important, she wouldn't have moved for the whole summer. Then my dad left and went to work.

I am nine years old, and now, I'm a gypsy. I live in the National Seashore campground in Frisco, North Carolina. Frisco is a town on an island, and this island is full of *danger*. My island has a nickname, and it is: The Graveyard of the Atlantic. This is on account of all the shipwrecks it's caused. So, that's one source of danger, things that cause shipwrecks, such as shifting shoals, which I learned all about from Mrs. Hammond in science class last year.

There are many other dangers, including: jellyfish, riptides, hurricanes, cactus, and brothers. My big brother, Nate, teases me all the time. I warn the tourists about sources of danger when I talk with them, but I leave out my brother. Mostly because he's not a *force of nature.*

It's a real big camper that we live in. You have to pull it with a truck. Aunt Fay stays in it all the time since she sold her house and hasn't yet got a new one. She says she likes it just fine. We're going to live here while our dad's busy with tourist season, since he'll be gone too much to take care of us. Dad comes to visit us most days before he goes to work at the restaurant. My mom has not yet come to visit. She's awfully busy being on the welcoming committee for the lighthouse movers from Buffalo, New York. That's another danger: erosion. That old ocean just ate away and ate away and ate away at the beach so much that the lighthouse (which is the tallest lighthouse in America) could topple over and wash off at *any second.* That's why it's getting moved. They're going to pick it right up and move it inland on a little train track, is what they're going to do. So it's very important to treat the lighthouse movers nice or else they might ruin our lighthouse.

No lighthouse would mean no tourists. Tourists *love* lighthouses. There's not a thing you can buy here that doesn't have a big old lighthouse on it. I've even seen dog hats with lighthouses on them. I wish I had a dog. But I wouldn't make it wear a hat, not unless it wanted to. Tourists love to buy things with lighthouses on them, but this is complicated. My dad says, "They are good for the economy." My dad works for a restaurant, and he feeds tourists every day. He works late, which is why he can't visit us every single night. He likes it when tourists buy things. My Aunt Fay says, "Tourists are a nuisance. Our economy did just fine for two hundred years before they started showing up." Aunt Fay has a bumper sticker on her truck that says, "If it's tourist season, why can't I shoot 'em?" I don't tell anybody, but in secret, I like the tourists. They make summer exciting. I spy on them all the time. I get real low behind a sand dune and I watch them. But there's been nobody interesting yet at the Frisco National Seashore campground. Just a bunch of boring old fishermen. It is only June, so maybe the interesting tourists aren't out of school yet.

The trick to spying is to stay very flat behind the sand dune while not getting cactus stuck in you anywhere. Cactus is a very real danger, and I know this because once I thought I had a cactus needle stuck in my foot for an entire week until my mom looked at my flip-flop and found a nasty needle buried in the plastic. I clear a space in the sand with both my hands for where I want to spy tonight. I make two circles and I fan them out and make a big heart. Then I hunker down. I hold up my pretend binoculars with one hand and move aside a couple of green sea oats with the other. I peep into campsite A-14. A red tent. No people. I skulk forward, looking through my binoculars for rhinos. I'm on the vast plains of Africa, just like in *The Lion King*. I've been crossing this giant desert for two days, but the path to the oasis isn't as short as I'd thought. I keep going when *bam*, from the corner of my eye I see not one, but three rhinos. They're big, hulky gray things with mean, pointed horns, and they're coming right at me. There's only one thing to do when you come face-to-face with three rabid rhinos, and that is to RUN. I run and run, tearing through the hot African sand, and just when I think I'm close to safety, I come up against a wide, black river. The current is strong, but I swim with hard, quick strokes. I kick my feet, and then I hear a voice from the oasis. "Evie," the voice yells. I can't answer because I'm swimming for my life. Then again, louder, "Evie!" The mud of shore squishes between my toes, gooey, and I slush up onto the riverbank and collapse for a second, breathing hard. A shadow looms over me. Just when I thought the rhinos were the worst of my worries, I see the evil face of Emperor Shang, the jewel thief I've just recently escaped.

"Dinner's ready," Emperor Shang says. He squints at me.

"I won't fall for your dastardly ploy," I say. I try to dash back to the river—to H-E-double hockey sticks with the rhinos—but Emperor Shang grabs my arm.

"You don't even know what dastardly means," he says.

"I do too," I say. I shake my arm away. Older brothers think they know everything. "It means wicked."

Nate strides toward our camper. I'm kind of hungry, so I follow him. "I don't want hot dogs again," I say.

"Talk to the chef," Nate says.

But Aunt Fay is not a chef. I've never seen her wear an apron or a big poofy white hat like the chefs in my dad's cookbooks, and she's never made anything other than hot dogs and SpaghettiOs in the five days we've been here. I follow Nate to campsite B-8. Nate runs up the steps to the camper and slams the door. Aunt Fay's standing at the grill, shooing away a seagull.

"Filthy wretch," she hollers at it. "No better than rats with wings."

Rats with wings. I get a real clear picture of that in my head. Rats with pointy yellow teeth and long slithery tails, wings flapping all around my head. I shiver a little. The seagull caws. "You took your shower yet, Evie?" Aunt Fay asks.

I go up and look at the grill. Hot dogs. "Nope," I say. "I couldn't get to the oasis."

Aunt Fay nods. She has short black hair and sharp brown eyes. Her hair blows around her head in the breeze. "Rhinos?"

"Three." I sit down on the picnic bench and pick at the silvery wood, peeling up a long strip to fend off any rats with wings. I wave it in the air to test it out. "Mom says hot dogs are full of chemicals," I say.

Aunt Fay reaches for a paper plate and stabs the hot dogs onto it. She looks at me, and I get cold-pricklies in my stomach. "Your mom's not here, is she?"

My wood strip makes *swish* sounds when I slash it through the air. Nate bangs back out the camper door and swings his long legs under the table. He reaches for a hot dog bun. "She's making a sacrifice for our family and our island," I say. This is what my mom has told me. After all, it's not everyone who gets chosen to be on a welcoming committee. I decide I'm hungry enough I want a hot dog. I reach for a bun, too.

Nate snorts. He squirts ketchup in a long red streak and eats half the hot dog in one gulp. "You shouldn't say things when you don't know what you're talking about," Nate says. He's got hot dog bun crumbs on his face.

I told you, older brothers think they know *everything*. "I know things just fine," I say. In fact, I know things better than him. I think that part, but I don't say it. He doesn't deserve me fighting with him. What is he, anyway, except for a rotten old no-good jewel thief?

One morning a ranger in a brown uniform comes up and tells Aunt Fay she has to move her camper. Rangers can be dangers if they try to tell the locals what to do, which they do *all the time*. Like moving our lighthouse; we didn't want it moved at all, but the Park Service up and said, "Too bad, it's getting moved or else it'll wash away." And then all the movers from Buffalo started coming to the island, and that's when my mom met her friend Bob. I think maybe Bob got her the job on the welcoming committee; I don't know. The ranger says Aunt Fay can only stay for fourteen days at a time, and they've overlooked that fact for five whole extra days and they can't overlook it any more. Aunt Fay raises a fuss. She says it's stupid that we have to leave when there are fifty empty campsites just lying around. But in the end the ranger wins. He says, "You just have to leave for a night or two, and then you can come back for another fourteen days." I have to take all the towels down from the clothesline and pack them up, and then I have to take down the clothesline, too. Nate rolls the awning up, and Aunt Fay throws the lawn chairs in the back of the truck. It's a gray old cloudy day, and I'm tired of camping. I'm tired of sand in my bed. "Why can't we go home?" I ask Aunt Fay. She's lying down underneath the camper, banging at the metal legs with a hammer to get them to fold up.

"Frisco Woods will be a nice change," Aunt Fay says. She says "nice" in the funny old way some people here do. *Noice*. She shakes some rust out of her hair. "All those trees for you to play under."

I roll my clothesline up into a giant clothesline ball. I don't care if it gets tangled. "I hate trees," I say. I throw the clothesline ball onto the camper floor. I want to go play with my friends. My friend Abigail had just gotten a new pogo stick when we left to go camping, and I hadn't even gotten to hop on it yet. It looked like fun. It looked like being a kangaroo.

Nate picks the stuff up off the picnic table and sets it in a bin. Palmolive soap. Clothespins. A big green sponge. My Mulan action figure that I got when we went up to Nags Head. "Do you have a looking problem?" Nate asks. He tosses Mulan at me. I miss the catch and she falls on the ground. "Do something productive," he says.

I stick out my tongue at Nate, grab Mulan from the concrete, and sit right down on the ground and stare at him some more. Then I make Mulan karate kick and chop the air. *Hi-yah*. Eventually Aunt Fay makes me get up and help, and we finish packing. She lets Nate back up the truck and hook the camper to the trailer hitch. I jump in the bed of the truck with the folded-up lawn chairs so I don't have to sit beside Nate. I wrap my arms around my imaginary dog. He's big and the color of red apple cider. His name is Jack, and he licks my face. I push his head to the side, but not in a mean way. "Stop that, Jack," I say. His slobber smells like tuna. A breeze kicks up and blows his pretty red fur around. Above our heads, the gray clouds puff and scoot along.

Nate sticks his head out the window. "Can I drive?" he asks Aunt Fay. Nate's fourteen-and-a-half. He can't drive.

Aunt Fay opens his door and stares at him. If you ask me, she's the one with the looking problem.

〰

I don't really hate trees. I just hate trees I can't climb. What's the point of a tree being there if I can't climb it? The trees at Frisco Woods are just *okay*. I can climb them, but they're not very high. I climb every tree in our campsite, which is a nice spot beside the sound that smells piney. There's a pool here, like a little spot of drip-drop blue glass. There's a store, a laundromat, phones, a table to clean fish, and hookups for water and electric so we have lights in our camper and dishwashing water in our sink. Plus I saw kids running around. I like it here fine, but Aunt Fay says it costs three times as much to camp here than in the National Seashore campground, so we can't stay. I want to go swim in the pool, but it's thundering, deep, fat, rumbles like an old man coughing, so I'm not allowed. I grab Mulan and call for Jack, and we run over to the sound. There's this one tree with roots that grab into the water like claws, so we jump from one root to another while Aunt Fay and

Nate finish setting up the camper. I make Mulan chop at the tree. She is one tough cookie. I hear shouting like kids playing, so we all get up to investigate. Jack trots behind me. He's a good dog and very obedient. He doesn't even have to wear a leash.

Five campsites over I discover the source of all the ruckus. There are no sand dunes here, so I press myself up against the rough bark of a tree to spy. Through my binoculars I see a boy about my size running around firing a water gun at a little girl with red pigtails. She shrieks and squeals. They look like they came from my mom's L.L.Bean catalog. I always wear a bathing suit in summer, since you never know when you'll get to swim, and I never wear shoes, but these kids have on shirts with collars, stiff-looking khaki shorts, and tennis shoes. "Tennis shoes" was the last word I got wrong on my spelling test this year. I spelled it like it sounds—"tenna shoes"—but that was not right at all. It's so dumb. People wear tenna shoes all the time, but they hardly ever play tennis. I've never played tennis before in my life, but I've sure worn tenna shoes. So I hate tenna shoes, and I never wear them anymore if I can help it. The boy with the water gun hollers and runs in a circle. I go up to him. "Want to play?" I ask. My mom always says it's best to be straightforward and clear.

The kid turns sideways and *pow pows* his gun. He has neat blond hair that's cut like a bowl. It lays down on his forehead all soft and perfect. My own hair is stiff and salty because I haven't washed it in three days. I don't like washing my hair. "We're playing bank robbers," he says.

Now, that sounds like just about the dumbest game I've ever heard. "We don't have bank robbers on Hatteras Island," I say. Then I tell them about some of the dangers we do have. I get up to the Portuguese man-of-war before the kid shoots me with his water gun.

"We're playing bank robbers," he shouts.

I sigh and say, fine, I'll play. I run in a circle and dodge when he shoots at me. "I'm Evie," I say. I karate chop a robber.

"I'm Jack," he says.

"That's the name of my dog." Then I giggle because this boy has a dog's name.

"You have a dog?" the girl asks. She has two missing front teeth and looks just like Pippi Longstocking.

That's when I realize they might not understand Jack is a pretend dog. I look back at the boy-Jack. "Is she kin to you?" I ask him.

Jack stops shooting and looks at me funny. "What?"

"Is she kin to you?" I ask again. I point at the little girl.

Jack puts his hands on his hips. Whenever I do that, my mom yells at me for sassing. "What are you saying?" he asks.

I start to feel real stupid. "*Kin,*" I say. I say it louder than before so maybe he'll get it this time. "Are y'all related?"

But old bowl-head just makes an ugly face at me. "I don't know what you're saying," he says.

I decide this game of robbers is just too silly to play any longer. Besides, kids who constantly wear *tennis shoes* can't be all that fun. "I think I hear my dog barking," I say to the catalog kids. And I run back to my own campsite where at least people know what *kin* means.

~~~

One afternoon a few days later I get ants in my pants. Not real ants—that's what it's called when I want to move and run around but can't. It rains and rains. Another source of danger here can be BOREDOM. When it rains and there's no beach allowed and no swimming allowed and no going out for sno-cones allowed, you could just about die of boredom. It's a genuine source of dan-
~~~

ger. Nate sprawls like a starfish on the bed reading some dumb comic book, and Aunt Fay just plays solitaire and smokes cigarettes. I write a letter to my pen pal in Ireland. His name is Eamon O'Shea, and where he lives they drink tea every afternoon and eat something called clotted cream. It sounds gross, but Eamon says it tastes good. I tell Eamon all about the new campground, but when that's done, I'm still bored. I draw him a picture of a starfish with googly eyes and put everything in an envelope, and then I am done with writing things. I try to think up reasons to go home. At least Jack and I could watch a video on TV or something. Finally I hit on a reason, and it's not even a lie. I get up off my bed and go over to the little stand-up and take-down table where Aunt Fay is slapping out cards. "I forgot my summer reading list at home," I say. I pick up a strand of my long, salty hair and use it to tickle her arm.

Aunt Fay sets down her hand of cards. "Do you need it?" she asks.

"It's vital," I tell her. V-I-T-A-L. I got that word right on my spelling test. "It's vital that I read twenty books from that list this summer so we get a pizza party when school starts back up." I shudder to imagine school starting back up.

"I suppose you want to go after it?" she asks. Aunt Fay leans back against the bench. It's red and your legs stick to it when you sit down. I wonder how bad her legs are going to stick since she's been sitting there all afternoon.

"It's for my education," I say.

Aunt Fay says she'll take me and, even better, Nate doesn't want to go. So me and Aunt Fay drive up to our house. It looks funny to see it after being gone. Our house is little and brown and square, and it's up off the ground on stilts. Nobody's home. Aunt Fay pulls the truck in the driveway and says, "Run up and get your paper."

I open the door, but I dawdle. "I might have forgot a few more things," I say. Rain spit-spats on my leg in little pings. "It might take me a minute."

I'm hoping Aunt Fay will come in with me, and then I can convince her to watch a video, but she just gets out a cigarette by going *tap tap tap* on the packet. She sticks the cigarette in her mouth and talks around it. "Do what you got to do," she says.

So I get out and dash up the steps like I always do, skipping steps three and eight. Nobody locks doors on Hatteras Island so I go right in. I stand very still for a moment. My house is quiet, just the soft pitters of rain on the roof and a *squawk squawk* coming from the fridge. Piles of dirty dishes cover the kitchen counter. I peek in the squawky fridge, but it's just beer and more beer. I'm about to go in my room and look for my paper when I hear a car door slam and then voices. I run to the window, and there's my mom, getting out of a blue car. I call Jack over and put my arms around him. Mom talks to Aunt Fay, and then my mom's friend Bob comes out of the blue car and stands by my mom. He puts his hand on her back and sort of steers her toward the stairs and up into the house. I let go of Jack and run to the door.

"Mommy!" I yell as it opens. I don't usually say *mommy* because that's for babies, but I'm excited. The last time Mom came to visit me and Nate was three days ago. She took us out for some Bubba's ribs and told us about how they're taking apart the lighthouse. Then we went and looked at it. It's all dug out and bricks are everywhere. It looks naked. It made my stomach feel sick. Her friend Bob took us in closer than most people are allowed since he's an important lighthouse mover from Buffalo, New York.

Mom hugs me. "Hi, Evie-girl," she says. She kisses my cheek and her lips are sticky with lipstick.

Bob pats my shoulder. "You been having fun camping?" he asks.

I step back and look at Bob. He's a big, tall person with a bushy beard. I feel shy, and I don't know why. "I guess," I say. Jack sits beside me and I pat his head.

Bob turns to Mom. "Mallory, why don't you go ahead and get what you need."

Mom smiles at Bob and then goes into her bedroom. I don't know what to do alone with this bushy-beard man. I look down at my toes. There's dark sand around my toenails. Jack shifts his paw. The door bangs open and there's Aunt Fay.

"I believe you'd best be setting your boots outside of my brother's house," Aunt Fay says to Bob. Aunt Fay's real little, and she only comes up to Bob's chest.

Bob raises his hands like Aunt Fay's sticking him up. *Give me all your money and nobody gets hurt.* He waves his hands back and forth a couple times. "Hey now," Bob says. "I don't want to start anything." He gives a little wave and then real quiet walks outside and down the stairs.

"You could've fooled me," Aunt Fay says to his back. She puffs on her cigarette even though Dad doesn't allow smoking in the house. Then she points it at me. "Get your things, kid. We're going home."

I don't want to. "I want to see Mom," I say. Then I run off into Mom's room before anyone can stop me. I hear her rattling drawers around. I stand in the doorway. Mom's got a whole big pile of clothes on the bed. Winter clothes with long sleeves and long legs and hoods. "Why do you need those?" I ask her.

Mom looks up and her mouth pops open. She turns back to the closet and shuffles some things around inside. A bunch of hangers fall on the floor and clang against each other. "It gets chilly at night," Mom says. She puts her hand up to her mouth, then rubs her forehead like she has a headache. She stops taking out clothes and sits down on the bed.

I go lean up against her. "Mommy, I'm tired of camping," I tell her.

"I know, baby," she says. "But sometimes we have to do things that are difficult. Sometimes it's not enough for things to just stay the same." She pats my hair. Then her hand gets harder on my head. "Have you not washed your hair?" she asks. Then she goes and gets that scoldy voice. "Evelyn, you have to wash your hair after you've been swimming. How many times have I told you this?" I pull away from her. She stands up and keeps on yanking things from the closet and tossing them on the bed. "Hair like seaweed," she says, all muttery.

"Evie," Aunt Fay calls from the living room. "Get your paper and let's go."

Mom lifts her head up and sniffs. "Is she smoking in here?"

I don't want to get Aunt Fay in trouble, so I don't say anything. I don't like it, being here with my mom's clothes all out of the closet. I decide that camping's maybe okay. "It's just for the summer, right? Camping with Aunt Fay?"

Mom folds up a bright pink sweater with a stretchy neck. "We'll figure it out soon," Mom says. "You'll be home soon."

I hear Aunt Fay stomping down the hallway, so I hug Mom and run out the door before she can get there. "I'm ready," I tell her.

Outside, Bob waits in the blue car. Aunt Fay and I get in her truck and she backs out, fast, without looking behind her. We drive down the twisty neighborhood roads and out to Highway 12. We swish through puddles. I think about how I forgot my book list of summer reading. I think that all I'll have to do is spy on tourists if I don't have any books to read. Then I get to thinking about something else. "Aunt Fay?" I ask. "If Bob's only here for work, but he's leaving after the summer, then he's not a tourist. So what does that make him?"

Aunt Fay snorts. She sounds like Nate when she does that. "A home-wrecker," she says.

I picture Bob on top of a great big wrecking ball, knocking over our little house on stilts. I imagine sharp pieces of wood flying everywhere. *Home-wrecker.* I don't like the way that word tastes in my mouth. I don't like it at all.

~

My dad comes to visit us at Frisco Woods that night, but he doesn't play with me or even talk much. Mostly he sits around at the stand-up take-down table with Aunt Fay and drinks beer. His face is all prickly, and I wonder if he's going to grow a beard like Bob. He doesn't come the next night, but he comes back the next. He talks with me a little bit then.

He drinks beer and says, "Evie, come tell your old man a story."

So I sit on his lap and tell him all about how Jack and I barely escaped some pirates on the beach today, and how Jack was braver than that dog Brandy in *Taffy of Torpedo Junction,* even if Jack didn't fight any Nazis.

I'm leading up to my big question of can I get a dog when my dad pats my head. He says, "Nazis are the least of our worries right now, kiddo."

"I told you, we didn't fight Nazis," I say. "We fought pirates."

Dad hugs me and rocks me back and forth. His beard prickles the top of my head. It itches, but I don't move.

"Do you need some warm fuzzies?" I ask him.

He doesn't answer, just squeezes me tighter in his arms. I'm all squished, but I don't say anything. I sit on Daddy's lap until he has to go home.

The next day, Aunt Fay says enough time's gone by for the rangers to not have burs up their butts, so we can go back to the National Seashore campground. I go search for the catalog kids to tell them goodbye, because my mom says always be polite, but their fancy RV is gone. I'm glad we're leaving. I hate it here at Frisco Woods.

~

The sea oats aren't green anymore. They're gold and fluffy and better for hiding behind. I find new trails in the woods around the campground all the time. My legs have scratches from yaupon bushes, but I don't mind. Scratches aren't true dangers. While I walk, I hatch schemes to get me and Nate back home with Mom and Dad. So far, it has not worked to: pretend to have malaria; say that I forgot stuff, even if it's vital to my education; get Dad to call Mom by being bad in his presence, either by stealing cigarettes and acting like I'm about to smoke them or by hitting Nate in the face; or try to get Aunt Fay's camper to fall on my leg to prove it's an unsafe environment. That camper won't fall for anything. I'm hiking today through the deepest jungles of South America, or wherever it is they crashed in *Swiss Family Robinson*. It is so hot. Even though it's five o'clock, it's so hot the air burns in my lungs. Parrots squawk in the trees and a monkey cries out, *ooh aaa aaa eee eee*. I swashbuckle some branches out of my way, and then, right before my eyes, I see a girl. And this girl is n-a-k-e-d. She's about my size, and she has hair that's even longer than mine, and she's spinning in a circle. Her red-gold hair flies out behind her like a sheet.

I step out of the jungle. "Why are you naked?" I ask the girl.

She jerks her head toward me fast and covers up her chest with her arms. Then she bends down to pick up a pink-striped towel and wraps it around herself. She pushes her hair out of her face. "I was waiting for a bath," she says.

"I never take baths," I tell her. "I find them boring."

The girl bends down and picks up some shells. "Why are you in our campsite?"

"I was hiking through the jungle," I say. I go look at the shells she's collecting. I show her what's what. I don't mean to brag, but I'm good at identifying shells. Coquina. Clamshell. Scotch bonnet. She says she wants to find a sand dollar, and I tell her the story of Jesus that goes in a rhyme about sand dollars.

She looks impressed. "I'm Charlotte," the girl says.

"E. V.," I say. Then I smooth it out and say it again right. "Evie Austin."

A little boy plods through the sand to where we are. He's got short legs to plow through all that sand. "Mom says it's your turn," he says to Charlotte. He's cute, maybe four years old. I want a little baby brother with short legs.

"This is my brother, James," Charlotte says. She points at me. "That's Evie," she says to James. Then Charlotte runs down the dune to take her bath.

~

I take a shower that night and wash my hair. Then I make Aunt Fay comb it out nice and put it in braids. I eat my supper fast and dash back up to where my trail comes out at Charlotte's campsite. I clear a fine patch of sand and hunker in. Charlotte's dad wears his bathing suit from the beach and no shirt, and he laughs and talks to Charlotte's mom. Charlotte's dad grills hamburgers and shoos away seagulls while Charlotte's mom cooks things on the camper stove and walks in and out setting the picnic table. Her mom laughs and shrieks when the napkins blow away, and Charlotte runs around gathering them up. Then Charlotte sets things on each of the four napkins—a salt shaker on her own, a pepper shaker on James's, a big stabbing fork on her dad's, and a can of soda on her mom's, so nothing blows away. For dinner, Charlotte's family has: Hamburgers. A nice salad. Green beans. Whole grain buns because whole grains are good for you. Juice or milk, you get your choice, or soda for Charlotte's mom but nobody else. A dessert out of a box. Charlotte's little brother James is so cute. He's got blond hair that sits just right on his head, but not like the Frisco Woods bowl-head boy. And he wears itty-bitty flip-flops, not tennis shoes. He swings his legs under the picnic table and asks for more green beans. Who ever heard of a little kid asking for more green beans?

I spy there for quite a while; then I slink back down to our campsite, unseen.

A few minutes later, along come Charlotte and James. Charlotte's holding James's hand. "Ask your mom if you can come take a walk," Charlotte calls to me.

I glance at the camper. Aunt Fay is inside, but I don't feel like asking permission. Besides, she's not my mom. "I can," I say. We all go for a walk as the sun sets and the Frisco National Seashore campground turns a soft gold color. Me and Charlotte each hold one of James's hands. He swings between us like a South American monkey.

During the next two weeks, Charlotte McConnell from Windsor, Ohio, and me become the best of friends. It's like we've always been this way. Most days, this is what we do: Meet up after breakfast. Play horses at the shower stalls. Charlotte's horse is Casey, and mine is Chestnut. We ride them up and down the beach, then make a loop of the campground, and we're done. Play Mulan, after she's a warrior. Play mermaids in the ocean. Build sand mermaids on the beach. Listen to Charlotte's dad and my Aunt Fay tell stories. Charlotte's dad's stories involve the *building blocks of the universe.* Play with Charlotte's cousin, Troia, who is as old as Nate but isn't mean and awful and who buys us popsicles. You say her name like this: TROY-uh. I think her name sounds nice. Much nicer than Evelyn. Troia is pretty. She looks like a fairy princess, or a mermaid; her shiny gold hair curls to her waist, and she has big blue eyes. We build campfires and sing songs. Play pirates. Sleep over in Charlotte's camper.

My dad keeps coming to visit a lot before work and sometimes after work if the restaurant isn't busy or he has time off, and he makes friends with Charlotte's dad. My mom hasn't come yet at the same time as my dad, but I wish she would. We run around and play tag while our dads drink beer, and during this time, Charlotte's mom reads. Sometimes we go lean against our dads and ask them to tell us stories.

I say, "Tell us about Blackbeard." And my dad tells us all about the pirate who got his head cut off on Ocracoke then swam around his boat three times with no head at all. We shiver at this and sit closer together on the picnic table. It's getting to be dusk, the sky streaking red and purple.

Charlotte says, "Tell us about the Big Bang." She shifts on her Dad's lap and pats his shoulder. And Charlotte's dad tells us about *general relativity* and the *expanding universe.* He points at the purpling sky, and I imagine it before there was anything there at all.

Charlotte says, "Tell us about the time you and Mom climbed

the Matterhorn." Charlotte's dad talks about how they had to turn around right before the top to help a man with a broken leg.

The first pinpricks of stars come out, and I say to my dad, "Tell us about how you and Mom met."

But instead of telling about the time he rescued my mom from a rip current, my daddy puts down his beer and says, "Honey, I can't tell that one right now." His face gets all scrunchy, and I feel like I'm going cry. Then my dad leaves. Charlotte's dad doesn't leave, except to go inside to read by lantern light. Sometimes I pretend Charlotte's mom is my mom, and Charlotte and I are long-lost twin sisters separated at birth, even though in reality we look nothing alike. Charlotte and I keep asking our parents to let me go back to Ohio with her for two whole weeks. We think it's only fair since she came to my home for two whole weeks. We think since our dads have become friends that the plan just might work.

One night I ask Aunt Fay if I can have Charlotte over to our camper for dinner and a sleepover. She says yes. Aunt Fay makes hot dogs, but this is fine. I've seen Charlotte's family eating hot dogs. Aunt Fay stands there and grills wearing this funny old t-shirt that's splattered with paint and rolled-up jeans. She's smoking a cigarette. Charlotte's mom walks Charlotte down to our camper. She stands at the edge of our campsite with her hand on Charlotte's back, and then she gives her a teeny push, like she's presenting her as a gift to Aunt Fay. "Just came by to say thanks for feeding the kid," Charlotte's mom says. She also has red-gold hair, and it makes me think of my pretend dog, Jack. I haven't thought about Jack in ages. I decide to tell Charlotte about him, and maybe we can play with him after dinner. Charlotte's mom's wearing shorts and flip-flops and a pink shirt with a lighthouse on it.

"Any time," Aunt Fay says. She waves her fork in the air like she's waving in a parade.

I go up and pull Charlotte into the campsite. I show her all my things, and we set the indoor table since it's real windy. Aunt Fay rustles around outside. Then she cups her hands around her mouth and yells, "Nate!" No answer. She does it again. Nothing. Then, "Nathaniel Jacob Austin, this is your last chance for supper."

"She's just joking," I say to Charlotte. But I know if Nate doesn't show up, we'll just eat without him.

Aunt Fay comes inside with the hot dogs. "You girls want to go see the lighthouse get moved tomorrow?" Tomorrow's the first day the lighthouse will move along on the train tracks. They'll move it one whole mile inland, but in tiny little spurts, Bob says.

Charlotte places a hot dog gently onto a bun. "Maybe," she says. Charlotte is afraid the lighthouse will fall over and be ruined. I've told her not to worry since my mom is making sure the lighthouse movers are being careful, but she's still scared.

"I want to see it get moved," I say. I pour some Kool-Aid. "Mom can get Bob to show us stuff."

"What's your mom's job?" Charlotte asks. I know that her mom is a mom all morning and teaches English to people who don't speak English in afternoons, and her dad is a geologist. That's how come he knows all about the *building blocks of the universe.* Charlotte fidgets on the red bench, and I hear her legs sticking. "May I please have a napkin?"

Aunt Fay looks around the camper. She hands Charlotte a beach towel. "We're out of napkins," she says.

"It's not her official job," I tell Charlotte. "It's a special job just for the summer. Like, to live up there and make sure everything goes okay."

Charlotte chews slowly. "Who hired her?"

"How should I know?" Then I think about this. Maybe it was

her friend Bob. Maybe it was the Park Service. It has to be the Park Service. I'm about to say this when Aunt Fay starts talking.

"Do you girls know about the Sea Queen of Connaught?" Before we can answer, she starts telling us all about this Irish pirate queen and her exploits.

I love pirate stories, and I bet my pen pal, Eamon O'Shea, knows all about that Sea Queen, but something keeps bothering me right now. "Aunt Fay," I say, interrupting. She doesn't yell at me, though. "Was it the Park Service that hired Mom?"

Aunt Fay's face looks tight over her cheekbones. She moves some plates around on the table. "You're going to have to talk to your mom about that," she says.

This makes me have a funny feeling in my stomach. "Why?"

Charlotte puts down her hot dog and picks at the bun. She makes a little pile of bun crumbs. "Did the Sea Queen have a sword?"

"I want to talk to her tonight," I say.

"Sea Queen's long dead," Aunt Fay says. "We'd have to have a séance to talk to her."

"I meant my mom." I have ketchup on my fingers, but I'm too embarrassed to wipe them on a beach towel. I smear my ketchup fingers on my shorts.

Aunt Fay shakes her head. "I'm not going out tonight," she says. "If your mom wants to talk to you, she can come here."

"Then I need a quarter to call her," I say. I push away my plate. It's a stupid plain white thing that sags if you pick it up. Charlotte's mom gives us food on thick cardboardy plates that have purple edges and flowers on them.

Charlotte finishes her hot dog and neatly wipes her mouth with the beach towel. I hate that beach towel. It's got some dumb cartoon cat on it. Charlotte turns to me. "Let's have a séance later and talk to the Sea Queen."

"If I have time," I say. I've got some important things to do.

My mom can't come see me. She says she's busy tonight, but she'll see me when I go watch them move the lighthouse tomorrow. Charlotte walks down with me to make the phone call, but I don't feel like playing with her after. I tell her my stomach hurts, and that maybe I'm having a bad reaction to some chemicals in those hot dogs. We go back to the camper with Aunt Fay. It's almost dark and Nate isn't back yet.

I want my dad and I want my mom and I want to go home.

Charlotte and Aunt Fay play cards until it's bedtime. I watch them. Charlotte and I walk to the bathroom and brush our teeth, then lie down in my bunk. I can't sleep, even if I pull the sheet up over my ear how I like it. Even if I listen to the ocean waves *shush* on the shore.

"I can't sleep," Charlotte whispers.

I turn over and look at her. "Me neither."

Charlotte's face is little and white. I can see her freckles in the moonlight. "I hate it that they're moving my lighthouse. I just know it'll fall over and be gone forever."

I move one arm out from under the covers. Until now, I hadn't really thought about the lighthouse falling. I thought my mom would keep it safe. Now I'm not so sure. Nothing feels safe anymore. Not even my very own family.

At midnight I wake up. I know it's midnight because Aunt Fay has a little windup clock and it says so. The campground is dark, and the only sounds are crickets going *CRICKit CRICKit CRICKit* and the soft thud of ocean waves plopping on the beach. I know what I have to do to fix things for my family. This isn't about rhinos or fake dogs or South American monkeys. This is serious. This is magic, and I have to be very precise. I reach over and shake Charlotte awake. She mumbles, and I tell her to hush.

"What are you doing?" she asks, her voice soft and sleepy.

I sit up in bed. "Come on," I whisper. "We have to go."

Charlotte asks where, but I pull her arm until she follows me out of bed. We crawl over Nate's empty bunk and slip outside, shutting the door very softly.

"Look at the moon," Charlotte says. She tips back her head.

But I don't care about the moon. "Come on," I say. "We've got to work a spell."

"A spell for what?" Charlotte asks. "What are we doing out here?"

I don't know if telling her will make it not work, if it's like a birthday wish or wishing on a falling star. I think fast. I need for her to help me. "A spell so the lighthouse won't fall," I say. Then I think maybe I also shouldn't lie or it might not come true. "A spell so when I come back from visiting you, my home will be back the way it should be." It's a good part-lie.

"What should we do?" Charlotte asks.

I take her hand, and we start walking. I head toward the boardwalk. "It's like a séance," I say. "Only part prayer, too, so God will fix things."

"I'm not allowed to go down to the beach alone at night," Charlotte says.

I stop walking, just for a second, and drop Charlotte's hand. "Do you want it to fall?" I walk on. Charlotte follows. We walk all the way down the boardwalk, then up the sand dune and over. My skin feels sticky with salt. I'm not sure how the spell will go, exactly, but

I do know that when you want to work magic, you have to do it on the beach at midnight. We stand for a second and watch the silvery, frothy waves in the moonlight. We're not alone, though. A campfire flickers and pops down at the high-tide line, black outlines of people sitting around it, smoking and laughing.

"What do we do now?" Charlotte whispers. She's standing very still.

I chew on my fingernail. It seems to me that important spells and things work in rhymes, like the Jesus rhyme on the sand dollar, or *Now I lay me down to sleep, I pray the Lord my soul to keep.* Only I don't like that prayer because it talks about *if I die before I wake.* Who wants to die before they wake? "It has to be in a rhyme," I say.

Charlotte moves closer to the campfire. "I think that's my cousin," she says. She yells Troia's name.

I clasp her arm and tell her to hush, but it's too late; Troia comes over to us. Two other dark outlines start to move, too. It's my stupid brother and his friend, Michael.

"What are you two doing out here so late?" Troia asks. She's wearing a pretty white dress that flaps in the breeze.

"We have to work a spell," Charlotte tells her, tugging on Troia's hand. "To save the lighthouse. Otherwise it's going to fall when it gets moved."

"How do you know it's going to fall?" Troia asks.

"Evie said so." Charlotte looks at me. "She knows because her mom works with the lighthouse movers."

I start to feel weird and cold-prickly. "We just have to say a spell," I say. "That's all."

But Troia gets all riled up. I told you, tourists go crazy over that lighthouse. She says if it's going to fall then we need to call somebody, and *now.* We can't let them move it tomorrow. We have to intervene and save a landmark of America. I feel the slow pulse of an idea behind my eyes. "We could call my mom," I say. "We could get her to come to the lighthouse and show her what's wrong."

Troia calls for Nate and Michael. They come running over and she tells them we have to get Mom.

"I'm telling Dad you smoked," I say to Nate.

But Nate just laughs. His laugh sounds different. "Like Dad cares," he says. Then Nate says it's crazy to call Mom, and he's sure the stupid lighthouse is just fine. He's real mean. "Why are any of you listening to *that*?" he says, and points at me.

Troia puts her hands on her hips. She's sassing Nate and I love it. "What harm can possibly come from calling your mother?" she asks.

And then, get this, Nate *agrees with her.* It's probably because she's so pretty. So Michael throws sand on the fire and we all run up the boardwalk to the campground phone and Nate calls Mom. "Tell her we have to meet at the lighthouse," I say.

So Nate says that to Mom, and then he's quiet, and then he says because I said the lighthouse is going to fall. He says, "I don't know where she got the idea." He rolls his eyes and it looks like he's going to give up. Troia rests her hand on Nate's arm. He shifts his feet in the sand. "Look, just meet us there," he says, his voice firm, like Dad's. He hangs up.

Then I put the next part of my plan in action. "Call Dad, too," I tell Nate. Nate stands there with his hand on the hung-up phone. "Why?" he asks. He slaps at a mosquito.

Again, I think fast. "I heard him and Charlotte's dad talking about the mechanics of lighthouse moving. Dad knows things, Nate. You have to call him. You have to get him to meet us up there." Then I look at Troia. I take hold of her arm. "Right, Troia?" Then she says yes, that is a good idea, and why doesn't Nate do that, and then Nate *calls our dad.*

Me and Charlotte run up to Aunt Fay's camper. Charlotte's upset, and I feel bad, but not bad enough to stop the magic. She bangs open the door. Aunt Fay is already awake, though. "The lighthouse is going to fall," Charlotte says. "Please, we have to stop it."

Aunt Fay stares at us. "What on earth are you girls talking about?"

"It's true," I say. I cross my fingers behind my back. "There's no time to dawdle. Mom and Dad have already been called. Now we have to get up there."

Aunt Fay stares at us some more. Then Charlotte starts to cry. I go stand by Aunt Fay. I look straight into her brown eyes. "Please," I say. And I mean it.

Aunt Fay sighs. She puts her hand on my head. "Get in the truck," she says.

And quick as lighting, Aunt Fay drives us to the lighthouse. Troia and Nate and Michael ride in the back of the truck. The parking lot to the lighthouse is all roped off, so Aunt Fay pulls over to a picnic table that sits in some pine trees. Charlotte and I jump out. Aunt Fay follows, and then the others climb out of the back. I can't wait for Mom and Dad to get here, but then I remember the spell.

But it's Charlotte who says it first. I swear, it's like we're sisters. "We have to do the spell," she says.

Having Charlotte here makes me brave and strong. I climb up onto the picnic table. "We do it here," I say. But then I feel less brave and strong. I don't know any rhyming spells. This *has* to work.

Aunt Fay climbs up on the table, too. She motions for Troia and Nate and Michael to get up. Troia and Michael do, but Nate just stands there with his arms crossed. "Thing is," Aunt Fay says, "everything's got energy. Plants. Animals. People. That lighthouse. So what we have to do is send some good energy out to the lighthouse."

I tug at Aunt Fay's hand. "It has to rhyme," I say. I close my eyes. I can feel the power. Soon Mom and Dad will be here, and everything will be fine.

Aunt Fay coughs, and then she starts the spell. Her voice gets real low and official. "Cats and dogs, pigs and hogs," she chants.

"That doesn't make any sense," I say.

Aunt Fay looks at me with one eye squinted closed. "Sturdy up the lighthouse logs," she continues.

I try it out. I make sure the real reason for the prayer is set in my head good. "Cats and dogs, pigs and hogs."

Aunt Fay chants it with me, "Sturdy up the lighthouse logs."

Charlotte starts in with us, and suddenly everything begins to make sense. "Cats and dogs, pigs and hogs. Sturdy up the lighthouse logs."

Troia and Michael chant, too. Nate stands there and watches. "Cats and dogs, pigs and hogs!" We chant it loud. "Sturdy up the lighthouse logs!"

We turn in a slow circle on that table and we shout it, shout it, shout it out loud.

The pine tree smell prickles sharp in my nose, and the midnight breeze is soft and salty on my arms, and it's working—I can feel it.

Any second now, two cars will come down that road.

Four

Dominican Al's Once-in-a-Lifetime Honeymoon Extravaganza, Sponsored by Dominican Al's Rum and Fine Spirits

— 2014 —

You are the lucky winner of a seven-day, six-night honeymoon at the spectacular all-inclusive Hacienda Paradisus Resort and Spa in beautiful Bayahibe, República Dominicana! You are a very single divorcée. Who do you choose as your all-expenses-paid traveling companion?

A.) Your five-year-old son.
B.) Walter, your aunt's Yorkshire terrier and your current best friend.
C.) Your former best friend, Charlotte, with whom you haven't had a conversation that lasted longer than five minutes in the past five years while you raised a kid and got divorced while she finished college and started graduate school, and who is now a poet who uses words like *pedagogy* and *pentameter* in her e-mails.

Answer: C. Your former best friend, Charlotte. You thought about taking the dog, but it would've cost $100 each way for his flight, and you're too poor for that. You're too poor for anything, which is why you entered every travel sweepstakes you could find this winter when things were slow at Outer Banks Realty. Your divorce was just finalized, and you needed to travel somewhere, anywhere, as long as it meant getting the fuck off of Hatteras Island. You did not win the Kitchens of India Sweepstakes to go to New Delhi or the Rax/Mountain Dew Country Music Songwriter's Competition for a trip to Las Vegas. The Outdoor Network's Monster Fish Contest to go salmon fishing in Alaska was a complete bust, and the obviously blind judges thought your son wasn't cute enough to win the Klassy Kids photo shoot in Des Moines, Iowa.

But you had a good feeling about Dominican Al's Rum and Fine Spirits. You liked his pink-and-green logo and the peppy music on the website, even though you had to turn down the volume so no one at work would realize you weren't working. You answered twenty trivia questions every day for a month to secure a spot in the honeymoon raffle. You were particularly proud of answering the final question correctly, that Spaniards originally sold potatoes as ornamental decorations rather than food. You won. You'd never won anything in your life, so you hadn't considered who would go with you for the Once-in-a-Lifetime Extravaganza. You're just hoping Dominican Al doesn't do a background check and find out you're divorced. Is "C." truly the best choice for a traveling companion? Only time will tell.

~

You step off the tiny airplane at the Punta Cana airport in the Dominican Republic (*República Dominicana*, you think in an imaginary Spanish accent that sounds strangely like Antonio Banderas) and the humidity greets you like a solid wall. You stumble against it, reaching out to grasp handfuls of hot, heavy air. It wraps around you like a cloak, thick and cloying. You squint in the sunlight and walk down the steps of the plane, shielding your eyes and scanning the runway for a tall, slender woman with red-gold hair and freckles to match. All you see is a thatch-roofed, wall-less building where throngs of tourists line up to get their luggage. You join them.

You're already sweating, which is ridiculous since you live on an island and should be used to heat and humidity, but this is different from home. You do a little excitement dance. You're a tourist. All around you Spanish flows like water, supple vowels, elastic *Rs*. *El Aeropuerrrto.* You get your paisley bag and are looking for the bus to the resort when you see a tall, slender woman with cinnamon hair that was once red-gold, hair that swings down her back in a glossy sheet. You wonder how it stays so shiny in this humidity. Your own hair is already fuzzy.

You pounce on Charlotte. She squeals and hugs you back, and you perform a tandem excitement dance. You feel like a little kid again, as if you were seeing Charlotte for the first time after she'd arrived on Hatteras for her annual vacation.

Charlotte brushes her hand across your forehead. "I love the side bangs," she says.

"I wasn't sure if they made my face look lopsided," you say. You and Charlotte walk through the airport. "Is that new luggage?" you ask.

Charlotte says she splurged last year's tax return in the hopes that she'd travel more if she had good luggage. "This is its debut," she says. Charlotte side-hugs you. You squeeze back.

You and Charlotte find the bus and wedge your way on board. It's packed, and you're crammed between Charlotte and a large man wearing a fedora. *Sombrero,* you think, your imaginary *Rs* beautifully rolled. The bus jostles off into the streets of Punta

Cana. You and Charlotte chatter and point out the window, remarking on the orange flamboyan trees, the glimpses of aqua water, the tall palms. You're sweating all over the vinyl seat and should've worn a sports bra because your breasts jolt every time the bus hits a pothole, which is often. You whisper this to Charlotte, but she's staring out the open window, her face sober. You look at her for a moment—the freckles you remembered so well are barely visible—then follow her gaze out the window.

The bus lurches and sways, swerving through throngs of people, past brightly colored, crumbling buildings and skinny, barking dogs; past dirty children crouching on door stoops. Thumping music pumps from store windows. You think the people look happy, calling to one another, elbowing their way down the street. Charlotte says, "The Trujillo regime used the word *parsley* as a shibboleth to murder Haitians in 1937." You don't know what *shibboleth* means, but you like the way it sounds. Shibboleth. You don't want to seem dumb, so you just nod. "The Haitians couldn't say the R in parsley," Charlotte says.

"I'd be screwed if I got shibbolethed," you say. "My Spanish *R*s only sound right in my imagination."

The bus winds its way out of the city, and now you look at fields of sugarcane, roadside stands where flies buzz around shanks of meat hanging in the sun, cows with protruding ribs.

Charlotte turns to you. She looks like she's going to cry, brow puckered, eyes glistening. "Do you see that?"

"I bet that sugarcane is good in mojitos," you say to Charlotte. You're trying to distract her from the sad, skinny cows. You can't wait to have some fun.

"I know I'm sheltered," Charlotte says. "But I've never seen poverty like this."

You tell her you agree. You've never been out of the country, either. And even though you've had to make meals of ramen noodles and hot dogs some nights, at least you don't live in a dirt-floored shack next door to a knobby-kneed cow and a squawking chicken. At least your son's never had to weave bracelets and sell them on the street to tourists. You picture Austin on the side of Highway 12, hawking his wares.

Charlotte says, "I just had no idea. And I hear that Haiti is so much worse." Then she turns and pats your leg. "Sorry, I don't mean to be a downer."

The bus pulls up to a set of tall, wrought-iron gates. They open, and just like that, the world changes. Fountains spray delicate mists of water into the air, pink and orange and white blossoms cavort in landscaped arcs, and a Spanish-tiled building with arched doorways comes into view. The bus stops, and you unstick yourself from the seat, get your bag, and go inside. Ceiling fans whirl, and even though the building is open to the outside, it's cool. You and Charlotte go to the desk.

"Evie Austin," you say to the girl at the counter. She wears a blue polo shirt with a yellow collar. She smiles at you. "I won a contest."

"¿Cómo puedo ayudarte?" she asks. The words trill and roll together. You don't know what she's saying, but it sounds beautiful.

"May we please check in?" you ask. You wait for a second. "It was the Dominican Al's Rum and Fine Spirits honeymoon contest."

"No hablo inglés. ¿Cualquiera de ustedes hablan español?" She half-smiles and her nose crinkles. "Permitamé conseguir alguien que habla inglés."

You look at Charlotte. Charlotte looks at you. You link your arm through Charlotte's. "Mrs. and Mrs. Evie Austin," you say. "Dominican Al's Rum?"

The girl at the desk motions over her coworker, an adorably round-faced man. His nametag says FREDDIE. Freddie speaks English and checks you in. You whisper to him that you and Charlotte aren't really married. He grins. You ask how to make a phone call home to let your family know you arrived, and Freddie says it costs ten dollars a minute. You call anyway and end up spending forty dollars listening to your son talk about Chutes and Ladders. You let him and your mother know you won't be able to phone again. Freddie wraps a yellow bracelet around your wrist, telling you not to take it off. He straps Charlotte in, too. You and Charlotte tap your wrists together like superheroes and follow Freddie to your honeymoon suite.

~

You've gained six pounds by the morning of the second day, or at least that's how it feels. Charlotte says the buffets of food and slushy machines full of piña coladas and daiquiris are stunningly ubiquitous, but all you know is that they're freaking delicious. You and Charlotte spent most of yesterday by the swim-up bar in the pool, testing out as many incarnations of Dominican Al's Rum and Fine Spirits as you could muster. You reminisced about the summer you met and caught up on what your families were doing. You might have gone salsa dancing; you don't really recall. You dimly remember telling Charlotte you were pissed she used the bath towel that was twisted into the shape of a walrus before you could take a picture of it. You're still salty about that, to be honest.

You and Charlotte both wake up with hangovers, skip breakfast, and go straight to the beach. You lie down on yellow lounge chairs under one of the thatch-roof umbrellas that spatter along the sand. You think that from the air, this beach would look like it was dotted with breasts. Tiny aqua waves lap at the shore, and palm trees wave their heads, tossing their fronds like a long-necked woman tossing her hair.

You squint against the brightness and fish around in your bag for your rhinestone-studded sunglasses.

"I like your bling," Charlotte says. Her own sunglasses are green with white polka dots. You got them for her as a birthday present two years ago.

"Thanks," you say. "I like yours, too. Whoever got them for you has excellent taste."

You watch a water-aerobics class. Most of the women are topless. "Let's go do that," you say to Charlotte, reaching around to untie your bikini top.

But Charlotte's digging around in her beach bag. She pulls out a pen and a stack of papers. "I totally blew off yesterday," she says. "I've got to work on this grading."

Charlotte had warned you when she agreed to come that she'd have to bring work, but you pout anyway. You poke out your lower lip and give her sad eyes, but Charlotte's not looking. You sigh and lie back down. You try to take a nap. You're bored. You bounce your foot up and down. "I'm going to get some food," you say.

Charlotte grimaces and circles something on a paper. "Why do they insist on using the letters *U-R* instead of writing out y-o-u-r?"

You traipse down the beach toward the fake lighthouse that's really a bar. It's fat and round with black-and-white horizontal stripes, cleaner than any lighthouse you've ever seen. You order a *hamburguesa* and walk around the resort nibbling on it. Music sways and trills from the buffet by the pool, and you do a salsa step you don't remember learning. You decide to go to the room and grab a book. You walk past the sprawling blue pool, the log with pink orchids, the gazebo with flamingos in front of it. You run into Freddie as you're walking down one of the open corridors lined with a pond and fountain. He asks how you're enjoying your stay, dimples flashing when he smiles. He's not staring at your bikinied rack, but rather at your hips. This unsettles you. You have a nice rack and you're used to men staring at it. You tell him you're having a lovely time and ask how they get the towels in such cute animal shapes. Freddie says the resort gives seminars on making animal towels. His favorite is the swan. He flirts with you, telling you about his apartment, his family, how beautiful his country is. You flirt back.

Freddie skims a finger down the side of your left hip. "Fuerte," he says. "Very strong."

You're a little weirded out, but not because he touched you. You never really think about your hips. "Thanks," you say. "I need to get my book." You scurry down the corridor. The air smells musty.

Charlotte's still grading when you get back to the beach. She's brought over a table and colonized it with stacks of papers weighted down with brain coral. She glances up. "Hey," she says.

You move her bag off your chair and sit down. "The craziest thing happened," you say. You tell her about Freddie's hip fetish.

Charlotte says, "It's a cultural thing."

You tell her you're used to your boobs being the body part that attracts attention. "If I'd gone to high school here, I wouldn't have gotten a reputation as Easy Evie," you say. "No one here cares if you have excessive cleavage."

Charlotte pauses her grading, pen in midair. "It wasn't just your rack. A lot of factors went into your reputation in high school." She goes back to her papers.

You cross your arms. "Enlighten me," you say. "Go on."

But Charlotte just shakes her head, still looking at her papers. "I didn't mean anything."

"I think you did. You meant I was slutty."

Charlotte looks up. She sticks her paper under a piece of coral. "Evie, that was a million years ago," she says. "Besides, people only thought you were bad because they had nothing else to talk about."

You just look at Charlotte, your arms crossed and eyebrows raised.

Charlotte sighs. "Do you want to go swimming?" she asks.

Dominican Al comes to the rescue. You spend a day and a half drinking rum and flirting with Freddie when he comes by the fake lighthouse bar while Charlotte grades papers and writes. Then she agrees to go on a day trip to La Isla Saona. It's a cloudy day, the tiny aqua waves bigger, but still nowhere near the height and power of a Hatteras wave. You and Charlotte board the boat and watch the fake lighthouse recede into the distance. You talk about other boat trips you've taken, how different this is from the ferry to Ocracoke, and Charlotte says boats still remind her of taking her father's ashes out to sea. She says she'll always remember the water changing as the boat rounded the tip of Hatteras Island, the way the Pamlico blended into the Atlantic and the waves roughened.

You land on Saona, which is a fake deserted island. It's a real island, but set up with buffets of food, picnic tables, and hammocks strung between palm trees. You and Charlotte sit beside a man with a white beard who turns out to be a professor of literature. He and Charlotte start talking about books. They talk about authors you've never heard of. *Márquez. Allende. Carpentier.* They keep talking. You finish your paella, your pastelitos, your tostones. By the time you finish your dulce de leche, Charlotte's talking about how uncomfortable the resort makes her feel, how it's as if she's participating in thinly veiled colonialism. "We as the heterogeneous white majority are exploiting the traditions and values of the citizens here just so we can have a nice vacation," she says.

You put down your spoon. "Tourism does good things for the economy, too," you say. "I've seen it firsthand."

Charlotte and the professor of literature exchange looks. "But it doesn't change the fact that wealthy Americans are swooping in, buying all the beachfront property, and making a killing while the local population works for a pittance," Charlotte says.

"It's a pittance they wouldn't otherwise have," you say. "Freddie says he has the nicest apartment of anyone he knows. At least he has a job."

"It's still an imbalance of power that has its roots in colonization," she says.

You stand up. "You mean the way you colonized my island every summer? How come that never made you uncomfortable? How come you think you have the right to exploit the locals there but not here?"

Charlotte stands up, too. The literature professor says he has to go find his wife and that it was nice meeting Charlotte. He scurries off. Charlotte says, "It's not the same thing. We all have the same rights at home, the same history. It's an equal playing field."

You stalk off and look at a pelican sitting on a log. Charlotte follows you. "You're on crack if you think you and I ever had an equal playing field," you say.

Charlotte looks genuinely puzzled, her brow puckering. "What do you mean?"

You sit down in the sand. It's damp. "You had the perfect little family, while I had a mother who fucked Bob the lighthouse mover from Buffalo. You had campfires with your dad playing games of charades and your mom leading sing-alongs in three-part harmony. I had asthma from Aunt Fay's cigarettes and a stoned older brother and a father who was drunk for half my childhood. How is that the same history?"

Charlotte starts to answer, but the crew from the resort is shepherding people back onto the boat. You climb to the upper deck and sit down. Charlotte sits beside you, her spine straight and stiff. The boat takes off, and you watch Saona fade away. The sky is blanketed with gray clouds, the water dark blue and choppy. "At least you've still got two parents," Charlotte says.

"That's not fair," you say. The dead dad card trumps anything you could say about how rough your life is.

"That's my point."

A crew member comes by and says they'll stop the boat above a coral reef if anyone wants to snorkel. Charlotte says she will. You go down and get a mask and fins, too. You'll be damned if Charlotte McConnell sees a coral reef and you don't. The crew member dips your mask in a bucket of chemical-smelling liquid, saying it'll keep it from fogging up. You put the mask on and it makes your eyes water.

The boat stops and piles of tourists jump into the Caribbean. You plunge in and swim hard for a few minutes, pissed. You see a bright yellow fish with a frilly fin and don't show Charlotte. You see pink-and-blue-striped fish, and you keep them to yourself. You kick and swim until you begin to calm down and breathe evenly through the snorkel. You love being underwater, love the sense of otherworldliness, the way everything above the surface disappears. You paddle and splash. You watch Charlotte dive again and again. She talks to a little boy holding a sand dollar and then dives some more.

You decide to look for a sand dollar, too. You dive down, down, down, the water pushing past your face like silk, the thrum of pressure mounting in your ears. You run your hands along the soft sand, feeling for the grittiness of a sand dollar. You dive seven times before you find one, thick and fat and unlike any sand dollar you've ever seen, and take it to the surface.

Now that your head is above water, you look around. You hadn't realized the sky was clouding darker, the water getting choppy. Most of the other tourists are already back on the boat, which looks far away. You hear thunder. You see Charlotte dive.

You wait for her to surface, treading water impatiently. "Get back to the boat," you shout. You start to swim toward her.

"Just one more try. I really want a sand dollar," Charlotte yells back.

"Trust me," you say. You tread water, legs bicycling under the surface. "I know the water."

But Charlotte's diving again. You wait. She dives three more times, and you finally shout, "I'm going now." Charlotte waves her assent. You begin the swim back toward the boat, Charlotte behind you. And just like that, the world changes. Thunder claps and rolls in a guttural Spanish *R*. Rain falls against your snorkeling mask, cold on your head. Waves rise and splash, rise and splash, the current pulling you away from the boat. You're a strong swimmer, a Hatteras islander, after all. You paddle and kick, fighting the water, fighting the storm, fighting it all. You swim solidly even with a fat sand dollar in one hand. You're almost to the boat before you think to look behind you. Charlotte's head is a small, blurry dot in between gray water and gray rain. You call her name. You're mad at her, but you can't let her drown. You turn back and swim toward her, your arms heavy.

"I'm getting tired," Charlotte says. She looks scared, her eyes round.

You grab her wrist and pull, swimming hard, kicking hard. Her weight drags, even though you can tell she's kicking, too, trying to help. Rain splashes and waves thrash. You pull and kick and swim. You lose a fin, break Charlotte's yellow bracelet. You kick each other. You keep your eyes on the boat, its hazy outline your only thought.

You climb up the ladder to the boat, reaching down to grasp Charlotte's hand and pull her on board. It's not until you and Charlotte are huddled under the eave of the boat's roof, wrapped in towels, shivering, that you realize there's still the broken, ragged edge of a fat sand dollar clasped tightly in your hand.

~

The next day, the weather changes. It's like there was never a storm, never even a thought of a storm. Small white clouds puff along the sapphire sky, soft ripples of teal water caressing the sand. The sand, still damp, is the only sign that anything ever went wrong. After you and Charlotte had recovered from the boat trip by sitting in the hot tub, you'd gone back to the room and taken a nap, then dressed up and eaten at a hibachi restaurant. Freddie gave Charlotte a new yellow bracelet. It looked crisp and starched next to your worn one. You and Charlotte didn't fight anymore, didn't talk about anything important. You thought saving Charlotte's life changed things, made her grateful to you, and that the trip would be fun from here on out. You went to a bar and watched soccer, yelling loudly with the rest of the crowd even though neither of you followed the game.

That day, you fall into a routine. Breakfast at the buffet, where Charlotte makes a big show of letting you go ahead of her in line and have the last serving of chorizo, saying she owes you, then head to the beach. Charlotte writes while you read a mystery novel. You convince Charlotte to go swimming topless by reminding her you'd saved her life. "Fine, you were right. I should've gone back earlier," she says. But she unhooks her bikini and bares her perky breasts; you take off your top, and the two of you stride into the sea. You feel brazen, exotic. You glide through the water. When you swirl to the left, your breasts follow. You and Charlotte eat lunch, topless, at the fake lighthouse and then put your bikinis back on and go to the pool. You swim and read, drink and eat. You talk about weather; you talk about food. That night, you and Charlotte and a healthy dose of Dominican Al go to the resort's nightly entertainment, which turns out to be a live game show called "How Well Do You Know Your Mate?" Freddie is the emcee, and he shines a spotlight on you and Charlotte, winking and asking the newlyweds to play. You think Charlotte will have stage fright and not want to, but she turns to you and grins. "Let's do it," she says.

So you both trot up onstage with Freddie, and he makes Charlotte go behind a curtain so he can ask you questions, explaining that she'll come back and answer the same questions and then compare the results. You're left with two brides, both young and tan and nervously smoothing out their sundresses. Freddie seats you all and cues some tacky game show music, then starts firing questions at you and the brides. *What's your partner's favorite season? Vacation spot? Food? What was the name of your partner's first pet? Of the two of you, who drives the worst? How old was your partner when he or she was first kissed? What's the last book your partner read?*

You've got this. *Summer. National Seashore campground at Frisco. Lasagna. Bear Minimum the teddy bear hamster. Definitely Charlotte. Sixteen. Poetry and Pedagogy: The Challenge of the Contemporary.*

Charlotte and the newlywed men are paraded out and shown to seats beside their partners. You nod confidently to Charlotte, and sure enough, when she answers the questions, you're off to a perfect start. You're asked to go backstage, and when you come back you answer that your favorite color is red, comfort food is Bubba's barbeque, flower is a daisy, that Charlotte takes longer to get ready in the morning, your car's four-wheel drive, you'd travel to Brazil if you could go anywhere, and your closet is a disaster. Charlotte's answered them all correctly except for the travel question. "I thought you'd want to go to the Himalayas," she whispers. "You used to want to be a Sherpa."

You whisper back that Sherpas are still pretty sweet, but ever since you watched a documentary about Carnival, you've wanted to go to Brazil. Your streak is broken. You guess that if Charlotte won the lottery she'd buy a house, when she'd rather take time to write and pay off student loans. She thinks you don't want any more children, your dream job is a biologist, your pet peeve is men who don't call back. Charlotte, it turns out, would rather go shoe shopping on an ideal weekend than see an art show, and she thinks you, if stranded on a desert island, could not live without your hair dryer. "Seriously?" you whisper. "There's not even electricity on a desert island."

"It was supposed to be funny," Charlotte says.

"Just because you don't need to blow-dry your hair for it to look good doesn't mean we're all so lucky," you snipe.

Charlotte rolls her eyes.

Freddie sends her backstage and asks you another question. "If your mate could go back in time and do one thing over in their life, what would they do?"

When Charlotte comes back, she does not answer correctly that she would decline to make your brother fall in love with her and then completely fuck him over.

You go offstage, coming back to answer the question "What is your biggest regret?" You say not finishing college, but Charlotte has expanded that into *dropping out of school to marry a controlling asshole*. You get partial credit.

You guess Charlotte will say her biggest fault is her pretentious use of big words and inability to have fun, while she answers a lack of assertiveness. Charlotte guesses the thing you'd change about yourself is your aimlessness and absence of ambition; you think you'd like to control your temper.

You lose the game. Freddie hands you each a bird of paradise flower as a consolation prize. Charlotte carefully places hers in a discarded water bottle and sets it on the nightstand, adjusting the flower so it looks toward her side of the bed. You throw yours at a flamingo.

〰

You stand in the lobby by a life-size metal sculpture of a bull, your bag packed. You and Charlotte have sufficiently ignored each other until checkout, and your flight leaves before hers. You stand there looking at the bull's flared nostrils, debating whether you should go back to the room and tell her goodbye *or* go back to the room and tell her goodbye, have a nice life, and fuck you very much. You're planning what to say when your stomach rumbles. Something isn't right. Your stomach rolls and growls again, a heaving pack of Spanish *R*s in your gut. Something is very wrong. You leave your bag and run as fast as you can back to the room, banging on the door until Charlotte opens it. You hurl yourself into the bathroom just as the explosive diarrhea begins.

"I think I have Montezuma's revenge," you say.

"I told you not to drink the water," Charlotte says.

You tell her you've been careful.

"That'd be a first," she mutters.

You throw open the bathroom door, but Charlotte's out of your line of sight. You can't get off the toilet, but you strain your neck around the door to see her reflection in the floor-length mirror. She's slung herself across the king-sized bed, arms crossed.

Your stomach cramps some more. "Why'd you even come if all you were going to do was work and tell me what an idiot I am?"

You crane your neck and see Charlotte sit up on the bed. "You *knew* I had to work. And you're not an idiot."

"I know," you say. "But you seem to think I am." Then you remember you are an idiot—you've left your bag in the lobby. Shit.

"I don't think that," Charlotte says. "Besides, you think I'm a pretentious snob."

You lean your head back against the wall. "Only a little." You sigh. "Would you go get my bag from the lobby and buy me some Imodium?"

Charlotte doesn't answer, just strides out the door. You sit on the toilet in your room at the spectacular all-inclusive Hacienda Paradisus Resort and Spa and have diarrhea for three solid hours. Charlotte's a snob, but she's a snob who brings you Imodium and a bottle of water; she's a snob who calls the airline and reschedules your flight. She brings you a crossword puzzle, a Sudoku game, and your mystery novel, and when those are exhausted, a copy of *Poetry and Pedagogy: The Challenge of the Contemporary.* You never realized how complicated teaching poetry was. You give Charlotte your credit card so she can call your mom to reschedule your pick-up time in Norfolk. When the four doses of Imodium have finally kicked in, you crawl out of the bathroom and curl in a ball on the bed. Charlotte sits beside you.

"I have to go soon, or I'll miss my flight," she says. She scratches your back.

"Do you think we should break up?" you ask dully.

"Why would we break up?" Charlotte asks.

"Because we're not the same people anymore." You bury your face in a pillow. It smells musty.

"It wouldn't be any fun if we stayed the same," she says.

You're not so sure. You miss the Charlotte you knew at the National Seashore campground; the Charlotte who watched Disney movies and ate Pop Rocks instead of discussing the commercialization of fairy tales in a heterogeneous society and the evils of high-fructose corn syrup. And you miss the Evie who turned wild cartwheels in strangers' front yards and imagined the campground into the plains of the Serengeti instead of answering phones at Outer Banks Realty all day; the fearless Evie who would've made out with Freddie instead of just letting him touch her hip. You miss them both.

In the end, do you:

A.) Stay best friends with Charlotte.
B.) Break up and go back to the imaginary friends of your childhood, Mulan and Jack the Golden Retriever, who sit and patiently wait, unchanged, for the Evie of the National Seashore campground to come and play.
C.) Realize you're different people, but when you're together, parts of you will always be those little girls on the beach eating sno-cones and making sand mermaids; parts of you will always be the same, no matter how much you change, and you'll always bring each other Imodium and pretend to be superheroes and swim topless and not let one another drown. And maybe that's okay; maybe that's enough; maybe that's all you can expect.

The answer is C. The answer is always C.

Five

The Big Book of Funeral Etiquette

— 2015 —

I stand over the body of my Aunt Fay, the body of the one constant presence in my life, and she looks nothing like herself. Aunt Fay never, not once in her life, wore thick pancake makeup with circles of rouge on her cheeks like a china doll. She slept flat-out on her stomach, not primly on her back, hands crossed neatly one over the other. Her hair was wild and windblown, sticking out in frantic tufts, not perfectly positioned in stiff, starched curls.

Prologue: Be advised that dead bodies may not fully resemble the people they once were.

Her death was expected; what wasn't expected was the wrenching pain in my chest when she went, the absolute, utter finality of the separation cleaving into me. I didn't expect to scream and hold on to her like a toddler when they took her body away. I didn't expect to recede inside myself. I didn't expect that at all. And so, I stand over her body, the dutiful niece, and begin to feel like I'm in a bubble, in the midst of a gaping emptiness.

My hair is pulled back neatly from my face, and I'm wearing a crisp black suit. I wonder, idly, if I can recycle the suit when I finally get my real estate license, or if that's just plain bad taste. Do real estate agents even wear crisp black suits?

"Mom," Austin, says, tugging at my hand. Austin is now six years old. I don't know if that's old enough to understand death, to understand that Aunt Fay's not just sleeping, that the creepy, pallid body in the polished box is not her. Austin wiggles his tie and tugs my hand again. "I think Walter just bit Grandpa."

I look away from Aunt Fay, across the dimly lit room crowded with people. It's warm, and the air smells of thirty different perfumes. Over by the guest book, Charlotte, who has flown in from Boston where she teaches poetry, tugs at the tiny, black, snarling mass that is Walter, Aunt Fay's beloved but ill-mannered dog, Yorkshire terrorist extraordinaire. Walter lunges at my dad and barks, sharp and high-pitched, and the hum of conversation stops. Walter latches on to Dad's pant leg and growls, shaking his head. For a moment the air is filled with nothing but sad, sad organ music. *On a hill far away stood an old rugged cross.* Dad kicks his leg until Walter lets go. Then Walter's posture changes, softens. People start talking again. My dad gives Walter a dirty look and goes across the room to hug someone. Walter glances up at Charlotte and wags his stub of a tail, as if he's expecting praise, then sits down and licks his chops. He never did get along with my dad.

I send Austin to my mom and walk over to Charlotte, my heels sinking into the too-soft carpet. I've never read a book of funeral etiquette, and I certainly don't know if there is one that covers proper behavior when the deceased's beloved Yorkie, specially instructed by pre-arranged agreement with the deceased to be present during funeral home calling hours, starts attacking mourners. For a second I picture a funereal massacre—scattered limbs, Walter's muzzle wet with blood, people stumbling over one another in search of missing body parts. Aunt Fay loved that stupid dog. When her diagnosis changed to stage four, she made me promise to bring Walter to say goodbye. She thought it would help ease his adjustment.

Charlotte kneels down to Walter, but he dodges before she can pick him up. "I think he's still out for blood," Charlotte says. She stands up. Walter takes his leash in his mouth and barks around it.

I wave my brother, Nate, over to Charlotte's corner. "Take Walter outside," I say to Nate.

Nate looks suspicious, or maybe that's just the look he gets on his face whenever Charlotte's around. Six years ago, Nate and Charlotte had a *thing*. Now what they have is a *history*. "You're the only one he doesn't bite," Nate says. I want to say "nuh-uh," to stamp my foot and insist that Nate do it. Being around my brother brings out the latent brat in me. He's right, though. Walter's a nutbag, but I can make him behave.

I take Walter's leash from Charlotte and walk outside. It's a windy spring Hatteras day, chilly and sharp, with a blueberry sky. Aunt Fay would've laughed at me if I'd said something like "blueberry sky" to her. She had no patience for fanciful language. "This is this and that is that, no two ways about it, kid." Walter huffs and looks up at me, expectant, as if he wants me to say, "Go for a walk?" He paws at the ground like a bull. "Not now," I tell him. I sit down on a stair step. My crisp black suit will get dirty, and my hair's already been messed up by the wind, but I don't care. The parking lot's full of cars and trucks, rusty old island vehicles with North Carolina plates and fishing poles sticking out everywhere. Charlotte's rental, a BMW with Virginia plates, looks slick and shiny and out of place. I want to take off my heels and run away. I want this fissure in my chest to stop pounding. The emptiness I first felt looking at Aunt Fay spills out again and seals around me, a sticky Grief Bubble. I don't know how I'm supposed to do this all day. I don't know what to do.

A car pulls up, and Royce Burrus steps out of it, polished loafers, adorable Buddha belly, and all. *Chapter 1: Funeral Visitors. For the bereaved, the arrival of one's former illicit lover may add an extra layer of complication to the grieving process. Try to maintain composure when coming face-to-face with the bodily incarnation of a past bad decision.* I've been thinking of Royce lately, mainly because whenever I drive up and down Highway 12, which, between going to work, picking up Austin, driving Aunt Fay to doctor appointments, and going to Nags Head for real estate classes, I do about eight thousand times a day, I see big signs that say, "Make Royce your choice." Royce is running for county commissioner. Two years ago, I made Royce my choice, and that obviously didn't end too well for me. Royce walks across the parking lot to me. He's carrying a bright yellow bouquet of flowers and the largest card I've ever seen. If he'd mailed that thing it would've needed ten stamps, I swear.

Royce sits down on the step. I rein in Walter's leash and put him on the other side of me. "Evie, honey," Royce says. He always did like to call me that. "I'm just really sorry. I know you and Fay were close." Royce pats my back. The ghost of our affair hovers between us, the ghost of all those times he touched me.

"Thank you," I say. Then I think that "thank you" sounds off. It's not like he just complimented my hair. "Thanks for coming." Only I don't know if I mean it. I stand up, and Royce and Walter and I go inside. Royce holds the door for me, and the warm, sicky-sweet air turns my stomach. Royce balances the giant bouquet and signs the guest book. I don't get the whole guest book thing. What do we do with it after? Charlotte catches my eye, and I mouth *Royce* and jerk my head toward him. She grimaces and comes over to steer Royce to a group of older men in fishing waders. Yes. Waders.

Chapter 2: Suitable vs. Unseemly. Even if the deceased did indeed enjoy both fishing and the company of fishermen, waders are never appropriate funeral attire. Walter and I walk over to Austin and Nate, who're both wearing dark suits and blue ties. They sit side by side, and I'm struck by how much they look alike. Maybe it's the outfits, or the way Austin adjusts his posture to match Nate's. I sit beside them, resisting the urge to pull Austin onto my lap. I pick up Walter instead.

"How's my kid?" I ask. I'm worried. Austin's never lost someone.

"Hungry," he says.

Nate ruffles Austin's hair. If I did that, Austin would have a fit. "We'll break for lunch soon and head back to Grandpa and Grandma's," Nate says.

Austin uncrosses his arms. He squints up at Nate. "Uncle Nate, can I ride with you?"

Nate doesn't answer because we're hit by a wave of condolence-givers, Nate's friends. He stands and shakes hands. A grasp and one solid pump. A back slap given. A back slap returned. I busy myself with Walter so I don't have to hug any of them. This batch of Nate's friends is the sort to carry soda bottles as portable spittoons.

"Honey, I want to give you this card." A hand on my shoulder. Kind eyes. Royce. "You open it when you get home." Royce massages my shoulder, his hand staying a fraction longer than comforting requires. *Hitting on mourners at calling hours is a faux pas; anything beyond the standard three-second pat is unsuitable and should be avoided.*

Nate slaps the last of his friends on the back and turns, extending his hand to Royce. "Thank you for coming," he says. Nate knows that Royce and I used to work together. He probably knows we had an affair, but he doesn't know it from me, and he doesn't show it, thank God. I know I should run interference between Nate and Royce. Chat about real estate. Talk about the time Fay brought my lunch to work and we all ate crabby patties outside. But all I can do is run my fingers through Walter's soft fur. That's all I can do for now.

~~~

Chapter 3: Providing Food for Mourners. When bringing a casserole to the bereaved, it is fundamentally inappropriate to include special directions related to the food container. I toss the pink 3 × 5 card bearing the words DO NOT BREAK along with Emma Midgett's address in the trash and sit down beside my mom at the inn's long dining table. Dad's set out casseroles, and Nate and Charlotte have stopped being awkward long enough to eat. *Do not take it personally if the bereaved discovers that the triple chocolate cake, the macaroni and cheese, or the green bean almandine all taste, in his or her distress, like lumps of wet cardboard.* Across from me, Austin stuffs lasagna in his mouth like he hasn't eaten in six days. I have a moment of panic—what if I was so trapped in the Grief Bubble that I forgot to feed my son breakfast? Then I remember fixing his Golden Grahams. Not too much sugar, but still tasty.

"Remember the time Fay bought that awful bus?" Mom asks. She's drinking her third mimosa, probably left over from the inn's Sunday brunch. *It is unwise to mix alcohol and grief when another set of calling hours awaits.*

"Only Fay," Charlotte says, putting her hand on my mom's just for a second. *See Chapter 2 regarding Appropriate vs. Inappropriate Touching.* Charlotte's good at this sort of thing. She always has been. If Aunt Fay were here, she would've defended her bus. "That bus was damned practical," she'd have said, slamming her fist on the table. "How many hours of enjoyment did your kids get out of riding that thing up and down the beach?" She'd have been pissed that we made the executive decision not to take Walter to afternoon calling hours. Out the window, the Pamlico Sound is all whitecaps and sunshine, and I just want to be outside. Or maybe it's that I want to be outside of myself. I don't know how to escape
~~~

the Grief Bubble, how to think about anything else. I feel trapped inside it. If I were a mime, I could place my palms against its sticky, waxy surface. I contemplate this as one of the funeral book illustrations: *Mourner Trapped in Grief Bubble*. Then I remember Royce's card. I excuse myself and go out onto the deck and sit in a swing.

Chapter 4: Cards and Gifts. If you haven't been in a relationship with the mourner for the past two years, it is generally considered unsuitable to bestow a large, glittery card bearing dueling proclamations of sympathy and abiding love. Proclamations of love may substantially impair the mourner's fragile mindset, causing her heart to pound with something other than grief. I tuck Royce's card back in its giant envelope and tap it against my teeth.

The door opens, and Charlotte comes out. She sits beside me, and her skirt blows around her knees in the breeze. "How is it we're not nineteen anymore?" Charlotte asks. She tucks her skirt under her legs.

"How is it we're not nine?" Charlotte puts her arms around me, and I breathe in her vanilla-Charlotte scent. "I think I might have sex with Royce tonight," I say.

"Royce, the sequel?" Charlotte asks. She sits back in the swing but keeps one arm around me.

I play with a strand of my hair. It's getting long. "I can't stand this."

Charlotte's quiet for a while, but not in a judgy way. We rock on the swing.

"If I sleep with anyone else, it'll up my numbers," I say.

"That's not really fair to Royce," Charlotte says.

I don't know how to explain it to her, how to say I need something, anything, to make me feel like me again. "Could you please not be so mature right now?"

Charlotte pinches my arm. I poke her in the side.

"You'll regret it if you hurt him," Charlotte says. "Trust me."

Nate pokes his head out the door. He's wind-tousled in two seconds.

Charlotte stands. "Round two?"

Nate nods. "Time to go sit in that room and cry some more," he says.

~

Chapter 5: Small Talk. Fitting topics of conversation to engage with mourners include, but are not limited to, the weather, fishing, games involving balls, the fullness of the life of the deceased, and happy memories. Unseemly topics include, but are not limited to, the last will and testament of the deceased, queries about putting down the deceased's bad dog, statements regarding the lovely appearance of the corpse, statements regarding how the deceased is in a better place now, and queries regarding the suffering of the deceased. She had lung cancer. Of course she fucking suffered. I just want to smack Loretta Gray in the head. How is that okay to ask? For the first time in Round 2 of calling hours, I cry. And this stupid black suit only has fake pockets—nowhere to stash Kleenex. I find a box of scratchy, generic funeral home tissues, but it's empty. I wipe at my eyes with my arm, smearing foundation on my suit sleeve.

Loretta Gray has me cornered. She's one of those women who wears pastel polyester suits. "What did you tell little Austin when she died?" she asks.

For the bereaved: try to retain your composure when faced with idiotic questions. "I told him Aunt Fay's body got sick and stopped working, and that she died," I say. "That's what all the websites said to do."

Loretta *tsk tsk tsks* and tips her head to the side. "Poor fellow. Do you think he understands?" She gazes over to where Austin sits on the carpet playing with race cars.

Let me just go over and ask him, Loretta: *"Son, do you understand that Aunt Fay is dead and that we'll never, ever see her again? Do you get that, kid? That she's dead, dead, dead? That she's never coming back?"*

"I don't know," I say.

Loretta purses her lips. She shakes her index finger at me. "What you need to do," she says, "is pick him up and show him the body. Make him hold her hand for ten whole seconds so he doesn't think she's just sleeping."

"Why would I do that?"

"You don't want him to think he'll go to sleep and not wake up, too." Loretta looks at me, eyes wide like I'm the dumbest parent in the world. "He needs to understand that Fay has gone to rest in the loving arms of Jesus."

"Right," I say.

She pats my arm. "The Lord never gives us more than we can handle," she says. "Keep your chin up." And she walks off to assault my mom.

I go to the coat closet at the front of the funeral home and root around in my purse for my cell phone. I'm going to call Royce and get out of here. I rustle and shuffle, and I can't find it. I can't find a goddamned thing. I pull out a brush, a tampon, a race car. I throw them all on the floor, and then I throw the purse down. "Very dramatic, kid," Aunt Fay says in my head. I kneel down beside my pile of crap and lean back on my heels. I feel empty, turned inside out. I shove everything back in my purse and sit down on the floor.

"Okay?" It's Nate. He's got his thumbs hooked in his pant pockets. Nate holds out a tissue. I take it, and he folds himself down beside me. We sit in the coat closet. When I look up, I see that Nate's face is red. I lean my head against my brother's shoulder and I don't say a word.

〰

The preacher, Dr. John, thinks it sounds extra holy to overenunciate the word *Lord* so it sounds like *Loo-ard*. I shift in the folding wooden chair and glance around. Dad leans forward, elbows on his knees like he's engrossed in a particularly tight football game. Austin gazes at the ceiling, his mouth moving in an absent *ba ba ba* motion like he's singing under his breath. Charlotte's hair falls over her face as she rubs her forehead. Nate slouches. And my mother heaves with full-on, shoulder-shaking, snot-running sobs.

Chapter 6: Weeping. While funeral rituals provide a socially sanctioned space for public displays of grief, mourners are obligated to weep in a manner that is not melodramatic. The Melodramatic Weeper may feel the need to be in the spotlight of the comforting action. I put my arm around my mom. She weeps into my shoulder. My black suit, which hasn't felt crisp in the last five hours, gets wet.

"'For to me, to live is Christ, and to die is gain,'" Dr. John quotes. I know he's quoting the Bible because he uses his special Bible-quoting voice, soft and precise. He stands in front of Aunt Fay's coffin in his preacher robe. "When I speak this verse, I can't help but think of Fay." Dr. John talks about the Apostle Paul and how he was in prison, chained to a Roman soldier as his guard. I wonder where they were chained. Ankles? Wrists? "Like Paul, Fay lived the last years of her life a prisoner to a body filled with sickness, yet she never complained." Dr. John has an earnest face. It looks like he truly believes this.

Mom wails. I glance at Nate. His mouth twitches. Aunt Fay was many things, but uncomplaining was not one of them. "Get that godforsaken blood pressure cuff off me," were her second-to-last words.

Dr. John lays his hand on his Bible. "Fay, like Paul, seemed to rejoice in her affliction."

This time Nate snorts. He turns it into a cough and covers his mouth with his hand. He squints. Mom shakes her head back and forth into my shoulder, sobbing in little *heh heh* puffs.

Dr. John talks about how the death of a Christian is a wonderful thing. "The problem is, we don't believe that," he says. Dr. John leans forward on his pulpit. "We think of death as some hideous monster come to cut off all our joys."

Austin sits up straight. He stops singing under his breath. Mom's weeping dials down a notch until she's just resting on my shoulder, breathing through her mouth.

"We live in a cruel world, and so when death comes to take us to the Loo-ard where we shall have perfect health, wouldn't you say that death is a friend?"

Austin's mouth moves again, but this time it's because he's chewing on his lip. He grabs my arm, then climbs onto my lap. I can't move.

Dr. John goes on, telling us how wonderful death is, and how God will give us all his beloved sleep one day. I wonder how I'm supposed to get any beloved sleep tonight when all I can think about is putting Aunt Fay's body under six feet of sandy earth tomorrow morning. The Aunt Fay in my head turns to me and winks. "You know what the opposite of death is, right?" she asks. "Death with his hooded black cape and sensual bony fingers?"

"Life?" I ask her back.

"Hah!" She pokes me in the ribs. "Sex."

I wonder if she's right. I wonder if being naked will disintegrate my Grief Bubble, or if an orgasm will. I think of Royce.

Chapter 7: Leave-taking. The funeral guest should keep in mind that mourners have just put in a full eight-hour day of public grieving. Lingering is inappropriate. Take heed when the funeral home stops playing sad, sad organ music. This is generally a leave-taking cue.

I wander around the funeral home waiting for the last stragglers to leave so I can go home and get Austin settled. I extract my phone and send Royce a message. "I've missed your Buddha belly." He sends one back. "The lucky Buddha's missed you." I write, "Thanks for the flowers. I used to only get them after sex." Royce responds, "I could bring you roses in the morning." I put my phone away and go over to the coffin. The Grief Bubble, which had gotten less sticky as I messaged Royce, circles back over me like a veil. I stand over Aunt Fay and wonder who selected the pink satin coffin liner. At least they didn't put her in a pink satin dress. Aunt Fay wears a nice pantsuit that is neither pastel nor polyester. I study her body. The caved-in jaw from cancer surgery. The gnarled hands. The short legs beneath the half-open coffin. She looks doughy, too soft, which is strange since she's probably in rigor mortis. I think again that this isn't my aunt. This isn't Fay.

"She was my family," my dad says, putting his arm around me. "She raised me." He pats my hair like I'm a kid, and it feels nice.

"I know," I say. "I know, Daddy."

Mom comes over and stands beside Dad. They hold hands. Charlotte and Austin walk up. Nate ushers the last straggler out, then takes the empty spot in front of the coffin. He picks up Austin. "Do you want to say goodbye to Aunt Fay?" Nate asks.

Austin doesn't answer. I don't think he wants to. I don't think any of us do.

~

Walter leaves three turds on my bedroom floor. "Thanks for that," I tell him. I flush the turds, wash my hands, and go back to my room. I've just gotten Austin to bed, and I hope the flushing doesn't wake him. Walter's asleep on my pillow. He lifts his head, then settles it back down on his front paws. I'm trying to decide what to wear to Royce's. Black panties—morbid or sexy? Charlotte knocks and sticks her head in my bedroom.

"I brought you some tea," she says. She sets a mug on my dresser.

I sit down on the bed and pet Walter. He opens one eye, then goes back to sleep. Charlotte sits beside me. "Can you listen for Austin tonight?" I ask. This shouldn't be too much of an imposition since Charlotte's sleeping in Austin's top bunk bed.

"Of course," she says.

I lift Walter, pillow and all, to the other side of me in case he wakes up and decides to get cranky. "I think I might have inherited a dog," I say.

"Maybe you could get on that dog whispering show." Charlotte stretches her legs out on the bed and leans back on her elbows. She opens her mouth to say something else, but just then a scream from Austin's room rips through the air. We both jump up and run in.

Austin sits with a rigid spine and screams and screams. It sounds like he's just been stabbed. "Baby, what's wrong?" I climb in bed and pull him into my arms. Charlotte sits and massages Austin's feet.

Austin stops screaming. He sobs instead. I don't know which is worse. "It's Skeletor," he says. His body shakes.

"How do you know about Skeletor?" I don't let him watch that junk.

"Dad and I watched it." Austin's face is red. His lip trembles and his hair sticks on his forehead in sweaty strips. He clutches his Batman comforter in both hands. "Skeletor's coming to take me. He said so."

I smooth his hair, kiss the top of his head. I rub his back and straighten his blue pajamas.

"Skeletor's just pretend," Charlotte says. "He's a drawing. He can't hurt you."

Austin shakes his head. "He's coming."

I rock him back and forth, back and forth. His small body collapses my Grief Bubble, and I'm flooded with the sharp pain of today until my chest literally hurts. Or maybe the Grief Bubble doesn't collapse. Maybe my Grief Bubble and Austin's merge.

Epilogue: It is the bereaved's ultimate challenge and responsibility to comfort fellow bereaved persons. Especially if the fellow bereave-ee is your son.

"Don't let him take me," Austin says. He clings to my waist.

I hold Austin's face in my hands. "No one's taking you. I promise." I hug him and cry into his hair. His body shakes against mine; mine shakes against his. We fit tightly together, me and this small body that was once part of my own.

Charlotte and I stay with Austin until everyone calms down. We put him in pajamas with Transformers on them since Transformers can beat up Skeletor any day of the week. We sing songs and read an old picture book that's too easy and drink warm milk, and finally Austin falls asleep. I smooth his hair one last time, and Charlotte and I slip back to my room.

I close the door softly and lean against it. "Thanks for helping," I say. I'm shaken. Austin hasn't freaked out like that since Stephen left. My phone's blinking on the dresser, and I sit down on the bed to read a message from Royce. "This little Buddha's ready to be enlightened."

Charlotte picks up the now-cold mug of tea. "That's why I'm here," she says. Then she sets the tea down. "If you need to go see Royce, I can take care of Austin if he wakes up. I'll be right there in his room."

Part of me wants to run out the door. To be anywhere but here, thinking of anything but death and burials and Skeletor. I stand up. "How does anyone ever figure this out?" I ask.

Charlotte shakes her head. "There are no rules," she says.

I nod. I put on my slippers and turn off my phone, then pick up my mug of tea. We pass Austin's room and walk down the hall to the microwave in the kitchen.

Six

Bad Dog

Walter is a bad dog. A Yorkshire terrorist. He: Pees on the floor. Runs away. Bites.

But he doesn't just *bite*. Walter: Waits until you're half-asleep, snuggled up with him on the sofa, watching Travel Channel, then turns and snaps at the remote.

He: Sneaks out of the house, running up and down the side of Highway 12 during ferry traffic so you have to chase after him with a butterfly net.

Walter pees on: New carpet; new shoes; real hardwood floors. He pees on the sofa you use to watch the Travel Channel; the bed; the ottoman your parents imported from Turkey. He pees on other dogs.

A brief story: You take Walter to the Petco in Manteo. He prances up and down the aisles like a prince, shiny black fur swinging. Then he shits on the floor. You're pricing Greenies and don't notice the small pile of excrement until an unsuspecting fellow shopper carrying a bejeweled shih tzu slips on it and falls to the floor. Walter, taking this as a territory challenge, lifts his leg and pees on the puzzled shih tzu, soaking its leopard-print tutu. The owner, whose J.Crew cotton-polyester jacket is now smeared with Walter-shit, is understandably offended. At this juncture, Walter curls his lip in an Elvis snarl and attacks her leather Coach handbag, which has been discarded during the poop-induced fall. He snarls and shakes and shreds and scatters. When management asks you to leave in lieu of calling the police, you and Walter politely comply, but before exiting the sliding-glass door, Walter succeeds in appropriating a catnip-filled toy shaped like a radish. You're too humiliated to return it to the store; besides, Walter growls fiendishly when you approach said radish. You decide to let him keep it. The radish does not leave his mouth for two days.

Seven

Postpartum

— 2009 —

You know you've lost it when you start writing letters to Dear Abby.

Dear Abby,
I look at my baby's squalling red face and I want to run away. What do I do?

Horrible in Hatteras

When the paper boy thunks the *Outer Banks Sentinel* against your door at seven in the morning, you go straight to the comics and TV listings, hoping Dear Abby will enlighten you. But she never responds. You have a birth certificate that says you're a mother. *Austin Charles Oden.* You look on the back for instructions, but there are none. You feel like the only horrible, unprepared mother in the universe. Your son cries, and for a minute, you pretend you don't hear him, scanning the page for your horoscope. You're pretty sure you've lost it when you read it and think, legitimately think, that the stars have aligned so you can leave:

Family members could be upset over frustrating events in their lives, and these moods could spill over to you. Today it would be best to leave them alone to work things out in their own way.

For the four days you've been home from the hospital, your mother has left your dad to handle things at the inn and come over to your little white house on Elizabeth Lane every morning. She arrives just after the *Sentinel,* and just after Stephen leaves to work in his father's hardware store. She comes grudgingly, but she comes. She's so efficient it's terrifying, changing your baby's diaper with quick, clean motions, handing him to you to feed. You press the baby to your breast, but he won't eat. You poke your nipple into his mouth. He won't take it. He's never taken it without a fight. He cries, his tiny face bunching and crinkling, pink mouth open in a howl that pierces your eardrums. He wails. He screams. He flails his tiny fists. Your incompetence burbles in your chest. You think he senses this and doesn't want to drink incompetent breast milk. Your mom sighs and takes the baby from you, jiggling him up and down.

You don't know what you're doing. You've never even had a dog.

~

You live on this scrawny, unprotected spit of sand between the Atlantic Ocean and the Pamlico Sound. A flat, sandy, cactus-ridden prison. You'd just escaped to college on the mainland, just fallen in love with biology and Shakespeare and Stephen Oden, who was even cuter in college than he was in high school, when you got pregnant. *Most Likely to Get Knocked Up and Move Back Home* might as well have been written in your high school yearbook. You lived up to your reputation. *Easy Evie.* You say it out loud as you stare down at your sleeping son, at his placid face and twitching baby fingers. His tiny nose encrusted with a fine, translucent rim of dried snot; his patchy, alien-scaled scalp.

What to Expect When You're Expecting never said that motherhood would feel like punishment, like solitary confinement. Your best friend, Charlotte, stayed with you while you were pregnant, but now she's gone back to college. All your friends have. Even the tourists are gone.

The baby wakes up, his eyes blinking and unfocused. He twists, writhes, and then the screaming starts. You pick him up. You spend your day bouncing, shushing, swinging, swaying—an odd combination of busyness and tedium. You try to sleep when he sleeps, like all the books say, but every time you close your eyes you see tiny limbs, umbilical stumps, and wide-open, screaming mouths. Empty. Waiting to be fed.

Stephen comes home, and it's as if you're looking at his high cheekbones and pale eyes through a sheer, gray film. He's covered, blurred, like everything else. When he takes over swaying duty, you hunker in the upstairs office and call Charlotte.

"I don't recognize myself," you tell her.

"I think I'm going to join a sorority," she says.

You write another letter to Dear Abby:

Dear Abby,

I made a mistake. I'm not ready to be a mother. I want things to go back to the way they were. What do I do?

Regretful in Hatteras

You don't mean to, but that night you fall asleep with the baby in bed beside you. You wake up sweating, trapped between your husband and your son, unable to move, your body pinned between theirs. You weasel yourself out of the covers and put the baby in his crib, sliding your arms out from beneath his body with glacial slowness, then go to the bathroom and stare at yourself in the mirror. You weren't kidding when you told Charlotte you didn't recognize yourself. Puffy-faced, dark-circled, greasy-haired. The baby starts to cry, but you sit down to pee anyway. You're still bleeding.

~~~

Dear Abby counsels a lazy husband, an excessive shopper, and a woman concerned with sneezing etiquette. By the time your mother stops by, you know you're required to say *bless you* out of politeness, even if you don't believe that her soul, in sneezing, leaves her body and is in danger of getting devil-snatched.

Your mom rocks the baby's cradle, a gift from her and your dad. It's yellow with a pattern of dancing elephants. Some of the elephants carry red umbrellas. *Has he eaten?*

You stare out the window at a lone puff of cloud in the glorious September sky. Even through the haze that films everything, you can tell the sky is stunning, the sort of blue-sky day you used to love to be outside in. The whiteness of the little cloud feathers out against the cerulean in a cotton ball puff, its edges ragged. You don't know why, but the cloud makes you teary-eyed. You blame it on sleep deprivation. "All he does is scream," you say. You've tried to feed him three times this morning, and he won't eat.

As if to back you up, the baby stirs and begins to cry, softly and staccato at first, then with loud, sustained, throaty wails. Your mom rocks and hushes, pats and sways. "Try to feed him," she says, handing you the baby.

You unsnap your nursing bra and poke your nipple into his mouth. He roots around and latches on, sucking and smacking. His nose is running, and snot gets on your breast.

"He was hungry," your mom says. She leans over and pats the baby's head, her long, dark hair falling into her face like a curtain.

Again, you feel like an idiot. "How did you ever learn to do this?"

"I didn't have a choice," she says. She looks up and pushes her hair behind her ear. "I didn't have my mother to teach me."
~~~

You've never really thought about the fact that your mom's mom died before your brother and you were born. You think about it now. You feed the baby and cry.

~

That afternoon you realize that, ironically, you've run out of milk. Cow milk. Milk for cereal and coffee and macaroni and cheese. You put on your maternity jeans and load your breasts into a jacket and head out the door to the Burrus Red and White grocery. You start the car and back halfway down the driveway before realizing you forgot the baby. You sit and think about driving away. Up Highway 12, across the Bonner Bridge, past Nags Head and Kitty Hawk and Kill Devil Hills to someplace on the mainland, someplace where your breasts could shrink to their normal size; where you could chop off your hair and change your name and start over. You could be a diner waitress, the mysterious woman with a shrouded past who ends up falling in love with the handsome town mechanic.

Dear Abby,

What's the most inconspicuous fake name one can adopt?

Ready to Run in NC

You turn off the car and haul yourself and your breasts back inside. The baby is quiet, and you're stabbed with the thought that he died while you were in the driveway. You run to the nursery, but he's just sleeping, tiny chest rising and falling inside his blue onesie. You think about what you'll need to take with you and pack it in a bag. Change of clothes in case he poops himself. Diaper. Wipes. Diaper cream. Changing pad. Powder. Ointment for circumcised baby weenie. Plastic bag to put dirty diaper in. Pacifier. Blanket. Rattle, even though he doesn't care about toys yet. You heft the bag onto your shoulder and head to the car. This time you only make it to the porch before you remember the baby's still inside.

You stand over his bassinet, debating whether moving him to his car seat will wake him up. You wonder if you should wrap him in a blanket or put a coat on him, or maybe his onesie is warm enough? You call your mom, but the girl at the desk of your parents' inn says your mom is outside tending to an issue with the pool heater, and can you call back later? You hang up, take a deep breath, and scoop up your son. His wobbly head still scares you. You tuck him in your arm and pick up the diaper bag. You make it to the living room before he starts screaming.

He screams all the way to the store. You park at the Red and White, go to the back door of the car, unlatch him from his seat, pick him up, and balance his wobbly head while you walk back around to the front seat. You sit down and begin the process of extricating your breast. The diaper bag with the blanket is in the back, and you don't want to get up and balance the baby again to go after it, so you lift your shirt with nothing to cover you. Your elbow bumps the steering wheel and honks the horn as you try to latch him. He cries and writhes. His tiny toes and fingers flex. He won't nurse.

Dear Abby,

My baby won't stop crying. This car is like an echo chamber, and I think I'm going to lose my mind. Is it rude to take a crying baby into a grocery store if insanity is the only other option?

Had It in Hatteras

You heft yourself, your breasts, and your baby out of the car and pace back and forth in the sandy parking lot. You remember that you haven't put your breast away. A woman walks by and stares.

Patricia Ballance, the mother of your high school boyfriend. You look down and try to latch him while standing, but he won't nurse.

You pull down your shirt, grab the diaper bag, and walk up the brick steps and into the store. The baby howls. A red-faced banshee. People stare. You try to put him in the cart but realize you need his car seat to do that. The diaper bag slides off your shoulder and smacks the baby on the head. He cries louder. It's then that you notice the smell of fresh shit. You panic. You can't even remember why you came here in the first place. You know the Red and White doesn't have a public restroom. You don't know what to do.

"Please stop crying," you whisper to the baby. For a second you contemplate placing the baby in the meat cooler to change his diaper. You could tuck him in next to the bacon and pot roast. At least he wouldn't roll away. You try to take a deep breath, but everything smells like shit. This is not calming. Your options are: The floor. The check-out counter conveyor belt. A bench on the front porch. The car.

You decide on the car and are turning around to run back outside when you spot your Aunt Fay. You've never been so happy to see her grizzled gray head in your life. "I need help," you say. The baby's shrieking climbs another decibel.

"You certainly do." Aunt Fay looks at you, then at the baby. "Is it supposed to smell like that?" Aunt Fay has never had children.

She puts her arm around your shoulder, plugs her ear with her other hand, and walks you outside. Together, you put the baby on a bench, take off his onesie and diaper, wipe and powder him, ointment his baby weenie, and put his clothes back on. You're covered in shit. You clean your hands with wet wipes, but there's poop on your shirt. The wipes just smear the shirt shit around.

You suddenly feel like you can't keep your eyes open.

Then the baby turns his head and pukes.

~~~

That evening you wait by the door for Stephen to come home from work. You hand him the baby before he can put down his keys and you run upstairs. You call Charlotte.

"I can't do this," you tell her.

Charlotte says she knows motherhood must be a difficult adjustment and to give it time. She tells you about the cute professor who teaches her world history class, how he puts his hand in his pocket when writing on the chalkboard and how all the girls ogle his butt.

You try to tell Charlotte about the Red and White poop debacle, but instead you hear yourself say, "I don't think I love my baby."

Silence on the other end of the line. "Of course you do, Evie. How could you not?"

You fiddle with the tassel from Stephen's graduation mortarboard that hangs from the edge of the desk. Your breasts hurt. You're so tired. "I guess so."

Of course you love your son. How could you not?

You hang up and mess around on the internet. You fall asleep halfway through a game of solitaire.

Stephen wakes you up by banging into the office. The neatness of his polo shirt and khaki pants infuriates you. He doesn't have a speck of shit or vomit or snot on him. "I've been working all day," Stephen says. He holds the baby out to you. "Why don't we have any milk?"

~~~

A month passes. Four weeks. Thirty sleepless nights. You feed that baby every two hours, every single two hours of every single day, no matter what. Your nipples crack and bleed. The baby sucks the life out of you. You become intimately acquainted with late-night TV. Lifetime, Television for Women, from midnight to two; a dead hour where you have a choice between *Miami Vice* and *Matlock*—you usually choose *Miami Vice*; *The Golden Girls* from three to five; infomercials after that. You know you've lost it when you order a Snuggie, swayed by the inclusion of a free dog Snuggie and $5.95 shipping. You don't even have a dog but think you could give it to Aunt Fay's Yorkie, Walter.

Your mom comes; your mom leaves. The baby eats; the baby cries. The baby poops. A lot. Stephen goes to work; Stephen comes home. You stop making dinner for him. You stop making dinner for yourself. One night, Stephen looks at you like he doesn't even know who you are. "What the fuck, Evie" is all he says. "What the fuck?" You can't afford a babysitter. You can't afford shit. You call Charlotte whenever you can pawn the baby off on someone else. She doesn't always answer, but when she does, she talks for long stretches, telling you about her classes and her dates and her sorority. Kappa Delta Delta. Their mascot is a panda. If you get her a gift for her birthday, she'd like it to be azure blue and Bordeaux, the sorority's signature colors, or sapphires, the signature jewel. You stop calling. She rarely calls you. Dear Abby still hasn't answered your letters.

Dear Abby,
Fuck you.

Irritated on Elizabeth Lane

The *Outer Banks Sentinel* piles up on your kitchen table, unread. You've even given up on your horoscope. Your mom comes in with three *Sentinels* in her hand and dumps them on the counter. She picks up the baby, holds him in one arm, and scrubs the stove with the other.

"He's eaten," you tell her. Your voice echoes dully in your head.

Your mom stops scrubbing. She puts down the sponge and stands beside your chair. "Have you eaten?" she asks. She jiggles the baby up and down.

You poke up some crumbs with your finger. You honestly don't remember. You muster the energy to shrug.

Your mom puts the baby in his cradle and sits at the table beside you. She pats your hand. "It gets easier," she says.

Your mom is not the sort to pat your hand and comfort you. You look into your mom's dark eyes, which are usually snappish but are soft now. "I'm not ready for this," you say.

Your mom pats you once more, then sits up straight and takes her hand away. Her eyes turn sharp again. "Do you think I was ready for your brother? For you? For your brother and you and your father working such long hours I don't think he even crapped at home anymore? But did losing it help? Did an affair help?"

"Your affair certainly didn't help me," you say.

Your mom tightens her mouth. She crosses her arms and stares at you, her gaze pinpricking your face. "What helped was remembering that no one forced me to marry your father, to get pregnant with one kid and then another. What helped was hard work—teaching you to ride a bike and talking Nate through his first breakup and buying that old inn and scraping paint and spackling walls and polishing floors until my knuckles bled. What helped was going to bed so tired I couldn't sleep but thankful as hell that this was my choice."

You push your hair behind your ears and cross your arms, a mirror of your mother. "The way it was your choice to leave for four months before you decided you didn't like living in Buffalo?" you ask.

"Evelyn, nobody likes living in Buffalo." Your mom grasps your face in her hands. She shakes your cheeks, like she's trying to wake you up. "This was your choice."

You turn your head away. You don't want to admit that she's right, that it was your choice. Ten months ago, you and Stephen had stood on a cold, windswept beach and had The Conversation about What to Do. You'd only been dating for three months, but you'd known each other your whole lives.

"Let's not do this," you'd said. "I can't do this."

Stephen took your hand. "It's your choice," he said.

You plodded through the sand, the wind in your hair like a wild thing. Waves crashed, spitting up gray-white spume that caught on the shore and blew like the tumbleweed you'd seen on TV. You and Stephen walked without speaking, all the way back to the boardwalk with no words, just the promise between you that together, you wouldn't do this.

That's when you saw them, tiny footprints in the sand. You stopped, frozen. Stephen stopped, too, and looked down. You closed your eyes and listened to the ocean. You imagined all the swells crashing on all the beaches of all the world; imagined slipping beneath the undertow, down to where the sunlight doesn't reach. You imagined the thick atmosphere rolling over your body and sucking you down. You imagined the baby inside you, your blood shushing around it like waves, the waters of your body shaking up and settling like snow in a glass globe.

"Let's get married," you said.

"Okay," said Stephen.

And you did.

It was your choice.

In the kitchen of your little white house on Elizabeth Lane, your mother takes her hands off your face. She goes back to scrubbing the stove. Your cheeks feel warm, like her hands are still there. Ghost imprints of your mother's flesh.

~

After your mother leaves, you pick up a *Sentinel* from the pile. Your horoscope from last Monday says: *You will feel more alive over the coming twelve months, as if you have woken up after a long sleep, refreshed and renewed and ready to take on the world. Don't waste that feeling. Use it to make real your dream.*

You toss the paper aside. Horoscopes are crap. You haven't slept in a month. *Make real your dream.* The *Sentinel* falls open to Dear Abby's comforting black-and-white smile.

Dear Abby, the letter reads. It's not one of yours, but you read anyway.

> *My coworker microwaves fish and fish byproducts, which, as you can imagine, makes the office smell dreadful. She also uses all of the coffee creamers. How do I deal with this person without making the work environment even more uncomfortable?*
>
> *Fishy Situation in Newark, NJ*

You think if you were Dear Abby, you'd tell Fishy Situation to leave some raw shrimp in her coworker's bottom left drawer to see how she liked dealing with that shit, but Dear Abby is apparently more mature than you. She writes:

> *Dear Fishy,*
>
> *You can choose your friends, you can choose your enemies, but you can't choose your coworkers. Sometimes the workplace calls for being graceful in ungraceful situations. In this case, buy some air freshener (consider a plug-in so the whole office can*

enjoy) and creamer and call it a day. If that doesn't work, speak to the HR department about the situation. But unless there are rules against fish in the microwave, there may be little they can do. Try to make the best out of your fishy situation.

You put down the column and smudge the newspaper ink off your fingers. The October sunlight filters through your kitchen window, streaking the walls golden. Your stove is clean and your kitchen smells like coffee, the only sound the low thrum of the refrigerator.

You try to imagine what Dear Abby would've said if she'd answered your letters.

Dear Evie,

Buck up and stop bitching. You're not the only person in the world to have a kid at nineteen.

Or maybe,

Dear Evie,

Things could be worse; at least your kitchen doesn't smell like fish byproducts.

Or possibly,

Listen kid, if you really want out, do it now. It's shit or get off the pot time.

You check on the baby. For once, he's asleep. You study his face. You check your hand for newspaper ink, then touch his cheek with your pinky finger. The baby twitches his head like he's trying to get rid of a fly. He opens his mouth then closes it. You look out the window; the sky is a pale, pearly blue. When the baby wakes up, you feed and burp and change him and decide to take him to the beach.

It takes an hour to get ready, you forget to pack baby wipes, and the baby screams all the way down the bumpy access ramp, but you finally park and get out and set up an umbrella and towel. You wrestle the baby and the car seat out and lay them in the shade. Then you sit down. The baby's still crying, shallow rasps of annoyance, thrashing his head side to side. "Hush," you say to him. "Listen to the waves." He clenches and unclenches his fists, grabbing baby handfuls of air. You jiggle his car seat back and forth until he quiets down. The breeze is soft and salty on your face, warm with a slight, autumn-cool edge. "Look," you whisper to him. "Those are sea gulls. Don't feed them or they'll never leave you alone." The baby turns his head toward you and yawns. "I'm tired, too, you little turd."

You rock the car seat back and forth, creating a shallow ditch in the sand, until he falls asleep. You lie down, and, keeping your hand on the car seat, fall asleep, too. You wake up to the baby's angry howl and jump to your feet without thinking, terrified the tide has come in. But the beach still stretches out in tan undulation, glassy waves lapping in the distance. The baby shrieks again and flails, and you look down to see the green iridescence of a biting fly on his arm. You swat it away. "Shit," you say to the baby. You unstrap him from the car seat and pick him up. His head wobbles less than it did a month ago. "I'm sorry. Those flies really hurt." You rub the spot on his arm. He cries and cries.

You pat his back and pace back and forth, whispering, "Shush, shush, shush." You match your whispers to the rhythm of the waves, *shush*ing as the water splashes on the shore. You walk and shush until the baby's cries begin to calm. You walk some more. The baby whimpers, sighs, then jerks his body away from yours, his arms pressed against your chest. He crinkles his mouth, but he doesn't cry. He stares. He looks at you with his big eyes, which are not blue anymore, but brown, like your mother's, like yours. He stares. A rush of breeze courses over you both, and you hold his head and look back at him.

You stand there on the beach in the breeze, you and your baby, looking at each other for a long time. The sun shines and the waves *shush* and you and your baby gaze. He opens his mouth in a round "o" and raises his downy eyebrows; he turns his head and blinks and gurgles something that sounds like *gerblah*. You carry him to the towel, sit down, and rest him on your lap. The two of you settle into the sand, facing each other. Still looking.

Eight

Women My Brother Has Loved

— 2017 —

The first one's easy—Nancy Drew. When he was thirteen and I was eight, Nate would pay me a quarter to check Nancy Drew books out of the library and bring them to him. It was my first business enterprise. I'd skulk around the aisles, pretending to be a spy in dark glasses and a trench coat. Sometimes I'd wear my yellow rain jacket and my sunglasses with the lenses shaped like daisies. In the beginning, I'd properly sign Nancy out, but then that got boring. I got bold. I'd grab Nancy, *The Hidden Staircase,* say, off the shelf, my fingers slick against her hard yellow cover. I'd tuck her in my waistband, dash out of the library, and ride my bike home as if I were being chased. Then, breathless and sweating, I'd knock three times on Nate's door—two quick taps and one long—to make the drop.

Nate would poke out his head.

"The eagle has landed," I'd say, sticking Nancy through the crack in the door.

Nate never had to rummage for quarters; they always smacked directly into my palm at the transfer of a book. Then his head would disappear, the door closing with a *click.*

It never occurred to me to save my quarters, so I'd use them to buy jawbreakers and gossip with the checkout girl at the Rod &

Gun. "I don't know what he sees in her," I'd say, shaking my head the way I'd seen my mom shake hers when talking with her friends.

I'd only read one Nancy book, *The Runaway Bride*. In it, Nancy went to Japan to solve a mystery. She was always changing her clothes, and at one point she dressed up like a geisha. I didn't know what "titian-haired" meant—I assumed it had something to do with breasts—and I only had a dim knowledge of geishas. All in all, Nancy annoyed the shit out of me. She was just so charming, so intelligent, so wealthy, and, above all, so very, very *good*.

After a while, I started having nightmares about the Hatteras Village librarians, especially Edna Owens with her stiff, gray curls and red-lined lips. I dreamed she chased me through the streets of Tokyo, running in quick, jerky steps on geisha shoes. But the nightmares were worth it for the thrill I got when absconding with a Nancy book. Never mind Nate. I was in love.

One day, I put on my raincoat and daisy sunglasses and knocked on Nate's door. Two short taps and a long one. Nate opened the door, his eyes narrowed. He hadn't yet finished *The Password to Larkspur Lane*, so he wasn't due for a new exchange.

"I deserve a raise," I said.

Nate stuck his head out, looked down both sides of the hallway, and then motioned me into his room. He sat at his desk chair, gangly arms slung across the faux oak of his desk. "State your case," Nate said.

I squinted. "The sum I acquire for keeping your secret is paltry," I said. I'd just learned the word *paltry* and was dying to try it out. It's what made me think of asking for a raise.

"You go to the library every other day, anyway," Nate said. "A quarter is plenty." He leaned back in his chair.

"You're supposed to be reading the Hardy Boys," I said. "Boys don't read Nancy Drew. Everyone knows that." I took off my daisy sunglasses and stared at Nate. I had him, and he knew it.

"Fifty cents," he said. "And not one penny more."

I accepted the deal, but every so often I'd extort Nate again. He'd refuse, I'd threaten, and in the end, Nate would hike my pay. I made it up to two dollars per Nancy delivery before Nate balked. Drastic measures had to be taken.

I waited until Mom set down the fried chicken and Dad said grace, then I speared a forkful of green beans and asked Nate if he'd read anything interesting lately.

Nate took a savage bite out of his chicken leg. "Just some stupid thing with a dragon," he said.

"How very *mysterious,*" I said. I cut a dainty piece of chicken breast. "Nothing else?"

Nate put down his fork. "Shut up."

"Hey now," Dad said. "There's no call for that."

I rolled my eyes and sighed. "Nate's just grouchy because he's in love."

"I said shut up," Nate said.

"With an imaginary woman." I salted my green beans.

Nate stood up, his leg jostling the table, and my iced tea sloshed onto my napkin. Mom gave him the stink-eye. "Sit down and finish your dinner," she said.

Nate sat. He glared at me.

"Her name is Nancy Drew," I said. "She has tits for hair. That's why he likes her so much."

Dad's eyes widened. Mom turned her head to look at Nate.

"That's not true," Nate said. "She's not—that's not why—so what if I like her?" He stopped and took a drink of tea. "And that's not true about her hair. It means redhead, you moron."

I sighed. "I wouldn't be calling the one person responsible for your happiness with Nancy a moron, if I were you."

Dad twitched his eyebrows up and down. "I'd like to hear more about this Nancy," he said. "She sounds like quite a catch."

Mom tried to summon her stern face, but her mouth flicked up at the corners. "Nate and Nancy does have a nice ring to it."

"Oh, I don't know if he's ready to be thinking about rings yet," Dad said. "Give the boy time. Although, that hair does sound pretty singular."

Nate looked at me then, his eyes deep and pained, his shoulders rounding in a slump. He stared down at his plate, tapping his fingers on the table. My stomach twisted; I didn't finish my dinner, not even the strawberry shortcake for dessert. I just kept seeing Nate's eyes. I just kept seeing how, for the first time, love laid him bare.

~

I know how to talk to my eight-year-old son about sex. Penis, vagina, whatnot. The mechanics are easy, and I have a book with little cartoon illustrations and everything. That conversation went fine. What I haven't figured out is how to talk with him about love. He's the same age I was when I had my first crush, and I wish someone had prepared me for it. How do I warn him about the rush, the geyser of endorphins that happens when *that* person walks into a room? How do I explain the way someone takes up occupancy in your mind, colors your entire world?

Austin and I stand outside Conner's grocery in Buxton waiting for Nate to finish buying a fishing lure. It's August, and the parking lot is frenetic with cars and trucks with license plates from Quebec, Ohio, Virginia, everywhere. Barefoot tourists and residents dodge around fishing poles sticking out of racks on the fronts of trucks, hopping quickly on the hot pavement.

Austin wipes his brow. "Sure is a hot one," he says. He squints.

I try to stifle my smile. He looks and sounds so much like my brother. I know it's not an accident, the way Austin mimics Nate. I know it's because Nate's more of a father figure than his actual father ever will be. I'm about to agree with Austin about the heat when I see Rick Garcia trotting across Highway 12. I just sold him the motel across from Conner's, and he's moving in today. Dr. Garcia used to be my English professor, and during the motel sale, we've become friends, though I still can't call him *Rick*. I wave, and he comes over to me and Austin.

"Have you seen a little girl?" Dr. Garcia asks. He holds his arm out, mid-chest. "About this tall? Brown hair in little, you know—" He makes pigtails with his hands on the sides of his head. "Thingies."

"Pigtails?" Austin offers.

Dr. Garcia snaps his fingers. "Yes. Pigtails."

I remember that his daughter was coming down today after having been with Dr. Garcia's brother in Chicago. "Fiona?" I ask.

Dr. Garcia runs a hand through his hair. "She's not handling the move well. She freaked out earlier, and I thought she went out back, but she's not there."

I touch Dr. Garcia's shoulder, briefly. His t-shirt's heavy with humidity. "We'll help you search," I say. "I'm sure she's around here somewhere."

Austin squares his shoulders. "Mom, I'm going to go look for her in the store."

I pat Austin on the head, but he shifts away and stands tall. "Sounds good," I say. "Why don't you cover the right side and Dr. Garcia and I'll check the left."

Austin walks into Conner's and turns down the aisle of lawn chairs and over-the-counter medication. Dr. Garcia and I go past the checkout lanes and wind our way to the ice cream section. Dr. Garcia takes quick strides, and I pace my gait to his. The only tenseness in the air between us is his worry for Fiona; otherwise it's neutral, not charged like when I walk with someone whose bones I want to jump. "She can't have gone far," I say. We walk past the bologna and turkey lunch meat, jostle a woman in a hot pink muumuu, cruise past the diapers and then the potato chips.

Nate runs into us as Dr. Garcia and I walk by the deli counter. My brother looks dissonant against the fluorescent grocery store indoors; his rumpled hair and tan skin and bare feet belong outside. "Austin's looking for you," he says to me. Nate motions over his shoulder, and we follow him past the canned vegetables and into the Coke aisle. There, sitting on a green plastic pallet, are Austin and a pigtailed little girl. Dr. Garcia rushes to Fiona, hugs and scolds her, and she starts to cry. But what makes my chest twist is the look on Austin's face, the softness and wonder in his eyes, the wide-open admiration as he follows Dr. Garcia instead of Nate to the door, then darts to Fiona's side.

His eagerness to stand beside her reminds me of the way Stephen used to wait for me after class in college, jumping out to grab my books like I was some schoolgirl from the 1950s, a delicate damsel just waiting for a big strong man. I don't want Austin to grow up to be the kind of guy who hurts women.

I should, I know, be more worried about him getting hurt, about seeing his endorphin geyser tamped down by a woman who doesn't feel the rush. But somehow, my own hurts are still so fresh. Somehow, all I can imagine is Fiona, ten, fifteen years from now, her face mottled from a different kind of crying.

~

When a female lobster wants to have sex, she pees, her urine a cloudy stream mingling with the salty waters of the ocean, to attract a dude lobster's attention. It works. The dude lobster arrives, clicking his dude lobster claws together in anticipation. *Click click clack.*

He whisks her into his lair, and she molts her hard outer shell, setting her bare lady lobster parts out for the taking. They get it on. Maybe it's good for the lady lobster. Maybe it isn't. Maybe the dude lobster romances her, makes her feel special. Maybe he doesn't.

And then, the lady lobster, naked, vulnerable, pink and bare without her armor, is forced to stay in the lobster lair until her shell regenerates. She can't hunt; she can't even go outside for a breath of fresh air. Maybe she likes the dude lobster's decorating style. Maybe she doesn't. Maybe his retro '70s shag carpet was charming at first but soon grew old. No matter her current opinion, she's stuck there, dependent on the dude lobster to bring her food, dependent on the dude lobster to protect her from the briny menaces of the deep. Dependent on the dude lobster for everything.

Because the dude lobster always keeps his armor on. Always.

~

Charlotte McConnell. She's the second woman my brother loved. Sure, there were girls in high school that Nate dated, one who crushed his ego by dumping him at his first school dance. There were girls in college, even one he brought home for an entire spring break. But he didn't love her. Nothing lit up inside Nate when he was around those girls. His eyes weren't sad and resigned when they broke up, his shoulders slumped toward his dinner plate. He didn't love any of them, not like Charlotte McConnell. He loves her still, I think. I love her still, of course.

How do I describe Charlotte, or at least the version of Charlotte that Nate loved? Think sea siren, all long hair and sad songs. But no, that's not right. Think delicate lady lobster, pink and bare. But that's not right, either. She wasn't purposely alluring in her fragility. She didn't mean to molt in front of Nate. I know that now. Think sad, pretty girl—smart as hell, funny as hell—lost, lost, lost. He wanted to take care of her, bring food back to the lair, kick the ass of any attacking octopi.

All she wanted to do was regenerate.

But I'm getting too abstract. It happened like this: Charlotte and I were nineteen. I'd just gotten pregnant, and her father had just died. It was a time period of large-scale fucked-up-ness. Charlotte ran away from home, basically. She said she couldn't stand to be near her mom and brother without her dad there. She withdrew from college and stayed at my parents' inn, where she worked for part of a year while I grew a baby. Nate had finished school, moved back to Hatteras, was trying to figure out what to do with his life, and there she was. Charlotte McConnell. Broken and raw and beautiful, standing there on our pier with her cinnamon hair blowing around her face.

I suspected something was brewing between them the day I got sick with some placenta craziness and Nate and Charlotte took me to the hospital. I wondered when Nate touched Charlotte's elbow in the waiting room, when Charlotte didn't pull away. But I was busy being sick, so I convinced myself I'd made it up. A few weeks later, when I was better and definitively back in the business of growing a baby, whether I liked it or not, Nate and Charlotte and I went to the Sandbar and Grille for dinner. It was one of those howlingly frigid Hatteras winter days, with the kind of wind that felt like it'd blow your skin off. We stomped inside and sat at the bar even though the restaurant was empty. Charlotte sat between us.

She twirled a piece of her hair around her finger. "I wonder what the soup is?" she asked.

Nate stretched across her and plucked a menu out from behind the bar. He placed it in front of Charlotte, flipped it over, ran his finger to the soup of the day. "Potato," he said.

"How Midwestern," I said. I didn't mean anything by it; it's just that soups around here usually involve some sort of fishy or clammy business. But Charlotte's from Ohio, and I guess mentioning the Midwest made her think of home. Anyway, something shifted in her body, a combination of stiffness and softening at the same time. The air around her changed. Her grief was so new at that point, surfacing unpredictably like a gushing freshwater stream in a salty pool. Nate didn't quite get it, though. He kept pointing to things on the menu that he'd tried, dishes he thought Charlotte would like.

She smiled at him, but it was the pasted-on kind. "How's the halibut?"

"You should try it," Nate said. "You know, just for the *halibut*." He nudged Charlotte in the ribs.

I rolled my eyes.

Charlotte laughed, but then it shifted into a little squeak. She lifted her hand to her mouth. "I'm sorry," she said. Her shoulders shook. "I'm sorry. I hate breaking down in public."

I turned to put my arm around her and tell her that everything was okay. I had a story ready about the time I peed my pants in the Red and White grocery when I was five, which was infinitely more embarrassing than crying in public. But when I reached out, I saw Nate's hand on Charlotte's shoulder, his fingers peeking out from under her hair. Charlotte was still, indrawn. She looked like a painting. She leaned into him then, closed her eyes, and took a breath as if she was absorbing something through Nate's skin. Then she shifted away, stood up, and went to the bathroom.

I asked her about it later. "So, you and Nate?"

Charlotte blushed in the way I imagined Nancy Drew would, a delicate pink flush blossoming across her cheekbones. "I don't know," she said. She shook her head and played with her fingers in her lap. She looked at me, her eyes clear for a moment, and then the stream of grief surfaced. "It's just that he's so solid."

I remembered that later, after Charlotte and Nate had had a *thing* for months, but then Charlotte fell in love with a research scientist living on the island and Nate found out. It was one of those tangled scandals that you'd read about in *Us Weekly* if they'd been movie stars and not just regular people. On the moonless evening when Nate first found out, he knocked on the door of my little white house on Elizabeth Lane.

"Did you know?" he asked.

I was uber-pregnant at that point, so I motioned Nate inside and waddled after him to the living room. We sat down. "I guessed," I said.

Nate nodded, slowly. "I really love her."

I patted his back. "I'm sorry."

My brother leaned his head back on my sofa, and we sat there, quiet, the air around him thick like tar.

The next day, I brought Nate a latte on my lunch hour to cheer him up, but he was brisk and quick-moving, tossing supplies onto his boat, jotting down reservations in a notebook. "It's fine," he said, when I asked him about Charlotte. "It's fine. It just wasn't meant to be."

Because Nate was solid. His armor had only slipped, gotten

cockeyed. Or maybe it was that he'd forgotten for a moment that he had any armor at all. That he didn't have to wait to harden back up.

~

A few days after we meet Fiona, Austin and Nate stand in the frothy water of the Atlantic, casting their lines into the sea. I'm sitting in the shallows just behind and to the right of them, drowsy, cool water rushing up and over my bare legs and then back again, the sun warm on my shoulders. Nate's line arcs into the water, barely visible, a silver fissure in the air. He squares his shoulders, settles his feet in the sand, and waits. Austin mimics him, casting, settling, standing. They look at each other and nod. The water *shushes* and I close my eyes.

"Fiona said she's never been fishing," Austin says to Nate.

"That so?" Nate asks. "Maybe we can show her the ropes sometime."

"What ropes?" Austin asks. I open my eyes and see that he's squinting seriously at Nate.

Nate jiggles his pole around. I imagine a school of tiny fish darting around for his bait. "It's a figure of speech," Nate says.

Austin nods. He and Nate stand quietly for a while. I release my body back onto my elbows and dig my fingers into the thick, wet sand.

Nate reels in his line. He looks at the naked hook, then walks to the truck, coming back with a plastic container of bait. He punctures a piece of chum and casts again.

For a while it's just waves and sunshine and the *caw* of seagulls. The sun sinks past my skin, its deepening warmth throbbing into my bones, my marrow.

"Only boys like fishing. Right, Uncle Nate?"

Nate shrugs one shoulder. "Your Aunt Fay was the best fisherman I ever knew."

"Why isn't it fisher*woman*?" Austin asks.

I've always wondered that, too. Fisherman. Postman. Mankind. Where's the credit for the ladies?

Nate shakes his head. "I suppose it should be. But people just say *fisherman*."

Austin tugs on his fishing pole. "I felt something." He reels in, but his hook pops out of the water empty.

"Must've got away," Nate says.

Austin cranks in the rest of his line and reaches for the container of bait. He hands it to Nate. Austin's been fishing since he could stand up, but he's never baited his own hook. He used to have nightmares about mutant ballyhoo, their fiercely pointed noses stalking his sleep. Nate weighs the container in his hand. He sets it down, reels in his line, and places his pole on the sand. Then he picks up the bait and holds it out to Austin.

"It's time you learned how to do this, man," he says.

Austin's mouth tightens into a straight line. "I don't want to," he says. "You do it, Uncle Nate."

Nate puts his hand on Austin's shoulder. "I know you don't like this part," he says. "But sometime you might want to fish without me."

Austin considers this. I shift to get a better look at them. I'm curious what Austin will do. He reaches into the container and pulls out a small silver fish. Nate hands him his hook and Austin stands there, ballyhoo in one hand, hook in the other. His thinking crease appears between his eyebrows, and I wish, as I often do, that I could get into his head. Finally, Austin takes a breath and punctures the fish onto his hook. "Like that?" he asks Nate.

Nate pats his back. "Just like that."

Austin looks up at Nate, his face serious in a way I've never seen it before. "If Fiona wants to come fishing with us, I can show her how to do it."

They both pick up their poles and cast out, arcing their lines into the sea.

~

There's weather underwater. Even at sixty feet, there's sunlight, choppiness, wind. Even at a hundred feet, you can tell when it's raining, when the skies change and the sun disappears. There's weather everywhere. Even in a lobster lair, where a bare lady lobster impatiently taps her claws against a rock, waiting, waiting, waiting for her dude lobster to return.

She's hungry. She's lonely. She's trapped, and she's starting to have second thoughts.

It had taken time to catch his eye. She'd waltzed past his lair, throwing her pheromones about. Because *this* lobster was *the* lobster. The dominant male. The dude. The one all the ladies want. She'd come calling at his door every day until he let her in. She'd surveyed the shag carpeting, the lava lamps, the glittery disco ball, and thought the dude was all she'd dreamed of. So she moved in. She shed her shell, and that's when everything changed.

The lady lobster wanted the sex, too, don't get me wrong. But somewhere in her heart, she also thought the dude would be super into her lady lobster brains. She realizes now, as she watches the weather from the window, that she got duped by pheromones. All that work to get the dominant dude and it turns out he's just a dude. And maybe there are other dudes out there who're better. How will she know if she stays in this shag-carpeted lair her whole life? What if there's a dude lobster out there in, oh, say, Australia, who doesn't listen to the Bee Gees and insist on feeding her fondue? How will she ever know what Australian dude lobsters are like if she stays with this one lobster dude?

She won't.

And so she has to go. But before she can leave she has to sit there, waiting, watching the weather swirl outside the window of the lair.

Waiting for her hardness to regenerate.

~

Monet Fairchild. She's the third woman my brother loved. Monet sported a tattoo of an angelfish on the left side of her neck. She was from Boulder, Colorado, but she said she'd always dreamt of the ocean, so she moved to Avon to work at Seaside Spa, where she created delicate sworls of custom nail color and taught hot yoga. This was just after Stephen left, and at first I blamed my dislike of her on that fact, thinking it was just my general state of gloom mixed with rage. Because Nate pulsated with happiness. He and Monet flounced about the island, arms entwined around waists, eyes gooey and gazing. My dad, who I could usually count on for a solid dose of snark involving Nate's girlfriends, doted on Monet like she was a baby pygmy goat. He even took a hot yoga class. My mom refused to do the dishes because she'd ruin her tie-dyed manicure, and Austin, who had just turned five at the time, began a sudden obsession with angelfish.

It was Austin, in the end, who undid things. He came a touch unmoored when Stephen moved to Raleigh, throwing screaming, red-faced tantrums each time I left for work, flailing bonelessly on whatever floor he happened to be near at the moment. He'd kick, he'd bite, he'd throw his *Monsters, Inc.,* folding chair across the room like a hopped-up movie star trashing a hotel. He'd refuse to eat, smearing SpaghettiOs on the carpet or spitting mushy, mangled mouthfuls of peanut butter and jelly on the table. It was during one of these pleasant Sunday lunches that Austin began to unravel Nate and Monet.

Monet, who was, of course, vegan, reached for the platter of tofu fries my dad had made just for her. The sunlight glinted off her highlights, and she stretched across the table to pat my dad's arm. "Thank you so much for preparing lunch, Mr. Austin," she said.

My dad, no lie, blushed. "Anytime, my dear," he said.

Nate rubbed a small circle at the base of Monet's spine with one hand and ate tofu fries with the other. "These aren't half bad," he said.

I wanted to make a joke about them being all bad, but Nate's relaxed posture and easy grin stopped me.

"Can I try one, Uncle Nate?" Austin asked. He'd been on company behavior for a while now because Monet was there, quietly mincing his hot dog into tiny bites and pushing the pink scraps around his plate. He hadn't thrown a fit in three hours, and I was getting nervous.

Nate began to hand a fry to Austin, but Monet whispered, "I don't think he'll like it." Nate put the fry back on his plate. "These really aren't your style, buddy," he said.

"Let him try it," I said. Anything Austin expressed interest in eating those days was fine with me.

Nate raised an eyebrow. "Do you think that's a good idea?"

"It's not like he wants to eat an entire pan of brownies," I said.

"Can I have a brownie?" Austin asked.

"No," I said.

Monet swallowed a bite of salad and said, "Of course, if you think it's okay. It's just that Nate mentioned Austin's been a bit—" Monet lowered her voice. "*Delicate* lately. I didn't want something new to—" Again with the lowering. "*Upset* him."

"He doesn't have consumption," I said. I couldn't help it. Austin had been acting like a shit, but he certainly wasn't delicate. I handed him a tofu fry.

Nate moved his hand to Monet's upper back. "Monet just wants us to keep having a nice lunch," he said.

Austin, his face a cherubic sheen of placidity, nodded and finished his tofu fry. "It's nice," he said. "It's a nice lunch." He smiled up at Monet.

"I'm glad you like it," Monet said.

We finished the meal without further incident, but when Nate and Monet said they had to go if they wanted to catch the last matinee, Austin started his meltdown.

"Don't go," he whined, tugging on Monet's hand with enough force that her shoulder dipped.

Nate looked at me with a conspiratorial grin, as if we were bonding over how very much Austin loved Monet.

Monet knelt down. "Sweetie, we're going to go see a movie. Do you like movies?"

Austin shook his head. *No no no no no.* "Don't go." His volume hiked a decibel.

"Uncle Nate and I will see you again soon," she said. She adjusted her purse on her shoulder and stood up, glancing at Nate. "Ready?" she asked him.

Austin buckled his legs beneath himself, his knees hitting the floor with a dull thud. He screamed, a throaty wail of anguish, and I moved to scrape him off the floor. Austin thrashed and flailed. The kid only weighed thirty-three pounds, but it felt like dragging a sodden, lifeless body out of the surf. He dug his heels into the carpet, leaving roughed-up streaks as I pulled him away from the door. "Sorry," I yelled over his hollering. "Have fun."

Austin regained his bones and stood straight up, his hands in small tight fists at his sides, red splotches on his cheeks. Maybe he did have consumption. "You can go, but don't take Uncle Nate," he said.

Nate tousled Austin's hair, and Austin collapsed to the floor again, yelling and banging. "I'll come see you tonight," Nate said. "It's nothing to freak out over, man."

"You won't either come back," Austin shouted into the carpet. "You won't either."

I splintered then, and Nate looked at me and I could tell he did, too. He sat on the floor and pulled Austin into his lap. "Don't you even think about biting me," he said.

Monet bent over and touched Nate's shoulder. "We're going to be late, hon."

Austin stopped pounding the floor, and his screaming changed to sobs, fat tears sliding down his face, snot smearing Nate's cargo shorts.

Nate rocked him back and forth, back and forth.

They didn't break up right then, of course. It took Monet a few months to get over Nate's pheromones, and it took Nate a few months to realize that one of the reasons Monet taught hot yoga was to have the sweaty, slippery attention of a crowded room three times a week. Monet started having dreams about Tuscany. She got a tattoo of a sunflower on her right calf and broke up with Nate and left not long after that.

~

I drive Austin up to Duck one rainy Saturday afternoon a week or so after he baited his first hook. We rarely venture this far north, but my dad wants some specialty cake-decorating tool that he could only find at a kitchen shop in Duck, and I need a strapless bra from the Belk in Kill Devil Hills, so I'd volunteered for the errand. We head up the narrow road, slamming headfirst into a traffic jam.

Cars clot the beach highway, a slow-moving snake of tourists trying to get to their posh rentals. We finally pull off at the Waterfront Shops; a fine drizzle mists down, and I throw the car into park. Austin and I'd stopped at Coquina Beach to swim earlier in the day since there's no public beach access this far north, so we're both sticky and sandy and wearing ratty t-shirts and flip-flops. We walk across the parking lot, and Austin jumps in a puddle, splashing me and grinning. I kick water back at him. A lady carrying a Burberry umbrella worth more than my car minces across the parking lot, looking at Austin and me with finely arched eyebrows.

"Come on, kid," I say, taking Austin's arm and pulling him to the steps of the shops. "Let's get this over with."

Austin takes the steps two at a time. "Hey, Mom," he says. He points at a latte-swilling couple dressed in polo shirts and khakis. "Can we get coffee, too?"

I swat his pointing hand down. I don't know where he got the idea that he likes coffee. I never let him have it. "Maybe later," I say.

Austin shrugs. "Can we go in the toy store?"

I tell him yes, and it's as we're browsing through the aisle of pirate accessories that Austin shouts, "Gee Gaw!" and runs over to my ex-mother-in-law.

On the scale of things I've never understood, hovering somewhere near the very top of the list is why any woman would ever request to be referred to as *Gee Gaw*. I turn up my lips in what I hope is a friendly smile at the coincidence. Stephen's mother is the sort of woman who wears polo shirts and carries Burberry umbrellas. "Hi, Mrs. Oden." I refuse to call her the g-words. Refuse.

Mrs. Oden gives Austin a side-hug. "Evie, why didn't you mention that you and Austin were coming up the beach today?"

I wipe some mud off my right calf with my left foot and kiss her on the cheek. "Oh, it was a last-minute thing," I say.

"Gee Gaw," Austin says, tugging at her hand. "Look at this." He pulls a pirate hat from the shelf. "I'm going to be Blackbeard for Halloween."

"How lovely," Mrs. Oden says. She looks at me, "Would your mommy think it's all right if Gee Gaw bought it for you?"

I protest, and she parries back until I shrug and smile and say that would be lovely. Also high on the list of things I've never understood is not only why any woman would request to be called Gee Gaw, but why she would refer to herself in the third person as such. Or refer to herself in the third person at all. "Would you like to join us for coffee or ice cream?" I ask. We walk to the register, and a woman in a polo shirt checks us out. I swear, there must be some inviolable Duck dress code.

"No, hon, I have to be heading back," she says. "But it was so good to see you both." Mrs. Oden pinches Austin's cheek and tells him she loves him. She starts to smooth down his hair, but Austin steps back to my side.

"You and Mr. Oden will have to come over for dinner soon," I say. And I mean it. Ever since we learned that we can't talk about Stephen, I've gotten along fine with his parents.

Mrs. Oden waves and walks outside, pulling her linen jacket up over her hair, and then she's gone around the corner.

Austin's quiet as we poke around the shops looking for my dad's utensil. He carries the bag with his pirate hat, careful not to bump it into people. We find the cake tool, and by the time we're done, the rain has stopped, so we walk along the shops' boardwalk on the Currituck Sound. There's a coin machine where you can buy whatever it is you feed to ducks, and I ask Austin if he wants to feed the Duck ducks. He nods, even though he's too old to really get a kick out of it, so I plink quarters into the machine until he has a palm full of pellets.

A mallard paddles by, and Austin selects a few grains, throwing them into the water. "Why did you and Dad get divorced?" he asks.

I blink, disoriented, as if his question has thrown me into a different place. As if I've been lurched onto a boardwalk in Brazil or Finland and have to shake my head to return to the northern Outer Banks where my son stands, calmly feeding a quacking herd of gathering mallards. He's never asked me this before, not so straightforward. "It's kind of a long story," I say.

Austin tosses a pellet. He nods, and again I see Nate. "I've got time," he says.

I sigh. I put more quarters into the machine until I have a handful of duck food, too. I toss some pellets to a small fawn-and-white duck. "Sometimes, even if they love each other, moms and dads just can't live together anymore," I say.

Austin rolls his eyes. "Is that what PBS taught you to say?"

"I think it was Dear Abby." The ducks paddle into one another, beaks opening and closing in a cacophony of quacks. I dump my handful of pellets in the water and turn to Austin. "We did love each other," I say. I close my eyes to remember if this is true. And yes, somewhere under all my resentment toward Stephen is a flicker of the love I once had.

"So why'd you get divorced?" Austin asks again. He continues to select pellets one by one to throw to the ducks.

Dear Abby never covered how to tell your son about how mommy and daddy were nineteen and didn't mean to get pregnant, and how they otherwise would've broken up within a year, and how they each had subsequent affairs. "We were very different," I say.

Austin hurls a pellet. "That doesn't explain anything," he says.

"We were young." I say it without thinking.

Austin looks at me, oblivious to the flurry of honking and feather-flapping below him. "You were old enough to get married."

"But we shouldn't have. We weren't ready to be the only person the other would ever be with. Does that make sense?"

Austin turns back to the ducks. "No. Not really."

I take one of his pellets and aim at a little white duck on the outskirts of the duck circle. "It's like your Uncle Nate," I say. "He loved other women before he met Aunt Jennie, but he didn't marry them because he wasn't ready. If he had, he'd probably be divorced, too."

Austin's thinking crease appears. "Are he and Aunt Jennie getting divorced?"

"No, that's my point. They waited until they were both ready to get married, so they probably won't get divorced."

Austin tosses the last of his pellets and dusts off his hands. He leans against the railing. "But then why did you and Dad get married if you weren't ready?"

I open my mouth and then close it. "We thought we were ready, but it turned out we weren't," I say.

"Then how do people ever know? That they're ready?"

"If you figure that one out, kid, you'd save a lot of people a lot of pain," I say.

Austin shakes his head. "I still don't get it."

"Join the club." I start walking down the boardwalk, then quicken my pace to a jog. "Last one to the coffee shop's a rotten egg," I say, calling the words over my shoulder. My feet thud on the wet boards. I look behind me but Austin's not there, and then he's swooshing past my side, laughing, running, the bag with his pirate hat bouncing against his legs, heedless of polo-shirted people raising their eyebrows, heedless of love. Running away, for a moment, from it all.

~

People think lobsters mate for life. It isn't true. After the lady lobster's shell has hardened back up, she tosses her hair over her shoulder, tramp stamps her lower back, and gets the hell out of that horrible retro lair. The dude doesn't try to stop her.

She packs her paisley suitcase and is ready to catch the next current to Australia, but something catches her eye. It's her best lady lobster friend, and she's all gussied up and prancing past the dude lobster's lair. Her friend twirls her hair and bats her eyelashes and is all set to pee when the lady lobster stops her.

"Look," she says, taking her friend by the arm. "I know he's the dominant dude, but you should realize that he's actually just a dude."

Her friend doesn't listen. She jerks her claw away and goes back to prancing.

The lady lobster thinks about this. The current comes, but she doesn't take it. Instead, she goes back to her old lair and waits, because she knows her friend will need her in a couple of weeks. While she's waiting, she thinks a lot. She thinks about why she thought the dude was so great to begin with. She thinks about pheromones. She thinks about the dude lobsters in Australia.

And then she thinks about how the dominant dude gently caressed her stomach when she was bare. She thinks about how he could've just eaten her but didn't. She thinks about how he could've dug in his claws and stripped her naked body into bloody ribbons. She thinks about how, even though she's over him, maybe he wasn't so bad. Maybe he wasn't all to blame.

A couple weeks later, the lady lobster's friend steams out of the dude's lair, hard-shelled and free. The two lady lobsters share some

Godiva truffles and merlot, laughing about the way the dude lobster played Marvin Gaye and seemed to think "boobies" was an actual word. They watch as another lady lobster puts on lipstick and begins sashaying past the dude's lair. And somehow, even though she never made it to Australia to check out the dude lobsters there, the lady lobster thinks that maybe things worked out for the best after all.

~

Jennie is the woman my brother married, the woman my brother loves. Jennie, like Charlotte, had vacationed on Hatteras her whole life, only Jennie came from western New York. Like Monet, one day she decided to live here, but Jennie moved with her boyfriend. She's a pastry chef, and when my dad decided to expand the inn's repertoire to include catering and selling muffins to local coffee shops, he hired Jennie. I'm the one who decided she and Nate should get married, even when she was still with Darth, a skinny guy with lank brown hair and a penchant for trench coats. Darth's parents were fanatical Star Wars buffs. That explained a lot, but not enough for me to forgive him for rolling his eyes when Jennie tripped on the carpet or honking the horn eight times when he came to pick her up one night. Really, who honks at all, let alone eight times? A guy named Darth, that's who.

I never trash-talked Darth while Jennie and I became friends, just pointed out how nice it was that Nate watched Austin on the nights I had to go up to Nags Head for school, how Nate's hair was naturally wavy like a sea captain's, the way Nate knew all about boats and currents and shifting shoals. I figured Jennie could notice on her own that Nate stopped by during nearly every shift she worked. Still, one morning, Jennie showed up in the inn's kitchen all splotchy-faced. She told me that Darth wanted to move back home. He told her she had to choose between this place and him. And she chose Hatteras.

Jennie sniffed as she cracked eggs for a quiche. "I know it doesn't make sense," she said. "He should be my home, right?"

"But you love it here," I said. I handed her an oven mitt with the sparkly outlines of the "Welcome to Las Vegas" sign on it, and Jennie took a tray of sheet cake out of the oven.

"I've never felt more at home anywhere." She set down the cake and stood with her mitted hand on her hip, brushing a stray curl out of her face with the other. "Maybe I'm just selfish. I'm supposed to want him to be happy, too."

I gathered a handful of eggshells and threw them in the trash. "But if you'd both be happier in different places, then you're not being selfish at all."

Austin clattered down the back stairs and into the kitchen, Walter on his heels. Austin and Jennie high-fived. "What's for breakfast?"

Jennie breathed deeply once, then took off the oven mitt and gave Austin the rundown on breakfast options. Walter pawed at Jennie's legs, stretching his back into an inverted arch.

I was waiting for Austin to finish getting ready for school when Darth showed up, Walter yapping in room-echoing barks at his arrival. Darth had dark circles under his eyes, and I almost felt bad for him. "Is Jennifer around?" he asked, walking into the inn's front room. I picked up Walter, and he lurched and lunged at Darth, scratching my arms.

"I think she's baking," I said.

Darth moved toward the kitchen, trench coat flowing in a shadowy trail. But Jennie came out, standing with one hand on the doorjamb. "Hey," she said.

Darth took Jennie's face in his hands. "Babe," he said, "we can't lose what we've got." Darth kissed her. "The Force is *strong* with us."

Austin thudded into the front room, his hair in his eyes. He was going through a Beatles phase. "Mom, where's my homework?"

I handed him Walter. "Take him upstairs, and I'll look down here."

"I don't want to lose you," Jennie said. Then, her voice cracking, "I'm sorry."

I looked for Austin's homework, picking and sorting through piles of coffee table books.

"Then come home. What do you even see in this piece-of-shit string of sand where everyone's always up in each other's business? Let's go home." I looked up to see Darth tug Jennie's hand toward him on that *home*.

Austin walked into the front room. "It's not polite language to say shit," he said.

"Sorry," I said, corralling Austin and pointing him toward a stack of magazines to search for his homework.

"Shit, Jennifer," Darth said, glaring at Austin. "Come home with me. Let's go home."

"It is *not* polite at all," Austin muttered. He threw a *Redbook* on the floor.

"Darth's just upset," Jennie said to him, coming over to help look for his homework. "He doesn't mean to be—" Jennie paused. She knelt down and set magazines on the floor, one at a time. "He doesn't mean to be impolite." Jennie unearthed a blue-lined sheet of paper and handed it to Austin, then stood up and turned to Darth. "I need to get back to work," she said.

"So we're done?" Darth asked. He ran a hand through his hair and a strand floated down to the carpet.

"We've been done for an hour and a half." Jennie turned and went back to the kitchen.

It took a few months for Nate and Jennie to start dating. Nate refused to ask her out for the longest time, stubbornly clinging to his heartbreak from Monet. But when he finally did, it was like they'd always been together. Like Jennie's fingers had always laced snugly around Nate's, like the crook of Nate's arm had always matched the curve of Jennie's neck. When Nate soaked Jennie with a water balloon at the Cape Hatteras School Festival of Fun, Jennie shrieked and wrapped him in a bear hug, shaking her wet curls in his face. When Jennie jumped on Nate's back, Nate hooked his elbows under her knees. They latched like puzzle rings.

A few months later, Nate, Jennie, Austin, and I drove up to Manteo so Jennie could woo the owner of the Front Porch Café into carrying our baked goods. We went to the waterfront, Austin running off to the playground with its kid-sized plastic pirate ship. Nate and Jennie held hands, swinging in tandem as we walked toward the squat, red-roofed replica of the Roanoke Marshes lighthouse crouched in the sound. Soft gray clouds scudded across the sky, and I zipped my windbreaker. I glanced back at Austin, who'd found a stick and was swinging it through the air, thrusting and parrying with an imaginary foe. "Put that down if another kid comes to play," I called to him. Austin didn't answer, just yelled something gutturally unintelligible and swung his stick harder.

Nate raised an eyebrow. "He's been pressing boundaries lately."

"No shit," I said.

"I think that's something kids need to do," Jennie said. Her hair blew into her face.

"But Dude Man's taking it pretty far," Nate said. We walked along the pebbly sidewalk, and Nate pointed out the weather tower to Jennie.

"How else is he going to learn?" Jennie asked.

I stared up at the flags flapping at the top of the tower. "Dear Abby says that kids push boundaries in their quest to mature."

"There's boundary pushing as a developmental phase, and then there's just plain old bad behavior," Nate said.

"Sure," Jennie said. "I'm just saying that if kids don't brush up against ways they're not supposed to act, they won't realize what's appropriate and what's not."

"I'm supposed to set and maintain limits and consequences to teach him skills for a productive life," I said. We walked toward Austin, who was thwacking the pirate ship's plastic slide with his stick. "Otherwise he'll grow up to be a douche bag."

"Growing up doesn't come easy," Nate said.

"But are douche bags born or made?" Jennie asked. "That's my question."

"And what's the statute of limitations on turning into one?" I asked. "I feel like by college, the die is pretty much cast. So maybe the cutoff is high school?"

We walked back to the pirate ship, the wind flattening my jacket to my back.

"I'm pretty sure I went to elementary school with some, though," Nate said.

Austin threw down his stick and ran over to us. "Uncle Nate," he said. "I just made up a joke. Want to hear it?"

Nate slung his arm around Austin's shoulders and gave him a noogie. "Absolutely."

"What kind of a sweater did the pirate wear?" Austin's hair blew in his eyes, and he shook his head to toss it back. "Arrr-gyle," he said. "Get it? Because pirates say *arrr*."

Nate groaned and Jennie laughed, but they kept holding hands as we all walked back to the car.

~

It's a couple of weeks after our trip to Duck, and Austin won't stop talking about three things: Blackbeard, divorce, and Fiona Garcia. School's started, and Austin and Fiona are in the same class and the same advanced reading group and have figured out that they both have divorced parents. This weekend, the Eastern Surfing Association's having a competition in Buxton, so I drive Austin over and we meet Nate, Jennie, Dr. Garcia, and Fiona at the beach. The day is chilly and still, waves tumultuously green-gray. Austin and I walk past the old lighthouse site, and he breaks away to run down the beach when he spots Jennie waving. I trundle through the sand to their blanket and sit down beside Dr. Garcia.

The beach is crowded, and a guy keeps announcing heats through a loudspeaker, but I get entranced by the crash of waves, the way the surfers' bodies carve water into fans of sea spray. I have one of those moments where I pause and step outside myself, just for a second. It's a precarious, fragile, ordinary moment, a moment that will never ever happen again. Just for a second, I see the way I fit into the geometry of our blanket, my legs perpendicular to Dr. Garcia's, Jennie and Nate at right angles to one another, Austin and Fiona sprawled on either side of them in arcs. For a moment, I sit outside my body, poised. And then the loudspeaker crackles and Fiona shrieks because she sees a sand crab and Austin shows her how to pick it up without getting pinched, and time streams back along in the ordinary fashion.

Jennie touches my shoulder. "Evie," she says. She beckons me closer and says into my ear, "You're going to be an aunt."

I shout and tackle Jennie to the sand, but when I sit up, it's my brother I'm looking for, Nate's eyes I search out. He's looking at me with a grin on his face. I tackle him, too.

Austin tosses down his sand crab and stands over us. "Why are you guys being weird?"

Nate takes his sandy hand and pulls Austin's ankle so he collapses with us and tells him he's going to have a cousin to look after soon.

"Isn't it going to live with you?" Austin asks.

"We thought we might keep it at your house," Nate says. He throws a handful of sand at Austin. "It won't take up that much space. You could empty out one of your dresser drawers."

Austin snorts and throws sand at Nate.

I scoot out of the artillery zone and sit up to look at the water. Somewhere under those rhythmically rushing waves, a dude lobster forages for food. Maybe, as the dude lobster uppercuts a marlin, he secretly thinks, *Must be nice to be a lady lobster and get to hang out at home*, not realizing how trapped she feels. Maybe he's one of those not-worth-it lobsters, the ones who're like, *I'm so lucky to be a dude lobster because I never have to shed my armor and the lady lobster is always going to be dependent on me*. Or maybe, as he pries a ridged mussel off a gray rock, he worries that his lady is getting bored back at his lair, bored with him, is fantasizing about lobsters in Australia. Even though, seriously, there's nothing special about Australian dude lobsters besides their crikey accents.

But maybe he decides to give her the plumpest mussel of the bunch. Maybe, as the dude lobster catches the current for home, he plans out where he and his lady will go for an adventure once she's hardened back up. Perhaps Australia; it does have that Great Barrier Reef he's heard so much about, and he likes throwing shrimp on the barbie as much as anyone. Maybe he doesn't even mention the marlin incident and instead asks her what she thinks of the shag carpet, and if she has any idea of how they should rearrange the beanbag chairs in preparation for the baby lobsters' arrival.

Maybe he realizes his fondue pot doesn't magically clean itself, just like mussels don't magically appear on their Formica kitchen table. Maybe, after the dude lobster takes off his coat and hangs up his hat, he gently puts his claw around his lady's pink, naked waist and spins her across the lair, dipping her to the music, swaying his lobster hips in time with hers.

Nine

Like an Eagle, a Real One

— 2016 —

Come with me to Vegas, the little Facebook message says. Facebook is a very valuable tool. It allows you to tell everybody you know that you ate a roasted red pepper sandwich for lunch; then, a few hours later, you can log on to tell them it gave you heartburn. Facebook will tell you when your ex-husband gets engaged to a twenty-two-year-old law student who insists your son call her "Mommie Casie," both spelled with an "ie." It'll show you advertisements for dating millionaires and meeting Mature VIP Singles and, if you're lucky, an ad for ordering a home STD testing kit. And it'll connect you with long-lost pen pals from back before there was e-mail.

Eamon O'Shea, my long-lost pen pal from back before there was e-mail, wants me to come to Las Vegas with him for a long weekend. Eamon and I started writing when we were nine years old as part of a pen pal project at school. I made my Aunt Fay, God rest her recently departed soul, tell me endless stories of Irish pirate queens, and then I'd write to Eamon for confirmation that the stories were real. We wrote off and on until I went to college. I even met Eamon once when we were sixteen. He'd come from Cork, Ireland, to visit me in Hatteras, North Carolina. Eamon was cute and had an accent. I took him to all the tourist destinations: the lighthouse, the shipwrecks, up the beach to Jockey's Ridge. We flirted. We kissed, once, right before he got back on the plane to Cork. But I haven't talked to Eamon in eight years, except for three reconnecting, pre-Vegas-summons Facebook messages, where I learned that he's now an investment banker living in Toronto.

No, I write back. *I can't afford it. Besides, it'll be weird.*

I pull out all of Eamon's old letters and spread them on my bed. His handwriting is small and precise, lilting in a tight cursive across the wafer-thin airmail paper. He talks a lot about soccer in his letters, which he calls football. I can't imagine I ever cared about soccer, but maybe I thought it was exciting back then. He talks about Ireland and books, and one letter deals entirely with the subject of clotted cream.

Eamon e-mails back. *I'm already going. I've one seminar to attend, and the rest is vacation. I'll pay for the hotel and the car and everything. Just get your flight and come!*

I make a list of pros and cons.

Pros:

- nearly free vacation
- nearly free vacation where, for a few days, I can be someone who doesn't have to manage rental properties and sell houses and raise a kid all at the same time
- chance to rekindle affections with tasty Irishman

Cons:

- tasty Irishman could have grown up to be a serial killer who just wants to get in my pants, whereas I'm at a point in my life where I need to not get murdered and not indiscriminately sleep with people with whom I am not in a relationship
- tasty Irishman was considered tasty by my sixteen-year-old self, who, in a few short years, would marry one of the biggest jackasses in the free world, who was likewise considered tasty
- plane tickets are still expensive

I take the list to show my mom. We sit in the new dining room she and my father just added to their inn, at a pretty table overlooking the Pamlico Sound. It's June, and tourist season is just heating up, but it's late enough in the day that we can sit and chat about the Vegas summons.

"Why would you think this is a good idea?" my mother says. She stabs at the cheesecake she's eating. My mother is little and wiry, and her hair falls in her face as she stabs.

I bite back my snappy retort. I've been talking to a therapist once a week ever since the day I shoved Austin. It was just once. And in my defense, he was acting like a real turd that day, absolutely refusing to put on his shoes when we were late, and I hadn't slept more than four hours a night for a week because I was studying, so I was already on edge, but I hate myself for snapping. I'm broke, but I'm charging therapy sessions to my Discover card. I'm working on anger management issues, though I refuse to admit to anybody that I have *issues*. "He says all I have to pay for is my ticket," I tell my mother. I steal a swirl of mango topping off her cheesecake. "And I need a vacation. And I want to see Vegas. And maybe I'll get lucky with Eamon." I don't tell her that, secretly, I'm hoping maybe, just maybe, lucky will turn into something more. I don't tell her that I'm lonely. I don't tell her that I don't care about upping my numbers anymore. Despite my reputation in high school, I've only ever technically slept with three men.

My mother grimaces. She still can't get used to me talking like I have a sex life, which, in all honesty, I haven't had in a few years. "You can't afford it," she says.

I know this. I know I'm a single, working mother. "Maybe I'll hit the jackpot," I tell her.

"Or else the jackpot'll hit you," my mother says.

"I have no idea what that means," I say.

Mom stands up and takes her plate toward the kitchen. "You've already made up your mind," she says, "so I guess I'm babysitting Austin." She shakes her head back and forth the way she always does, the way that means *my daughter is a fool.*

Well, maybe so. Maybe I am a fool.

"And don't you dare," my mother yells from the kitchen, "come back married."

But the way I figure it, you don't win the crapshoot if you don't blow on the dice, or something like that.

"Even if the minister is Elvis?" I ask her.

I'm a fool on her way to Las Vegas.

~

When I see Eamon O'Shea at baggage claim, the first thing I notice is that he's wearing carpenter jeans. I'd expected him to wear khakis and an Oxford cloth shirt with the sleeves rolled up, or else a suit—something investment bankerish. And they're *stonewashed* carpenter jeans. This violates my code of fashion. Carpenter jeans are only okay for a guy to wear if he's doing actual carpentry and has a hammer thrust into the little side loop thing. Aside from the pants, Eamon is not unattractive. He has dark hair and blue eyes, a long nose and a square jaw. He sees me and opens his arms. "Hi, Evie," he says, and smiles. "It's you." The voice gets me, the way he says my name with a slant, *Eavie*. What girl isn't a sucker for an accent? All in all, Eamon is rather good-looking. Tasty, even.

I give him a hug and do a quick assessment of sexual sparks based on skin-to-skin contact. Inconclusive. Though he smells nice, like man-pheromones coming through travel-worn deodorant. "So we're in Vegas," I say.

"Four days and three nights," he says, and he kicks his bag into rolling position and starts walking toward the door.

"I've got to get my bag," I say to his retreating back.

Eamon wheels around. "Right," he says. "What does it look like?"

I see my bag trundling around the circle and point. "The one with the paisley that looks like amoebas," I say. It's also got duct tape holding the right top corner together, but I don't want to call attention to that.

Eamon grabs for my bag. If he'd been Stephen, my ex-husband, he'd have let me pull the bag down myself. "And duct tape," he says, placing the bag at my feet. He runs an appraising finger over the corner of my bag.

"Whatever," I say, but then I realize this is an angry response to what I see as a personal attack on my inability to purchase a new set of luggage. I remind myself that getting angry will not fix anything, and may in fact make the situation worse. "It's all the rage in Paris," I say.

"I'll show you the Paris casino," Eamon says. He takes off for the door again. He walks fast, but maybe it's just that I have short legs. "It's right next door to our hotel."

I can't tell if he says *our hotel* in a way that's creepy or exciting, since I don't yet know if I want to sleep with him. I settle on exciting. I can't wait to see someplace new. Eamon and I make our way to the shuttle, out of the air-conditioning, through a slap of dark night heat, and then into the iciness of the bus. He doesn't help me pull my luggage up the steps, but he does lift it onto the shelf-thing. We sit together and our legs touch.

A few more people sit down, and the bus starts moving. I swear, this airport is bigger than eight of my hometowns. I say this to Eamon. He nods and looks out the window. "I didn't realize Vegas would be this spread out," I say. "It looked so big and flat from the plane."

"You're going to love it," Eamon says. He looks out the window again, but I don't see anything but more airport.

The bus rolls along. I jiggle my leg to see how it feels against Eamon's. I wonder why he's being so quiet, then think that maybe he has jet lag. "How was your flight?" I ask. Eamon had a nonstop flight from Toronto.

"Yeah, it was fine," he says. He gives me a half smile and looks away.

I wait to see if he'll ask about my flight. Flights, I should say, since I had to get up at six in the morning, drive three hours to Norfolk, and then change planes twice. But I did get to see the George Michael episode of *Behind the Music* on the last plane. I love airplanes, but I hardly ever get to fly. Eamon is quiet. I have a seven-year-old son. I'm not used to quiet. "Did they feed you anything good?"

"I ate," Eamon says. He crosses his arms.

I give up. I text my family to let them know I arrived, and then I look out the window, too. We're finally pulling out of the airport, and the tall buildings and flashing neon of the Strip twinkle brightly in the distance. I jiggle a little, in excitement this time.

Eamon points out the window. "The Welcome to Las Vegas sign is coming up," he says. He grins like a little boy.

I crane my neck out and up, way up where I think all the flashy signs will be. The bus rolls on, and almost too late I see the sign, much lower than where I was looking, a sparkly alien-shaped thing with a crowd of people out front taking pictures. "It's so little," I say.

Eamon looks personally affronted, his lips a straight line. "Well, it's old," he says.

I make a note to never refer to anything a man is excited about as being *little*. "I didn't mean it wasn't nice," I say. "It's a lovely sign."

I stare up at the flashing hotels and casinos and the steady march of people going up and down the street, some with big plastic bong-looking drinks hung around their necks. I want to walk around with a bong-looking drink around my neck. I don't see any wedding chapels yet, but I don't ask Eamon about them because I'm afraid I'll make a joke about getting married, and that was one big *Don't* on the Travel Channel's *Top Ten Vegas Do's and Don'ts* show. One should never joke about getting married in Vegas because it's too easy to make it happen. We get to the Flamingo, I pull my duct-taped bag from the rack, and we roll off the bus and into the hotel.

The Flamingo smells musty, and then, as we roll our bags down to check-in, like cigarette smoke. There's pink everywhere, flamingo pink, stuck-on-the-inside-of-a-Pepto-Bismol-bottle pink, Barbie pink. I think that Mattel should've made a Flamingo Vegas stripper-showgirl Barbie with a headdress and lots of bling. There's a small line of people at the desk even though it's nearly one in the morning, and Eamon and I wait and wait and wait, and then, because we had to wait and wait and wait, we get upgraded to a Go Room. It has stripy walls, a big flat-screen TV that Austin would kill for, and white patent leather headboards. At least Eamon was honest about getting two beds. At least maybe he doesn't *just* want to get in my pants. "I'm taking this one," Eamon says, throwing his stuff on the bed closest to the big window, where you can look down and see the fountain show at the Bellagio. "Do you mind?"

I'm annoyed with this, and I'm also annoyed that the room smells like the inside of an ashtray after a long party full of swingers, or mobsters, or hipsters, or some other chain-smoking "er"-ending group. I can feel the cells in my lungs turning black. I cough a little, but I make sure to reframe the situation, because logic defeats anger. My lungs will pink up again after this weekend, and it'll be worth it to look out at the dancing fountains every half hour. "Not a bit," I say in a tone that I hope is nonchalant, even-keeled, and serene.

~

Eamon wakes me up the next morning by banging shut the sliding bathroom door. He stays in there for forty-five minutes, and when he comes out, he brings with him a billowing waft of AXE body spray. He smells like a pack of prepubescent boys. I pull the covers over my head, not ready to be awake after my fifteen-hour trip.

"Evie," Eamon says, and I get a kick out of the way he says my name. "It's time to get up." He pushes a button and the curtains slide open.

"Says who?" I ask. But I sit up, a little dance of excitement in my stomach.

"We've got a lot to see," Eamon says. He bangs around the room a little more.

I get up and pee, and when I come back, Eamon is standing in front of the closet in just his boxer shorts. They aren't even cute boxer shorts; they're plain yellow and kind of dirty-looking, and if these are the boxers Eamon O'Shea plans to seduce me in, he's got the wrong plan. I pull some clothes out of my amoeba bag and head back to the bathroom, sliding the frosted-glass door shut.

From the other room, Eamon clears his throat. "Evie," he says, "You woke me up in the night."

I look at myself in the mirror and pull at the bags under my eyes. "Oh?"

"You woke me up when you went to the bathroom."

I paste up my toothbrush and run water in the round, raised sink. "I'm sorry," I say through a mouth of foam. I spit and get dressed and come back into the room.

"It's just that you woke me up and I couldn't get back to sleep," Eamon says. This irritates me, it really does. What does he want me to do? Go back in time and not pee? I apologized, right? Eamon's sitting in a chair looking out the window. I remember my therapist Judy's advice about feelings of rising anger. I breathe deeply, from my diaphragm; breathing from your chest won't relax you. I picture my breath coming up from my gut. Then I picture my lung cells gasping from the smoke smell. In my mind, they look like amoebas. Little, death-black amoebas.

Eamon turns in his chair. He smiles a little. "Maybe next time, if you get up in the night, you could not flush." He says *flush* like *floosh*.

"Sure thing," I say, making a mental note to restrict fluids near bedtime.

~~~

Eamon informs me that we should go to McDonald's for breakfast, which is fine with me because it's cheap. Then he informs me the McDonald's is at the other end of the Strip, and that I probably shouldn't have worn the shoes I'm wearing, which are pink flip-flops with a little heel. He informs me of this after we've wound our way out of the labyrinth of the hotel and stepped out into the 101-degree morning and started walking.

Eamon throws his arm around my shoulder, and we cross the street in the jumble of a crowd. "You're here!" he says, jubilant. This is rather adorable. "What do you think so far?"

What I think is that when people say, *It's a dry heat*, they neglect to mention that convection ovens also emit a dry heat, and so do hair-dryers, and so do broilers. I think I can feel the dying cells in my lungs basting. It's nothing like the heat at home, which is thick and damp and salty and alive. But I look around and point at a big
~~~

fake hot-air balloon beside a fake Eiffel Tower. "That's pretty," I say. "And I love the fountains."

Even at nine in the morning the Strip bustles with crowds of people. We jostle and shuffle and walk and walk and walk. Eamon walks fast. He steps off the curbs ahead of me and scans for traffic, then guides me across the streets, his hand on my back. By the time we hit fake New York, I feel like I'm going to throw up from the heat. We reach McDonald's, and the air-conditioning stings it's so cold. I get an Egg McMuffin, but I'm too queasy to eat.

"What's the matter?" Eamon asks through a mouthful of hashbrown.

I push my McMuffin away. "I feel sick," I say.

Eamon snaps his fingers. "Right," he says. "I meant to tell you to drink lots of water before we left the room. You're probably dehydrated from the flight."

"Dehydrated sucks." I put my head down. My stomach hasn't felt like this since I was pregnant. I have a moment of panic before I realize I haven't had sex in three years and two months.

"I'll get you some water," Eamon says. He goes to the counter and comes back with an ice-cream-sundae cup. "We'll just have to refill it," he says.

I drink and drink. Eamon refills my cup four times. He pats my back each time he returns to the table and tells me about the time he got dehydrated in Death Valley. "It's the worst I've ever felt," Eamon says. I forgive him for forgetting to tell me to drink before we left the hotel. I drink and drink until I can go up and refill the clear plastic cup on my own, then I drink and drink some more. Finally, I smash down some McMuffin.

It's during the smashing-down portion of breakfast that Eamon looks at me and says, "You used to be really thin ten years ago, didn't you?"

I stop chewing. I don't have to do any anger management techniques because I'm too stunned to be angry. I swallow my bite. "I guess so."

"I mean, like, *really* thin," Eamon says. He takes a drink of coffee. He raises his eyebrows, questioning.

I want to throw my cold McMuffin in his face, but instead I say, "I was sixteen." I don't know what he's getting at—I'm not big now, and I wasn't unusually skinny then—but if I try to find out I'm afraid I won't stay calm. I've already forgotten to breathe from my diaphragm. I put down my McMuffin. "Let's go," I say. He walks out the door in front of me. I think, *Ten years ago you had the sense not to wear stonewashed carpenter jeans,* but I don't think my therapist would like it if I said that out loud.

We walk around the Strip, and I see fake Camelot, fake New York, fake Egypt, fake Paris, fake Venice, and some real lions at MGM, which doesn't have a fake theme except for the movies. It's hot, and it gets hotter. I tell Eamon about Walter, my inherited dog. I tell him how I'm worried Walter's going blind, and Eamon says you can get cataract surgery for dogs. He says he's sorry about Aunt Fay and tells me how much he enjoyed the painting lesson she gave him that time he visited.

We go to In-N-Out Burger for dinner, and Eamon hands me the ketchup before I ask for it. He points out a kid in a powder-blue leisure suit, and we make up stories about him. Eamon asks me how I'm doing financially, and if Stephen pays alimony and child support or just child support, and if I have any investments, and if my parents have any investments. Then he asks me if I'm seeing anyone, and how long it's been since my last boyfriend. I start to feel like I'm getting interviewed by a reporter from *Us Weekly,* or at least *Star.*

Then Eamon asks me how much my Aunt Fay suffered before

she died a year ago, and if I blame her because she used to smoke. It's at this point that I start making a list of all the things Eamon does to piss me off. I figure this is a way of replacing my overly dramatic, angering thoughts with rational ones, in simple list format. Throughout the rest of the evening he:

- snaps at me to turn my cell phone off, then gets pissed when his rings a moment later, before he realizes it's his own
- tells me that I can't play penny slots because it's pointless and I'll never win
- asks me again if I get alimony

I figure he's done at least six things by the time we get back to the hotel room, so I start at seven when he asks me if my bed is comfortable and can he try it. I mean, really, get a more creative line than that. But still, I let him lie down beside me. I'm curious about what will happen next. When I compare him to Stephen, Eamon's offenses seem less awful. Seven isn't such a high number. Maybe I'm just being critical. I'm just being critical.

"Come here," Eamon says, and he kisses me.

It's been a while. I kiss him, and all my old Easy Evie instincts come flying in and I'm back in the baseball dugout with Zack Gray letting him feel me up. Eamon and I make out hard-core for a while, and then he starts to unzip his jeans, and I realize he thinks I'm going to have sex with him, and in that same instant, I realize I don't want to.

"Wait," I say. I sit up and pull down my shirt. "You haven't passed my entrance exam."

Eamon doesn't play along. He's supposed to say, "Is it an oral exam?"

I say it for him. "It's an oral exam." I raise an eyebrow. My oral exam is fun. It's administered before any guy is allowed in my pants and involves such questions as: *Do any of your self-descriptors involve the words* drug-dealing fiend? and *Are you currently on parole?* and *Have you ever just bluntly asked to stick your finger up a woman's ass, just for a second, just to see how it feels?* If the answer to any of these questions is *yes*, then I reconsider letting the guy in my pants.

"What do you want to know?" Eamon asks.

I think for a second. The Facebook ad pops up in my head. "Do you have any STDs?"

Eamon's mouth crinkles like I've asked him if he'd like a bite of rancid sweetbreads. "Of course not," he says.

I sigh. "It's just that I don't know you well enough to have sex with you," I say. Because I'm not Easy Evie anymore, dammit.

Eamon looks puzzled. "We only have the weekend," he says.

"I'm not the kind of girl who comes to Vegas just to get laid," I say. *Anymore*, I think.

"Then why bother coming to Vegas?" He shifts in the bed, tugging at his jeans. "Come on, Evie," he says. "I'm uncomfortable enough as it is." And Eamon starts to kiss me again.

And this is where things get complicated. Because even though Eamon O'Shea has been a jackass all day and is currently coercing me into sex, he's a good kisser. I don't feel threatened. I think that if I tell Eamon to stop, he probably will. And it does feel good to kiss someone; it feels good to be wanted. I kiss him back, and I let him take my shirt off, and all the while I'm arguing with myself, debating whether being in Sin City and sex-deprived is reason enough to get it on with a jackass or whether I should obey my newfound, grown-up, no-indiscriminate-sex-with-jackasses rule.

I'm about to give in when Eamon pulls off his stonewashed jeans, and suddenly, out of nowhere, I see an image of George Michael's butt in the "Faith" video. I hear the lines, "Well, I need someone to hold me, but I'll wait for something more." That does it. I know for sure I can't have sex with Eamon O'Shea. I'm not sure what to do. I feel like I've led Eamon on, mostly because I've led Eamon on. Then I have a zing of inspiration. "I have to go to the bathroom," I say into Eamon's mouth. "I'll be right back."

The bathroom still smells vaguely of AXE. I sit down on the toilet, hoping that Eamon will think I'm putting in a diaphragm. Do people still use diaphragms? I take a deep breath, then start to curse. "Shit," I say, quietly at first. Then, louder, "Shit!" I walk back into the room and put my hands on my hips. "My period started," I say. "And I didn't pack anything." I push my hair behind my ears.

Eamon looks disappointed and a little confused.

I pull on my shirt. "I'm going down to get some tampons," I say. I hope that saying *tampons* out loud will make him realize that this is the only thing going into my vagina. I grab my flip-flops and my room key and walk out into the hall.

~

Things a man can do to make sure he does not get into my pants:

- always use the bathroom first, and always leave the toilet seat up (I know I should refrain from thinking that someone *always* does something that makes me angry, but it's true; he does it every single time.)
- ask me if I'm serious when I joke that we should order an $1800 bottle of wine from room service
- tell me I need to marry rich
- continually wear the same pair of stonewashed carpenter jeans in 112-degree heat

Eamon does all these things today, and finally I escape to the pool and he goes to the spa. I don't know why anyone would pay twenty dollars to sit in a sauna when all you have to do is step outside, but that's beside the point.

I vulture around until a recliner in the shade opens up, and then I order fruity drinks and charge them to Eamon's account. I'll pay him back later, but it feels good to drink on his tab. I call home and tell Austin about the MGM lions and the fountains at the Bellagio. I imagine Judy, my therapist, saying in her soothing voice, *Use imagery; visualize a relaxing experience, from either your memory or your imagination.* I try to picture myself on the beach on a nice sunny day, but that doesn't work, so I move to my imagination and visualize myself riding along on a horse behind Legolas the Elf as we go off to shoot Orcs. It's not exactly my own imagination, but it works.

By the time Eamon comes back from the spa and joins me at the pool, either the drinks or the anger management exercises have made me much more forgiving because I start to think about the nice things he did earlier today. He:

- held doors for me
- helped a child in a wheelchair get unstuck from a sidewalk ramp
- took my picture in front of a flamingo
- said *hello* to a little lizard we saw

I pretend that Eamon O'Shea has only ever done nice things like saying *hello* to a little lizard. I lean back in my recliner and try to relax through the thumping music and crowd of people. I think I've seen more people these last couple days in Vegas than I have in my whole life. If you took every tourist who ever visited the Outer Banks and smooshed them together into one place, that'd be what Vegas is like. A fake palm tree mists water over me, and I let the heat settle into my bones.

Eamon doesn't try to get in my pants again tonight. He watches CNN from his own bed in his yellow boxers and a Nirvana t-shirt. Still, I make a point to rustle around in the bathroom and pull off the maxi pads I've been wearing with great gusto. I decided they make more noise than tampons. I wrap them in lots of toilet paper and leave them crumpled in the wastebasket. It annoys me to have spent $7 on a box of pads, but I remind myself that I'm not wasting them, that they're being sacrificed for the good of my sexual self-esteem.

~

Eamon decides we're taking a tour to the Grand Canyon West. We leave early so he can get back in time for his business meeting. It's nice of him, since I've never seen the Grand Canyon. He tells me once we're on the bus that we've eaten a big breakfast and will therefore not need lunch. "Why would we not need lunch?" I ask him.

He looks at me like I'm stupid.

And the sick thing is, I start to feel stupid.

"Evie," he says, and I'm tired of the way he says my name. "We just had a huge breakfast. And I have the apples I took from the spa." He shows me two green apples and two red apples.

I start to think I'm just complaining too much and that I'm silly for wanting lunch and that maybe he's right, that of course he's right. "Okay," I say.

"That's my girl," he says, and despite myself, I get a little thrill at the praise. I know it has a name, what I'm feeling—it's that thing kidnapees feel for their snatchers. Munchausen by Proxy? Stellan Skarsgård Syndrome? I know how I feel isn't right, and it isn't me, and it isn't okay, but I watch the desert go by outside the bus window because I'm trapped.

"Beautiful, isn't it?" Eamon asks.

Personally, I think it's flat and boring and ugly, and very, very beige. Beige isn't my color. I think the desert would be okay if it had an ocean, but I don't say this to Eamon. "Beautiful," I echo.

~

Eamon's seen the Grand Canyon three times, but when we get to the Hualapai Indian reservation, he takes the window seat on the small tour bus to the Skywalk bridge. We place our bags in a locker, listen to the spiel about not going on the bridge if you have a heart condition or extreme fear of heights, and put white booties over our shoes. I feel like a surgeon. I tell Eamon this, but he doesn't smile. We walk through a little maze and step out onto the bridge.

Now, I've never been afraid of heights before. I've climbed the 208-foot Cape Hatteras lighthouse too many times to count, and I've never been scared. But when I step out onto that glass bridge and look down, down, down into the striped canyon below my feet, I want to throw up in my mouth.

Eamon extends his arm like he owns the canyon. "Isn't it magnificent?" he says.

I scoot over to the edge of the bridge where the glass is frosted. I can't look down, so I look at Eamon. "I think I'm going to throw up in my mouth," I tell him.

Eamon's eyebrows pull together. "Buck up," he says. And he strides out into the middle of the bridge. The bridge is shaped like a big C out over the canyon, and Eamon struts it back and forth, finally settling on a spot as opposite from me as he can get. He stands there and looks out, leaning over the railing.

I inch my way to the center of the arc, staying on the frosted glass. I grab the railing; it's hot beneath my sweaty hand. The sun beats down. The only thing between me and a four-thousand-foot drop is four inches of glass. I try to look at the canyon. There's a giant eagle-shaped rock formation, red and tan and beige, and I feel like I'm right in the middle of a Jeep commercial. Someone asks if I want my picture taken, but I'm too focused on not barfing to answer.

"Jump up and down," the same voice says. I look. It's a tour guide, and he's wearing a traditional Hualapai shirt with a name-tag on it that says HANK. He has long, black hair and a long, black mustache. Mustaches usually violate my code of fashion, but I think this mustache might be ironic because it's so long. Ironic mustaches are okay for short periods of time and strictly for the purposes of irony.

I cling a little harder to the railing. "No," I say to Hank of the mustache. He's carrying a walking stick and wearing a headband. I wonder how hot his head gets, absorbing the sunlight all day.

Hank thumps the stick on the glass. He comes closer to me and puts his hand under my elbow. "It's solid," he says. "Jump on it." Hank jumps up and down, and Hank is a big man, let me tell you.

I manage a tiny, wussy jump. Somehow, Hank's hand on my elbow connects me to the earth, and I feel more solid. I jump higher.

"Touch it," Hank says.

I give him a look.

Hank grins. "I know, right," he says. "That's what she said." He kneels down, pulling me with him, and runs his hand over the glass.

I sit. The glass is warm. It appears to continue to hold me up. I look down, but this is a mistake, so I look back at Hank. He sits beside me, and we stare out at the Jeep eagle.

"I don't think your boyfriend likes me talking to you," he says, glancing at Eamon. Eamon's squinting out over the canyon, leaning as far as he can over the railing.

"He's not my boyfriend," I say. "And as far as I can tell, his face always looks like that." My legs are sweating onto the glass. I look down at them, then down, down, down into the canyon, down to the brown river at the bottom.

Eamon comes and kneels beside us. He clears his throat. "I was wondering what your people think of that eagle," Eamon says to Hank, gesturing out over the canyon. "What do they see as the difference between that eagle," again, he gestures, "and a real eagle?"

I look at Hank. Hank looks at me and gives me a nudge. "That one doesn't move as much," he says, more to me than to Eamon, jerking his head at the Jeep eagle.

Eamon sits down, cross-legged. He nods as if Hank has just said something profound. He and Hank and I are the only people on the bridge. I wonder if my legs will leave sweat marks on the glass. I turn to ask Hank who has to clean it, but Eamon says, "Do your people believe in the power of the eagle?"

Hank launches into a long story about his ancestors and their spirit animals. I'm pretty sure he's making it up for Eamon's benefit, both because Hank glances at me during the particularly outrageous bits and because the story sounds like something I once saw on Discovery Channel.

Eamon says, "Do your people—"

"Why do you keep saying *your people*?" I ask Eamon. "It's not like he's from Mars."

"That would make him an alien, wouldn't it, Evie?" Eamon says this in the tone I usually reserve for scolding small animals. "In which case I wouldn't be saying *people* at all."

"Don't talk to me like I'm an idiot," I say.

Eamon sits ups straight and presses his lips together. Then he slowly turns his head away from me to gaze at Hank. "As I was saying before we were interrupted," he says, and he rolls his eyes at me, "do your people believe in the legend of the canyon?"

Hank puts his arm around my shoulder as he answers, and then Eamon says it's time for us to go. Hank writes his name and e-mail address on my admission bracelet, and I follow Eamon off the bridge.

~

Eamon and I walk to the edge of the canyon where there are no railings. I wish he'd fall off the side, that a gust of wind would come along and blow his sweaty body and his stonewashed carpenter jeans down, down, down, so I could enjoy my last night in Vegas alone. I hate him and my hatred of him pounds in my chest, and for a second I'm afraid I'll push him. Eamon doesn't talk to me or offer to take my picture. We sit on a hot beige rock, and Eamon asks if I want an apple. I say yes, and he hands me a green one.

"Can I have a red one, please?" I ask.

"I was going to eat the red ones," Eamon says.

I look at him. He pulls out the red apple and takes a big chompy bite. Eamon has two red apples in his bag. I know this.

All the diaphragm-breathing and fuzzy bunnies frolicking through rainbows aren't going to help me now. "That's the most selfish thing I've ever heard," I say.

Eamon stops chewing his red apple. "What do you mean?" he asks.

I stand up and pace along the edge of the canyon. "What do you *mean*, what do I mean? You have two. You have two red apples, Eamon."

Eamon looks mildly puzzled. "I like red apples better," he says.

"And I've just clearly expressed that red apples are my preference as well."

"Then maybe you should have brought some," Eamon says.

Of course that would be Eamon's answer. Of course it would.

"My seven-year-old son knows enough to share," I say. I kick a beige stone, and it careens into the canyon. I'm pissed. I wonder if Hank can see me. I wonder if he'd turn me in if he saw me shove Eamon over the edge.

Eamon tosses the apple core into the canyon and wipes his hands on his jeans. "Why didn't you go on vacation with your son, then?" He asks it through a mouthful of apple. Then he snaps his fingers and points at me, quick. "Right, because you can't afford it."

"Fuck you," I say.

Eamon snickers. "That was rather the idea, wasn't it?"

"Yeah, well, I don't fuck douche bags." I cross my arms and stare Eamon down. The sun thumps on my head, and somewhere out near the Jeep eagle a real bird circles and caws.

"The bus is coming," Eamon says. "I've a meeting to attend." He gets up and walks to the parking lot.

As I watch his retreating back it hits me—Stockholm Syndrome. That's what I've been suffering from. There's no other way to explain how I gave Eamon this much of a chance for this long. Something else hits me, something Judy has said—getting angry won't solve anything.

She's right.

What solves things is revenge.

~

We're back at the hotel and Eamon says he's taking a shower first, that he's all sweaty and he has to get ready for his seminar. This is fine with me. I change into a push-up bra, a low-cut black shirt, and a tiny skirt. Then I fluff up my hair and put on some lipstick, red. I lie down on my bed with one hand under my head so my cleavage falls together. Eamon comes out wearing a towel. The waft of AXE follows him.

"Is it my turn?" I ask him.

"Sure," Eamon says. He looks at me appraisingly. "All yours."

"Thanks," I say. I rub my legs together. They're sticky from sweating all over the Grand Canyon.

Eamon rattles an Oxford cloth shirt off a hanger. I roll onto my other side to face him. I squish my breasts together a little more. "That was some canyon," I say. I lower my voice a little, trying to sound husky. "It was so deep."

Eamon digs a new pair of boxers out of his suitcase. "I bet you learned all about it from your tour guide friend," he says. He looks at me. "You two looked pretty cozy."

I sit up and cross my legs, hoping that my underwear shows. "I'm not into men with mustaches," I say. I play with the hem of my skirt.

Eamon walks over to me. He loops a tie around his neck and shimmies it into place. "Is this straight?" he asks. His eyes move from my cleavage to my legs and back up.

I stand up and tighten the tie's knot, then massage his shoulders and run my hands up and down his arms. I walk over to the window, making sure my gait accentuates my hips. "The fountains are on," I say. Eamon stands behind me, close enough that I can feel his erection. "It's amazing how high they shoot up." I lean back against him.

Eamon turns me to him. "I knew you'd come around."

I press my breasts against his chest and let him grind his penis into my hipbone. He's about to kiss me when I say, "You're going to be late for your meeting."

"Shit," Eamon says. He looks at his watch and grabs a pair of khaki pants off a hanger. Eamon stumbles into them, shoving his penis down and zipping with a wince.

"I won't forget where we left off," I say. And I kiss him, deep, with tongue, and then guide him out the door.

I stand there for a second, breathing in the AXE and smoke smell of the room. It's quiet. I think about the Irish pirate queens. Gráinne Ní Mháille, the Sea Queen of Connaught, didn't take shit from anyone. She would've shoved Eamon off the Jeep eagle canyon and been done with it. I call room service and order the $1800 bottle of wine and a steak and lobster dinner, charged to Eamon's account. I stuff all of my things into my amoeba bag and roll it right up next to the door, then sit down and send Eamon a text message that just says *wet*.

Eamon's dirty yellow boxers lay crumpled on the floor near the closet. I pick them up and rip them in half, then tear them again and again. The fabric feathers down into a little canary heap, a sad nest for a flightless bird. A text comes in from Eamon, *ur such a hot little bitch*. I hate it when people use "ur."

I remember all my toiletries are in the bathroom, so I go in to get them. Eamon's left the toilet seat up. I put the lid down, hoping he'll pee all over it. I zip up my cosmetic bag, and I'm almost to the door when I see his stupid bottle of AXE. It's black with the word VICE scrawled across in red graffiti letters. I unscrew the top and dump it down the sink. It makes a satisfying glugging noise. I stuff my toiletries in my amoeba bag and text *mmmm* to Eamon.

By the time I've eaten dinner, showered, drank two glasses of wine, and ordered an X-rated movie to the TV, which I mute, night sparkles outside the window, lit up in carnival light and color. The Bellagio fountains shoot up in their lacy synchronized dance. I text Eamon again. *You're going to be so surprised when you get back to the hotel.*

I unmute the TV and orgasmic moans fill the room. No orgasm has ever felt better than this, this power, this liberty, this sense of flight that fills my chest and rises, rises, rises, until I'm free. I walk over to the door, grab my bag, and stride into the neon Vegas night.

Ten

An Open Letter to Patricia Ballance

— 2008 —

Evie Austin
Dr. Garcia
ENG 101

An Open Letter to Patricia Ballance (and Her Stupid Fat-Headed Son Ronnie, Who I Know Will Read This Anyway Since He's Such a Mama's Boy) on this the Twenty-Ninth Day of September 2008, in Fulfillment of the Assignment to "Write a Letter to Someone Who Has Wronged You, Employing Ethos, Pathos, and Logos"

To: Patricia Ballance, mother of Ronnie Ballance, the boy who broke up with me eight days before our high school graduation because you (Patricia Ballance) didn't want your son dating a girl with a reputation as bad as mine, even though you went to school with my parents and know my family is a good family, but still didn't want Ronnie hanging around me because I'm that bad of a bad girl, or at least you think I'm that bad of a bad girl, even though I'm really not, as this letter will soon prove using astounding rhetorical means.

From: Evelyn Ann Austin, who's not really all that bad, as you will see, and even though I don't want to date your stupid fat-headed son anymore, you'll be sorry you broke us up because you could've ended up with me as your daughter-in-law one day instead of potentially getting that insipid Molly Morgan who can't even spell *insipid,* much less define it, and I know this by experience because we're in English 101 together here at East Carolina University, and boy, is she ever dumb.

RE: Badness
Dear Mrs. Patricia Ballance,

It's not like I was the stinky kid. It's not like, when Ronnie and I sat together at the Blue Table in kindergarten, he would've come home and complained about me, and you would've had to call Ms. Fasunight and had Ronnie moved to the Yellow Table so he didn't have to smell my stinky bad-girl self all day. And it's not like I wasn't over at your kitchen eating Fruit Roll-Ups after school at least twice a week like all the rest of Ronnie's friends from our class, and it's not like Ronnie didn't know that my mom was one of the safe moms to get a ride home with if you happened to be working late one day at the Red and White or needed to run up to Nags Head for a new set of patio furniture or to have a cavity filled. It's not like I was always the Bad Girl, but I can tell you how it all started, and it all started with Mike Tyson.

Or maybe it started before that.

Maybe it started one day in July on a sand dune at the National Seashore campground in Frisco, the summer Nate and I lived there with Aunt Fay because our parents were experiencing marital difficulties because my mother was screwing Bob the lighthouse mover from Buffalo. That one day in July, a day that was so hot the heat was all mirage wavy, like you could gather it up around you and make a chair out of it and sit down and lean back, that day I climbed up a sand dune and made friends with a girl from Ohio, a little tourist girl with a little tourist brother and the nicest little tourist family you ever did see. She was pretty. She had freckles and red-gold hair to match. No one ever told me specifically not to make friends with tourists, but I sort of got that implication, perhaps because they all go away at the end of the season and you're left without them and all the hard work you did to make friends in the first place is wasted. So maybe I made friends with Charlotte because I felt like it was frowned upon, which isn't doing much to convince you that I'm not a bad girl. The point is we made friends, and later that same summer, maybe because of the aforementioned marital difficulties that were then afflicting my parents, I was allowed to go home with Miss Charlotte McConnell of Windsor, Ohio, and stay there for two whole weeks.

Now, you should understand this, Mrs. P. Ballance, when I tell you that, for a little Banker girl like me, two weeks away from the ocean and home could have been quite the traumatic experience. I could have cried and cried every night because I felt so lonesome for the soft shushing sound of the waves. I could have tried to call my mother every two hours because I had a stomachache, not that my mother would have answered on account of her preoccupation with Bob the Man from Buffalo. I could have felt so claustrophobic up in all that grass and land that I died, just *died* so I could get back home. But I didn't. I didn't do any of those things because I had Mike Tyson.

Let me tell you about Charlotte's pretty little town—it was like those coloring books, the ones with the Holly Hobbie girls in their gingham dresses, and they're always standing in front of these pretty little white churches, or walking around in pretty pretty fields with pretty pretty horses running around. There are bricks for sidewalks and tall trees with green leaves and a covered bridge to walk through, and everybody is *nice* to everybody else, and everybody says stuff like, "Oh, it is so nice to meet you, honey," when you get introduced at the Golden Dawn grocery store in neighboring Jefferson. That's the kind of pretty little town it was. And who do you think happened to live right next door to Miss Charlotte McConnell of Windsor, Ohio? Well, I'll tell you. It was one Don King, boxing promoter extraordinaire. And who did Don King happen to manage, but the one and only Mr. Mike Tyson.

Iron Mike.

Kid Dynamite.

The Baddest Man on the Planet.

Every day Charlotte and I and her friends Sarah N. and Sarah M. would go play freeze-tag around the statues on Don King's front lawn. We played with Don King's grandchildren, too, so it wasn't like we were trespassing. We wouldn't have gotten *shot* or anything. We weren't doing anything illegal. Mike Tyson and the other boxers—I know there were others, but I don't remember their names—trained in tents in the backyard, punching and jabbing and floating and stinging like birds or bees or whatever. We made them stop to watch us do cartwheels. My cartwheels sucked. I never took gymnastics. Charlotte's, of course, like everything else in her life, were perfect, and she always remembered to point her toes and make wings out of her hands when she finished and stood back upright. But the point is, Mike Tyson never failed to stop jib-jabbing to watch me and applaud, and so I thought he was a pretty nice guy.

When I got home and school started up, of *course* I told everyone that Mike Tyson was pretty much my best friend. I may have been slightly prone to exaggeration when I was younger. In the third grade, I told Jessica O'Neal that I had a bionic toe. She believed me for a whole year. Okay, so maybe the toe thing was less of an exaggeration and more of an outright lie, but you get the picture. Mike Tyson called me on the phone with his little-girl-voice and wished me happy birthday. Mike Tyson baked me a batch of fudge brownies with swirls of caramel. Mike Tyson won me a goldfish at the county fair. For a whole year, I was the coolest person in the fourth grade. I was practically *famous*. Not only had I gone off-island for two whole weeks by myself, but I came back best friends forever with a world-famous sports star. I swear, Misty Garber was on the verge of overlooking our five-year feud just so she could hear me talk about Mike Tyson. I would have forgiven her, too. I would have been just that magnanimous.

And then, after one full year of basking in Mike Tyson's glory, it ended. This was fifth grade, and I was still on a Tyson kick. I think what I was saying then was that Mike Tyson might visit me and we'd go out and eat Bubba's ribs. But what I didn't know was that earlier that summer, Mike Tyson had raped a girl. I didn't know this at all. My classmates and I were at lunch, and it was Thursday, pizza day, the first pizza day of the entire school year. And right there in the lunch line in front of everyone, Misty Garber busted out with what she'd been wanting to bust out with all through math, reading, and recess. It went like this: there I stood in my white ruffled skirt, neon pink leggings, and the fuchsia polka-dotted Keds my mother had let me get. She'd come back home by then, but I think she still felt guilty about Bob the Man from Buffalo. We'd gone all the way up to Sound Feet Shoes in Kitty Hawk, and she let me pick out whichever new school shoes I wanted, and even though she told me nothing would go with fuchsia polka dots, she bought them for me nonetheless. I loved those shoes.

You should've heard how jealous Charlotte got. That was before cell phones, and I had to use my allowance to buy a phone card to call and tell her about my shoes. But it was worth it to hear her just about scream because she had to get boring brown loafers and wasn't even allowed to get the ones with pennies in them. Of course, I knew deep down that she was happy that I had the Best School Shoes in the Universe.

So there I was, all decked out and feeling pretty grand about life in general and pizza day in particular. This was before I cut my own hair off, so it was sticking at the back of my neck because I was sweating a little in the pizza-smelling cafeteria. That was back before they put air-conditioning in the schools. Misty Garber sauntered up to me and cut in line and said to Stephen Oden, who was standing next to me picking at a scab on his forearm, "Did you know that Evie's best friend Mike Tyson is a rapist?"

And if you think kids don't know what that word means, you'd be wrong.

I mean, you wouldn't be *exactly* wrong. Little kids might not know precisely what it means, but they know enough, and they know that it is B.A.D.

But Stephen Oden stood up for me, and for a second I wasn't yet BAD. "What do you know?" he asked Misty. "Did you meet him?" And he punch-punched at her a little.

Boy, did that ever make Misty mad. Her face got all red under that stupid puffed-up hair of hers, and she sort of stamped her foot, because she is *exactly* the kind of girl who saunters and stamps her foot, and she said, "My mom saw it in the newspaper, and that means it's true. He was in prison and everything. He's probably going back to prison soon."

Stephen Oden considered this. Then he just shrugged and went back to picking at his scab.

That could have been the end of it, but Misty didn't stop. She kept on telling everyone that Mike Tyson was a rapist, and she'd sort of hiss the word "rapist" so it went "ray-pisssed." And she said it loud, too. Ray-PISSSED. So by the time I got to the front of the line and the lunch lady put my pizza and corn and chocolate milk on my tray, everybody knew. I wanted to wilt down into my fuchsia polka-dotted Keds.

The worst part of it was that I didn't really even know what ray-pisssed meant, so I defended my friend Mike Tyson. I said to Misty, "So what if he's a rapist? I bet your dad is a rapist, too." I said this right into Misty Garber's face. You can bet that did nothing to patch up our feud. "Maybe everyone is a rapist from time to time," I said, all explanatory-like, to Stephen Oden, who was getting his lunch card punched. "Maybe I *like* my friends to be rapists," I said to Ronnie, your very own Ronnie Ballance, as he requested chocolate milk instead of plain even though he had chocolate allergies. (I bet you didn't know that about him, but it's true.) I said stuff like that to everyone. I was tired of feeling like wilting down into my Keds. I really was.

What happened next was that Misty went and got a dictionary after lunch, and she looked up *rapist,* only she couldn't find it in there, but she sure found *rape,* and she read the definition out loud to the whole class. It was right before Mr. Fink came back into the room to teach us about the ancient city of Ur. This is what Misty read, her mouth moving all sanctimonious-like under that stupid puffed-up hair: "Rape," she said, clearing her throat a little.

I squirmed in my hard yellow seat and lifted the lid of my desk up and down, up and down. "Nobody cares what you read," I said. I knew I was lying, but I said it anyway. I guess in a way that was bad.

Misty cleared her throat *again*. "N. One." She said it just like that, too, I'll never forget. She didn't make it "noun" or anything.

Just "N. One." She wasn't the brightest bulb in the pack. Then she went, "Forcible seizing and violation; ravishing." Everybody (because everybody really did care what she was reading) went "oooh" when she said "ravishing." She made it sound real bad, probably worse than the word really means. *RAV*ishing. Then she said, "Two. Carrying off by force." That one was kind of boring so people stopped paying quite as much attention, and I slammed my desk down hard to make everyone look at me and giggle instead of listening to Misty. But then, loud as all hell, louder than the rumble of twenty kids talking after pizza-Thursday lunch and before they got down to the most serious business of studying the ancient city of Ur, she said, "Force to have sexual intercourse." And she closed the book with a smack and put it back on the shelf, smug as all get-out.

I think she must have been skipping around to find the most awful of definitions of that word, because I've since looked it up and found there's one in there about a plant grown for fodder and oil, but Misty never once mentioned that, because she knew she was losing her audience. She went straight for the "force to have sexual intercourse."

That was the turning point. That's how I got to be BAD. I thought a bad man was a good man, and I bragged about it to everyone on the planet. Kids don't let you forget things like being best friends with a rapist.

And when you're best friends with a ray-pisssed, people make out like fuchsia polka-dotted Keds are the worst thing in the world, even though the day before they were positively coveting them.

I walked from my Aunt Fay's all the way to the Frisco Rod & Gun that night to buy a new phone card to call Charlotte and tell her about my utter humiliation, but instead I ended up talking about other things, Ur mostly, except that I was really too upset to learn anything of value about Ur, so what I did was say, "Ur," a lot, like I was thinking about what to say next, and Charlotte would say, "What did you study today?" and I would say, "Ur, Ur, Ur . . . oh yeah, Ur!" And I bragged about my shoes a little bit more. The thing was, Charlotte didn't know I was now the bad kid, and I wanted to keep it that way. She still, to this very day, nearly nine years later, thinks I'm a nice girl, and I'm quite content to just let her think it.

The next thing that happened to make me bad happened in the ninth grade. As you'll see, this also took place because of Mike Tyson. I swear, that effing Mike Tyson just about ruined my life. Imagine high school. By this time I'd cut my hair and grown it out about ten times, but in ninth grade it was shoulder-length and shaggy and cut like Jennifer Aniston's. I loved it even though it never stayed the way it was supposed to. I was about the same size I was in fifth grade, the same size I am now, which is: small. But I had some knockers at that point. Those I did have, and they were bigger than Charlotte's. She hadn't had any come in yet back then and was super-jealous of mine. Most girls were, I have to admit.

So there I was, all Jennifer Aniston-ed out, walking down the hall on the very first day of school, walking a little bit bouncy so my new boobs jiggled, looking for my locker. Well, I found it, all right. Wouldn't you know that someone had gotten there early and taped pictures from Mike Tyson's ear-biting fight with Evander Holyfield all over my locker? Blood and sweat and ear-lobes everywhere. I never did find out who did it, but I have my suspicions. I mean, for crying out loud, the ear-biting happened in *June*, and it was now *August*. But like I said, kids don't let you forget. Everybody in the hallway laughed at me, I'm not even exaggerating, especially the girls. Girls are so mean. I was still pretty upset about it at lunch, so I ate my sandwich real quick and then went out to the baseball dugout just to get away. It was a pretty day, still summer-warm but with a little bit of autumn poking at the air, saying, *Let me in, I want to come in*. That's my favorite kind of weather of all time, and I just wanted to be outside in it. Apparently, so did Zack Gray, who was a junior and a Popular Boy. He was already in the baseball dugout, eating an apple and just looking out over the Pamlico.

Now, you know that Zack Gray is a cute kid; I don't have to tell you that, Patricia Ballance. And you also know that he and Abigail Krawchuck have been together since sixth grade. Everybody knows that. But you don't know how Zack Gray looked at me that day in the baseball dugout. How his eyes lingered a second too long on my new boobs.

"I hate this place," I told him. I sat down and swung my Jennifer Aniston hair over my face. I might have leaned over a little bit and squeezed my arms together so as to create cleavage, but not in a way that was obvious.

Zack Gray crunched down on his apple. He chewed slowly. "Why do you hate it?" he asked. A breeze answered the poking little bit of autumn and said, *It's still summer, back off!* It blew Zack Gray's hair around, and I found that too adorable.

I pushed my own hair back behind my ears, then realized this wasn't the way it was supposed to look on TV, so I put it back and leaned my elbows on the bench seat. "People are so close-minded." I said it like I was the oldest, wisest person in the world and the people here made me so tired with their stupidness and immaturity.

"I know what you mean," Zack said. He finished his apple, stood up, and threw the core out of the dugout. It landed in some reeds and made a *plish* sound. He wiped his hands on the butt of his jeans (he had a really cute butt in those jeans) and smiled at me. "Do you know that Abigail thinks she can get pregnant by going to second base?"

"That's ridiculous," I said. I arched my back a little and sat up straight. "People don't really think that anymore, do they?"

Zack walked over and sat down beside me. "Abigail does," he said. He reached out his hand like he was making to touch my left boob. "Gonna get you pregnant," he said.

I pretended to be scared and grasped my arms over my chest. This is another move that causes cleavage if you position your arms right, and I positioned my arms right, let me tell you. I liked that Zack Gray. He was fun. "Oh, no, Zack," I cried, all mock scared. "I'm not on birth control. You'll have to put a condom on that hand."

We laughed and then it was quiet for a second. Then he reached out and really did touch my left boob. "You got pretty, Evie," he said. He moved his hand all over my left boob. It felt good and I let him do it.

"Thanks," I said. My voice sounded funny in my own ears.

Then he kissed me. I let him do that, too. We kissed until the lunch bell rang and we had to go inside.

During school, Zack Gray pretended not to know me in the hallway. He walked around holding hands with old Abigail Krawchuck like he had never fondled my left boob at all. He never said *hi* or broke up with her or anything. He didn't get to touch my right boob until the next day, when I went out to see if he would be sitting in the dugout again. He was.

That's when the girls started to look at me funny, as if they had *heard things*. I'd walk down the hall and see Misty Garber whispering something to Emma Midgett, and they'd both stop talking when I came close and I just knew they were talking about me. I don't know why people listened to old Misty Garber in the first place. She only moved here when she was four, whereas my family has been here since some goddamn shipwreck back in the Dark Ages. And even in high school she had that stupid puffed-up hair. I still am none too fond of Misty Garber, if you want to know the truth. I hope she's having fun selling fishing lures and t-shirts to tourists.

But I guess the point is I always thought Zack Gray'd break up with Abigail and realize he wanted to date me. But he never did. By then other guys who had respectable girlfriends had heard I was easy, and sometimes I got lonely and let them make out with me, too. Charlotte said I was overcompensating for an insecurity complex, but I don't know about that. All I know is that boys can be really nice when they want to make out with you. Sometimes, I'd make out with them because it was fun, and sometimes because I liked to see them get all horny, and sometimes because I hated their pretentious girlfriends who wouldn't talk to me. Sometimes I liked them and hoped they would like me back. I never even had sex with all those other girls' boyfriends. I just let them feel my boobs and sometimes, well, never mind. Which isn't so bad if you consider it. And of course I stopped all that when I became a respectable girlfriend for a few weeks, before you made Ronnie stop talking to me.

If you want to know the truth, Mrs. Patricia Ballance, I was just so sad when Ronnie stopped talking to me eight days before graduation. I remember when he started talking to me, I mean talking to me in a different way than before. You were there, you should probably remember, too, unless you were busy chaperoning. It was after the last performance of *Carousel*, in which you will recall that your Ronnie played Mr. Bascombe, and since I'd helped paint the sets, I was invited to the after-party at Rocco's Pizza. I'd just tried a bite of anchovy pizza and decided it was disgusting and spit it into my napkin. Ronnie saw that and grinned at me. It was hot in there, especially with all of us crowded around, and Ronnie still had his stage makeup on, and it was sliding around his face because he was all kinds of sweaty. He looked ridiculous.

"Fish don't belong on pizza," I said.

Ronnie scooted over closer to me. "What do you call a fish without an eye?" he asked.

I put down my pizza and pushed my hair behind my ears. "What?"

"Fsssshhhhh," Ronnie said. Then he laughed.

Then I started laughing because he was laughing, and then I choked on my Diet Dr. Pepper and Ronnie banged on my back. I looked up after I wiped off my eyes and I saw you staring at me with a funny look around your mouth like maybe you'd have to sterilize Ronnie's hand for cooties after he'd touched my back, but I didn't really think anything of it. I was too excited because that was when Ronnie and I started dating. Not really, of course. But that's when things changed. We started to talk at school, in homeroom and study hall, and then we sat together at lunch, and then he asked me to prom.

I should have known something big and bad was impending when I showed up at your house to take pictures and you opened the door and said, "Hello, Evie. That's an interesting dress." And you got that funny-mouth look again, like my dress was a total harlot outfit, when in reality it was only a very short red gown and not trashy at all. Charlotte said I should get it because red is always classy and will never go out of style, but then again, she's the kind of girl who can wear a very short red gown and not get looked at like she's wearing a total harlot outfit because she's a good girl and has never been bad.

Anyway, I was wearing heels, so I was standing up extra tall, and I just said, "Thank you, I got it at that little place up in Buxton" and walked right into your house like I had been invited. Ronnie and I stood by the fireplace and had our pictures taken, and for a while your mouth relaxed and got normal and so I thought everything was okay. Ronnie and I had such a good time at the prom, and he was a real gentleman and got me punch. We danced, and he was a good dancer and he looked sharp in his tuxedo. All in all, it was *A Night to Remember*, as our theme foretold. I won't tell you all about what happened afterward at the bonfire on the beach, but I'll just say that we had a good time. Not *too* good of time, though, if you know what I mean. And he gave me his ring, and we decided to go steady. Even though Ronnie was just a drama geek, somehow the fact that such a nice boy as Ronnie Ballance liked me turned me into a Very Respectable Woman. And that made me happy.

So when Ronnie stopped talking to me, and I didn't have that anymore, do you know what I did? I started taking quizzes online. I found out that maybe the reason he didn't call me back was because I wasn't interesting or feisty enough. I started reading articles like, "Living Alone and Loving It." I started imagining reasons why Ronnie stopped talking to me—that maybe he saw me biting up baby carrots and spitting them out to put on my salad instead of getting out a knife and cutting board. It sounds disgusting, but let me tell you, it's effective. Or that maybe he suddenly decided I had insufferable halitosis of the breath and smelling me talk was far too painful for him.

It was a day like any other day when Ronnie stopped talking

to me. An almost-graduation day. A have-an-assembly-in-the-gym-about-caps-and-gowns day, so maybe a little less than ordinary, but sunshiny and hopeful and nice all the same. All of us who were starting up at ECU in the fall decided to sit together, me and Jessica O'Neal and Stephen Oden (I think that Stephen Oden grew up to be quite cute, and ever since we've been here at college, he hasn't been nearly as jerky as he was in high school. In fact, he just now poked his head into my room and said hi, exactly like we were old friends. It wasn't all his fault he was jerky in high school—that's what being a popular kid'll do to you, in my opinion. There's a good chance it'll make you jerky, which is why I'm kind of glad I wasn't a popular kid after all) and Joe Meekins and Sam Gillikin, but not Ronnie, no Ronnie, no Ronnie at all. We'd been going steady for five and a half weeks at that point, and I wanted to sit next to Ronnie. So I went all around looking for him, and when I found him he was sitting with a whole other group of people, ones who were not bound for East Carolina University, ones who were destined to be Tar Heels or Wolfpack-ers or whatever, but certainly not Pirates.

"We're sitting over there," I said to him. I was wearing my Gap blue jeans I'd mail-ordered that Mom had hemmed up for me because I can never find jeans that are short enough. They were my favorites, and I was wearing them and red flip-flops and a little red t-shirt that said, "I Hate Myself and Want to Die" over a happy rainbow and some cartoony hearts. That shirt cracked me up. I still wear it all the time. So anyway, Ronnie just acted like he didn't hear me. I said louder, "Come sit with us," and poked him in the arm. Ronnie looked at me and his face was all funny, and he sort of glanced away like he never heard me either time I said anything. So I gave up and walked back to my spot on the bleachers, but my stomach was all wrong and the inside of my mouth felt like I'd just sucked on a great big wad of smashed-up cotton balls.

All through the assembly I couldn't pay attention, and wouldn't you know, I got a too-long gown—only I didn't realize it until the last minute and so my mom didn't have time to take it up. So I duct-taped it and that's how I graduated from Cape Hatteras Secondary School, Home of the Hurricanes. With a duct-taped gown. But at least my hair looked good. I flat-ironed it twice on account of the humidity. Not that Ronnie even noticed, since by then he hadn't talked to me for eight and a half days straight. It wasn't like he was just busy, either, because we were doing the same things, graduating from high school and all. He was very definitely ignoring me.

This is what I did next: after we were all graduated with our caps thrown into the air, I walked right over to Ronnie Ballance, and I said, "Why aren't you talking to me?"

He looked very uncomfortable, maybe because I'd asked him this every day for the past seven days now, and he knew he'd have to answer me pretty soon. "I'm sorry, Evie," he said. He gave a little sigh, and I wanted to punch him. "My mom said I had to break up with you."

"Your *mom*?" I said, as incredulous as can be. "Why on earth does your mom care who you date, and furthermore, why would you listen to her?" (That's right; I was trying to usurp your influence, Mrs. B.)

"She didn't want me to get a reputation," Ronnie said. A gust of wind came along and blew his hair all around his head, and for the first time, I didn't think he looked cute. So I just walked away, but I was steaming mad.

The worst part of it was when I called Charlotte about it (by this point I had a cell phone so it was easier), she didn't really care, and I can't say as I blame her because her dad was very sick and in fact just died this August, and how does a boy not talking to me even begin to compare to that? It can't. So I felt even more all alone.

I'm not saying this is why I did what I did next. I'm not saying that at all. But maybe it was part of the reason. A girl doesn't get so mad she spreads rumors that Ronnie Ballance, all-American Good Boy, took advantage of her at a bonfire, which forced her to then go have a secret abortion for no good reason at all. I suppose you've heard those rumors, but you didn't know they came from me, and that I did it to make Ronnie seem bad. I guess I wouldn't have gotten so upset if Ronnie hadn't been the first boy to treat me like a person and not a total slut-bag. If he hadn't given me a taste of what it felt like to be legitimate instead of the girl who makes out with other girls' boyfriends in the dugout out behind the school.

Anyway, Mrs. Patricia Ballance, as you can clearly see, this badness reputation wasn't all my fault. Mike Tyson had quite a lot to do with it, and the mean girls at school, and their stupid boyfriends who liked my boobs. It wasn't all me. And, come on, it's not like Ronnie's a saint, either. Besides the whole drinking chocolate milk despite being allergic to chocolate thing, did you know he was pretty much always the one to get hold of beer to take to bonfires? Did you know he smoked weed? It's true. I never did that, even though I know you won't believe it. He also once told me that he was scared he wouldn't get a good score on his SATs and was seriously contemplating cheating. I don't think he did, though. But I never thought about cheating on my SATs. Those kinds of things don't occur to me.

Before I go, here are some things about me that you might like to know:

1.) I'm making a New Woman of myself here at college. This is kind of hard to do since half my high school also goes to college here, but I'm doing it. The other day, guess who came along and, all on his own accord, sat beside me in the dining hall? Stephen Oden, that's who. I may have said it before, but he's a Popular Boy. Not as much of a Popular Boy as Zack Gray was, but still pretty high up there. Anyway, we had a nice lunch of Cinnamon Life cereal and talked about home and our classes (his favorite is sociology while mine is biology), and then we each made a waffle. I think he might like me.
2.) Then, tonight, Stephen Oden came by my room, and we took a walk. I thought to myself, *things are looking up.* If you must know, I've been homesick since I got here. I've missed the soft shushing sound of the waves. I've cried myself to sleep. I've called my mother every two hours. My mother hates it when I do that. She's too busy to listen to me complain about being homesick. But Stephen Oden isn't. He listened to me complain about being homesick for two whole hours straight tonight. We walked around and didn't even hold hands or anything, just walked around under the trees and talked. And then Joe Meekins walked past and saw us, and he gave Stephen Oden a *look,* and I said, "Well, hell. Here we go again." I said it right out loud.

Stephen looked over at me. He reached up and pulled some leaves off of a tree and then tossed them on the ground. "What's wrong?" he asked.

I crossed my arms (but because I was mad, not to create cleavage). "Aren't you ashamed to be seen with me?" I asked him.

Stephen just put his hands in his pockets and walked along. "You can't let them get to you like that, Evie," he said.

At the time it kind of pissed me off, because what does he know, but I think he may be right. And he's also very cute. I didn't really answer him, just walked along and changed the subject to rhinoceroses, because in my opinion, if you ever find yourself in a conversation going somewhere you don't want it to go, just bring up rhinoceroses.

And so then Stephen walked me back to the dorm and very nicely kissed me goodnight on the cheek.

I think I'm going to like college.

3.) In summation, my ethos is that I'm actually a nice girl who just got a raw deal on account of Mike Tyson, mean girls, and boobs. My pathos is to make you, Patricia Ballance, feel bad about telling Ronnie he had to break up with me. If I was a man and I made out with girls in the dugout, you wouldn't have cared at all. It stinks that you're a grown-up woman who should know how these things work and you're the one perpetrating this myth that I'm bad. My logos is to show you the logical progression of Mike Tyson making me into a seemingly bad girl and all the other stuff that went into my so-called reputation.

4.) And just so you know, I was the only one in my school who could have pulled off that prom dress. And red never does go out of style.

5.) I have moved past all this now, and so should you.

6.) Sincerely (and not badly) yours,

Evelyn Ann Austin

Eleven

For His Part

— 2018 —

The key to getting someone to buy a house is to make them fall in love. It doesn't matter if the house is wildly impractical or thousands of dollars out of their price range—if they fall in love, that's it, they're hooked, and they're buying. I've gotten pretty good at it, and in the three years since I've had my realtor's license, the best case of falling in realty love was when I got my former English professor, Dr. Garcia, to buy the Cape Isle Motel. He'd just inherited some money and was looking for a midcareer shift. He'd already fallen in love with the Outer Banks, and when I showed him the motel—a brick building with a circular driveway, a little blue jewel of a pool, and plenty of space out back for his daughter, Fiona, to play—he fell in love with that, too. I'm good at making people fall in love because I know it's a trick. Once their hearts start to pound, reason has no pull. They just leap. But I don't trust that gaping, awful tumult. All I trust is logic, slick and hard.

I pull into the driveway of the Cape Isle Motel to pick up my son, Austin, from his play date with Fiona. I'm still in my realtor costume, a button-up shirt and khaki pants and cute little brown heels. I have a bobbed haircut and bangs (bangs or Botox, I always say, though I'm mostly joking because I'm only twenty-eight and look younger) that make me into the epitome of a professional lady. My image is ruined when I step into the ninety-degree August afternoon and trip over Wilbur, the Garcias' bulldog. He slobbers on my pant leg.

"Jesus, Wilbur," I say, and reach down to pat his head and wipe the bulldog spit off my slacks.

"Mom!" Austin runs out of the motel lobby, barreling at me like he barrels at life. My son is dark and sharp and feisty and smarter at nine years old than a dozen of me and Stephen put together. Nicer, too, but I think he gets that from Nate. "Daniel taught Wilbur to skateboard," Austin says, bending down to scratch his knee. I can tell he's debating whether or not he's too cool to give me a hug, and he glances to see that no one's looking before he throws his arms around my waist.

"Awesome," I say. "Show me." I wonder who Daniel is.

Austin runs back to the lobby. He's getting gangly. He'll probably need new pants soon. Austin comes back with Fiona and a broad-shouldered, dark-haired man. The man carries a battered skateboard, and Wilbur barks and runs toward him, pink tongue flailing. The lobby door bangs open and shut again, and Dr. Garcia steps out, trailed by Orville, their other dog. Orville is a whippet. He's the flattest dog I've ever seen. I like him because he never says anything and rarely slobbers on me.

"Check out the new trick," Dr. Garcia says. He's told me a million times to call him Rick, but I still can't do it.

The guy with the shoulders bends down and rolls the skateboard toward Wilbur. Wilbur jumps on and pushes with his back leg, barking madly the whole time.

Austin and Fiona clap their hands and cheer. They chase after Wilbur and try to get the skateboard, but Wilbur picks it up and runs behind the motel and the kids follow. "Was the mayhem this intense all afternoon?" I ask.

"Much worse," new guy says, and he looks at me for the first time. His eyes are dark and liquid. He smiles. One of his lower teeth crooks behind the others. "I'm Daniel," he says, holding out his hand.

I reach out to shake it just as Dr. Garcia slaps Daniel on the shoulder, and we miss the connection. "This is my brother," Dr. Garcia says.

I'm a little bit flummoxed by Daniel's adorableness. "Hi," I say. Then I remember not to trust emotions. "Evie Austin." I reach out and shake his hand firmly and professionally, like I'm there to sell him an A-frame.

"So your son is Austin Austin?"

I feel myself blushing. I hate this question. *Of course* I'm not dumb enough to name my son Austin Austin. "I gave him my maiden name. I took my last name back after his father and I divorced. Austin has his dad's last name." I stare at Daniel. Jerk.

Dr. Garcia rubs his hands together and nods. Then he pats Daniel on the back. "Daniel's staying with us for a while," Dr. Garcia says. He says it in a way that makes me think Daniel is recovering from a long stint in prison or a near-fatal illness.

Austin and Fiona and Wilbur thunder around to the front of the motel in a cacophony of legs and wheels and barking. "We'd better get moving," I say to Austin. He looks like he's about to whine for more playing time so I give him the stink-eye.

"Fine," he says. He walks to the car, dejected, slump-shouldered, feet dragging. He throws open the door and slams himself in.

"It was nice to meet you, Evie," Daniel says.

Austin sticks his head out the car window. "See you, Fiona," he shouts.

"Evie," Dr. Garcia says, snapping his fingers like my name is his brightest idea yet. "You're the perfect one to show Daniel around the island."

I narrow my eyes. He's trying to set us up, and I'm not falling for it. Daniel's hair shines, sleek under the heavy August sun. "It's a small island," I say. Daniel looks at me with those eyes, and there's something sad behind them. I forgive him for thinking I'd named my son Austin Austin. Maybe he really is recovering from a near-fatal illness. Maybe I shouldn't do anything to upset him. And it is a small island. A little tour is no skin off my nose. "But if you call me sometime I'll show you around."

~

Stephen texts me to say he's thinking of moving back to Hatteras. We generally communicate better with a sheen of technology between us. I know it's not smart, but I can't help but get a little *zing* of excitement at the thought of Stephen coming home. Things are never boring when we're together, that's for sure.

I'm sitting with Nate at our parents' inn, having tea on the deck after an early dinner. I show him my phone. "Stephen might move home," I say. I prop my feet on the deck railing and fish my sunglasses out of my purse. The inn's guests splash around in the pool and swing in hammocks. The inn itself sits on the marshy edge of the Pamlico Sound, the water diamond-sparkly in the late afternoon sun.

Nate swallows his tea and sets the mug on his chair's armrest. He nods and narrows his eyes out at the Pamlico. Sometimes I think he's practicing to play the role of Stoic Sea Captain on a made-for-TV movie. It'd air on Lifetime, Television for Women, and Nate would play Captain Morgan Stern, gruff but softhearted, unlucky in love until he meets the secretly cancer-ridden heroine with a murky past. In real life, Nate's married, with a baby daughter, Lara. He has no cause to squint narrow-eyed at the sound. "Be good for Austin," Nate says.

I nod. I try a squint-eyed gaze to see how it feels. *I'm just a stoic man.* "I hate to get Austin all riled up if he doesn't actually do it," I say. Stephen and I have managed to forgive each other for past wrongs. We're better at co-parenting than we used to be, but I don't quite trust him yet.

Nate runs a hand through his wavy hair. "May be better to not mention it," he says.

I stand up and lean over the deck railing. The Pamlico gleams as the sun creep-inches its way down the sky. "I think Stephen's lonely," I say. Ever since Stephen got dumped by the latest of the little chippies he's dated since breaking up with his fiancée, he's been calling and texting daily, sometimes just to tell me about a particularly delicious batch of French fries he'd eaten or a funny license plate he'd seen.

Nate stands up beside me. "Lonely might be good for Stephen. Make him figure out what matters."

Maybe it wouldn't be so bad to have Stephen back, if he figures out it's us that matters, me and Austin. And my life could use a little *zing* right about now.

~

There's nothing like coming home to a puddle of dog pee. I stop by my house to let out poor geriatric Walter and step right in it. It's the first day of school, and I've taken off work early to get Austin, even though I know he won't appreciate this and probably won't even notice.

"Dammit, Walter," I say, even though I know he can't help it. Walter is sixteen and blind. He wanders over and bumps into my leg. Walter is the main reason I made sure our house had laminate floors—I didn't want our home to turn into Pee Carpet Palace. It's the first time Austin and I've had our very own place, one we didn't share with Stephen or my parents. I throw my shoe in the sink and grab the spray bottle of cleaner and some paper towels. I'm annoyed because those are the only shoes that go with today's realtor costume, and I have two minutes before I need to leave to pick up Austin. I shove my feet into the pair of orange Crocs I keep by the door and hightail it to school.

The parking lot is hopping, and it's too hot to sit in the car, so I get out and stand with the other moms near the entrance, hoping nobody notices the cloggy ugliness of my shoes. First generation Crocs really are god-awful. I nod to Emma X, who's been married so many times no one can keep track of her last name. She used to be Emma Midgett. It's still a little weird to me that this school, the site of my childhood taunting, is now Austin's, though they remodeled it a few years ago. It looks like a great big beach cottage now instead of the brick squatness of my day. I'm glancing down to see if there are noticeable sweat stains on my blouse when I hear my name. I look up. It's Daniel.

"I think Fiona has shoes like that," he says. He's wearing tan cargo shorts and a green t-shirt, and he still has those eyes and that face and those shoulders.

"They were a gift," I say. "From my mother. The dog peed on my other shoes, my real shoes." Flummoxed, I run my hand along the beachy planks of the school building.

Daniel puts his hands in his pockets. "I just meant that you looked nice," he says. He smiles and the crooked bottom tooth makes my heart flit against my rib cage, which irritates me. I'm not sixteen, for crying out loud.

"Are you here for Fiona?" I ask. Then I curse myself for saying something so stupid. Of course he's here for Fiona.

"Being together helps both of us, I think," Daniel says. "She's still a bit flummoxed about the move."

Daniel actually says *flummoxed*. "I was just thinking that," I say. I wonder why Daniel needs help.

"About Fiona?"

"About flummoxed," I say. I shake my head. I'm not making any sense.

"It's a great word," Daniel says, like this is the most logical conversational progression ever.

The bell rings and kids stream out the front doors, wild and raucous. It takes us a second to find Austin and Fiona. All the kids look alike with their backpacks and first-day-of-school clothes. I spot Austin and wave. He grins and runs up to me, then remembers that he's cool and slows to a walk. "Hey Mom," he says. "You took off work early."

"It's your first day," I say. I'm pleased he noticed. "How'd it go?"

Fiona has found Daniel. He rests his hand on her head. Fiona squints up at me. She's a cute little thing, freckled and green-eyed with dark hair in a messy ponytail. "Our teacher has a sweet voice," she says.

"That's a good thing," I say.

We all walk to the parking lot, Austin and Fiona chattering and giggling. I turn back and see Emma X watching us. She whispers something to Jackie Ballance. I know they're talking about me and Daniel. I know I have ugly Crocs and no dinner plans, and I'm sweating like a wildebeest, but none of that matters right now.

"Why are you smiling, Mom?" Austin asks. He shimmies his backpack around on his shoulders.

I mess up his hair, and he pulls away. "I'm glad you had a good first day," I say.

Daniel stops walking and points at a blue sedan parked right beside my car. "This is us," he says. Fiona climbs in, her backpack bumping the doorframe. She looks like a turtle. "How about this weekend for a tour?" Daniel asks, removing Fiona's backpack and tossing it in the back seat.

"Sure."

Austin and I climb in the car and drive away, singing along to the radio. "Mom, how old does someone have to be to go steady?" Austin asks over the music. I roll down the windows and my hair blows back from my face.

"I'd say nine is a good age." I glance at Austin in the rearview mirror. He grins, and we sing louder. *Ba-Ba-Ba, Ba-Barbara Ann.* There's a buoyancy inside me, something bright and arch and new. I drum my hand on the steering wheel as we turn onto Highway 12.

~

Stephen texts me that evening. *What illness did everyone on the Starship Enterprise catch?*

What? I text back.

Chicken Spocks.

That's illogical, I write. Then I call him. Austin's asleep, so I keep my voice low and the TV on quietly in the background. "I think Austin's about to make his move on Fiona," I say.

Stephen groans. "Welcome to the realm of relationships, kid."

"I think it's cute," I say.

"Is she pretty?" Stephen asks.

"She's nine," I say. "But yes, she's adorable. Sweet, too." Walter ambles over and bumps into the sofa. I pick him up, and he settles on my lap.

"They say boys choose mates who're just like their mothers," Stephen says.

I roll my eyes. But I'm pleased. Stephen goes on to talk about his family, and how his dad's ready to retire and let Stephen take over the hardware store in Hatteras. "I could make it turn a good profit, Evie," he says. "I've learned a lot."

I wonder just what Stephen's learned. I wonder if he's changed as much as I have, if we're really different people from the ones who got knocked up and married too soon and had matching revenge-affairs, or if we're still the same idiots, only older.

"I was an idiot," Stephen says.

"I was just thinking that," I say. Then I brace myself for Stephen to yell at me, but he just laughs. "I didn't mean it like that," I say. "I was thinking how dumb we both were at nineteen."

"And twenty."

"And twenty-three," I say.

Stephen clears his throat. "I didn't know what I had until I lost it," he says. "It's time I focused on family. On what matters."

I pet Walter's silky head. "On living long and prospering," I say. *Zing.*

~

Nate and I meet for coffee the next morning at the inn. I've just discovered mail-order Dunkin' Donuts coffee and I wonder where it's been all my life. It's windy and a little chilly, and fat gray clouds plump along the skyline. All the guests are inside, but Nate and I sit on the deck. My phone rings, and I jump. I don't recognize the number. I answer. It's Daniel, and before I can think, I'm agreeing to show him the island today. I hang up.

"Hot date?" Nate asks.

"Shut up," I say. "I'm just showing Dr. Garcia's brother, Daniel, around. It's professional courtesy."

"I thought you were hanging out with me and Lara today," Nate says.

Shit. He's right. "I'm sorry," I say. I stand up. "I forgot."

Nate shakes his head. "You would drop everything for some man."

This pisses me off. I turn to Nate. I'm taller than he is since he's sitting, and I like this. "I'm not the girl I used to be, Nate. I'm not going to let a pair of nice shoulders fool me again."

Nate shrugs.

"Don't be a dick," I say. Then I feel bad because I'm the one breaking our plans. "Let's do dinner instead."

Nate agrees, and we take our coffee mugs into the kitchen. "Remember to show Daniel the new baseball dugouts."

"Smartass." I punch Nate in the shoulder and leave.

When I drive up to the motel, Daniel's standing at the entrance beside the sign, one foot crossed in front of the other. He waves, and he looks like the Vegas Vic cowboy, minus the hat. He gets in the car, and we drive north to the lighthouse.

"The Cape Hatteras lighthouse is the tallest in America," I say, in full tourist-guide form. But this is boring. This is the stuff everybody knows. I change my mind. "Have you heard about the Cora tree?" I ask.

"No," Daniel says. He shuffles his stuff around, and I notice a fancy camera.

I keep driving north, telling Daniel the story of how long ago the witch Cora was tied to a tree, about to be burned, when she vanished in a flash of lightning that emblazoned her name into the trunk. I pull into the parking lot of the National Park in Buxton and curve around to the lighthouse, which rises in front of us like a giant, striped barbershop pole. "Want me to take your picture?" I ask.

"Absolutely," Daniel says. We climb out of the car, and he hands me the camera and shows me what button to push. Daniel stands in front of the lighthouse; he gives a thumbs-up and a big grin, and I click.

"There's a museum if you want to see it," I tell him.

Daniel takes his camera and goes back to the car. "I'd rather see the Cora tree if you don't mind," he says.

So we head south to Frisco, turning in at Brigand's Bay, a pretty little subdivision of residential and rental houses. We get out and walk along Snug Harbor Drive, searching for the right tree among the row of twisty live oaks. "This is it," I say. I point out the spot in the bark.

"I think it says coma," Daniel says.

"It does not," I say. "What kind of a witch is named Coma?"

"Because the lightning put her in a coma?" Daniel asks.

I tip my face to the sky. "Speaking of lightning," I say. The fat gray clouds from earlier have spread across the entire sky. The wind blows my bangs into my eyes, and I shiver. It's going to pour soon. We get back in the car.

"What now?" I ask. Then I remember that Daniel doesn't know anything about the island, so of course he wouldn't know what now because that's my job. "Now is time for a Hatteras-style sno-cone," I decide.

Daniel asks what this is. I pull onto Highway 12 and turn right, telling him it's ice cream on the bottom and flavored shave-ice on top. "The owners have been here since the 1950s," I tell him. The rain starts, and I flip on the wipers. We get to the shave-ice place and hold our arms over our heads and run through the rain to order. I get chocolate chip cookie dough on bottom and black cherry on top, and Daniel goes for a classic vanilla topped with orange. He pays even though I protest. We sit in the car and eat, and I'm freezing. Daniel shudders a little, too. I turn on the heat, but this makes the shave-ice melt, so we eat fast, slurping and crunching and shivering the whole time.

"What brings you to the Outer Banks?" I ask. I adjust the heater so it blows on my legs.

"A few things happened at once," Daniel says. He pushes at the sno-cone with a spoon, flattening the top. "My father died, I thought I got cancer, and I got fired."

"Wow," I say. I wipe a drip of black cherry off my arm.

"I know," he says. "Scott Bakula would play me in the made-for-TV movie."

"I love Scott Bakula," I say. "I love any man whose name rhymes with Dracula."

"Vampires are pretty awesome," Daniel says. He bares his teeth and makes his fingers into fangs.

"Anyway," I say.

"Anyway," he says. "It turned out I didn't have cancer, just a benign thyroid tumor. But it made me reevaluate things, like how the company I was working for was doing some unethical stuff. The short version is, I called them on it, and I got fired."

I crunch some shave-ice. "What's the long version?"

"I'll tell you about it sometime," Daniel says.

I try to decide if this is fishy or not. I finish the shave-ice and move on to the cookie dough. "So now you're here," I say.

"Now I'm here. You know Rick got some money from our father. That's how he bought the motel. I got some, too, so I can stay for a while as I figure out my next step."

"And help with Fiona," I say.

"And help with Fiona."

I sit quietly for a second. I wonder if my lips are stained from the shave-ice.

"Family's really important to me," Daniel says.

"Me too," I say. I don't mean to tell him how Stephen and I didn't plan to have Austin, but it slips out. "He's my favorite person in the world," I say.

"He seems like a great kid," Daniel says. "I know Fiona loves him."

"He has a crush on her," I say, leaning my head back against the seat. "I hope Stephen does move home, just so Austin has his dad close when he starts trying to figure out girls."

Daniel eats the last of his ice cream and squishes the paper cone around the spoon. He tucks it carefully into the cup holder between us and wipes his mouth with a napkin. Then he takes my hand. I let him. We sit and listen to the rain.

~

Stephen calls during dinner. Nate and Jennie are over with the baby. I've made shepherd's pie (I always tell Austin it's made with real shepherds), and Jennie feeds little spoonfuls off the top to Lara, who bangs her fists on the high chair tray and squishes potatoes out of her mouth until they run down her chin. I see Stephen's number and pass the phone to Austin. "It's your dad," I say.

Austin jumps up, bright-eyed. No pretending to be cool here. He grabs the phone and runs down the hall. "Dad!" he says, followed by a rushing string of sentences that fades away as he closes the door to his room.

Walter stumbles across the dining room and thuds his head into Nate's chair. Nate reaches down to pet him. "Did Daniel enjoy the dugouts?" he asks.

Jennie and I are friends; she knows my history with dugouts. She stops feeding Lara to give Nate a dirty look. "Seriously?" she asks.

"If you must know," I say to Nate, "I showed him the Cora tree and we ate a sno-cone and went to the maritime museum. It was entirely innocent."

Jennie hands Lara her sippy cup. "What's Daniel's story?" she asks.

I feel weird telling her Daniel's out of a job and doesn't know what he's doing with his life. Aimlessness is not a highly recommended quality in a new guy. "He's here to help out with Fiona," I say. Then I remember I'm not starting a relationship with Daniel. "He's between jobs right now."

"Sounds stable," Nate says. He leans back with his hands laced behind his head. Jennie swats him in the stomach.

Austin runs down the hall. He trips over Walter, and Walter yelps. "Mom," Austin says, waving the phone at me. "Dad wants to talk to you. He's coming home!" Austin jumps up and pumps his fist in the air.

I get up and take the phone. "What's up?" I say to Stephen.

There's a rattling noise, like Stephen's blowing his nose or driving through a tunnel. "Austin's pretty excited that I'm moving back," he says.

I walk down the hall, out of earshot of the table. I kick at a loose baseboard I've been meaning to fix. "You know you have to do it now, right? Did you quit your job?"

"I took care of it. I've sold my house," he says. Stephen pauses, and the rustling sound gets louder. "Evie, I'm coming home."

Home. It sounds funny coming from Stephen, who always wanted to leave the island and make a new home somewhere else, somewhere less isolated, somewhere landlocked. "I guess you are, then," I say. I get the *zing* again. Stephen's coming home.

"I think we should spend time together as a family," Stephen says. "I'm realizing how much I need you guys."

I think about Austin's fist-pumping, face-alighting reaction. It makes me smile. "I think we need you, too," I say. "You know. Austin does." We chat a little more. Then I hang up and walk back out to the table. My shepherd's pie is cold. "Stephen will be moving back in about a month," I tell everyone.

"Yes!" Austin shouts.

Nate raises his eyebrows but doesn't say anything. He picks the strangest moments to be stoic. Jennie telegraphs me a look that says, *We'll talk later.* Lara yells something that sounds like "bababaaba" and smashes potatoes in her hair. For his part, Walter lifts his hind leg and pees on the floor.

~~~

Daniel calls me the next day. We talk for four hours. He tells me about his first girlfriend when he was ten, how he's researching medical school applications, how he once wanted to be a jockey before he knew they were only four feet tall. He tells me about his company's involvement in insider trading, how he was afraid of losing his job and didn't talk for the longest time, and how he still feels guilty. I tell him about my inordinate love of rhinoceroses, the time I met Mike Tyson, how I stumbled into realty but really love it. I tell him about how my first boyfriend broke my heart, how his mother wouldn't let him date me because I was the Bad Girl.

It would be completely illogical for me to fall for Daniel. We've seen each other precisely three times. I'm a smart woman, and I've been burned by love or lust or one of those L words that's not *logic* too many times to let a dark-eyed, broad-shouldered man sway me from my convictions. It's just infatuation. Weak knees do not a healthy relationship foretell.

~~~

Keep an ear to the ground for deals on residential houses, k? Stephen texts.

I write back, *Which village?*

I'd prefer Hatteras, but Frisco or Buxton would be okay.

I think about texting Stephen that he wouldn't be having this problem if he hadn't prostituted our little white house on Elizabeth Lane to a developer who tore it down and built a pastel vacation rental, but I can't muster the snark. *Will do,* I text.

You're beautiful, Stephen writes.

Hey, it's my job, I text back.

No, Stephen writes. *I mean it. You're beautiful.*

This time the *zing* shivers its way up to my heart.

~

I borrow Nate's truck and drive Daniel to the ends of the earth. The village of Hatteras is the last bit of civilization on the island, but if you drive onto the beach access ramp and keep going south, the land stretches along for miles, nothing but sand and sea and dunes. A person can drive right out to the tip end where the ocean and the sound blend together. In evenings this late in the summer, there's usually no one out but a fisherman or two, sometimes some kids and dogs. You can watch the ferry boats on their way to and from Ocracoke, and it's a good place to look for dolphins. There's no one out tonight—Daniel and I are alone on the edge of everything.

"I just feel comfortable with you, Evie," he says. We're sitting on a blanket watching the sun set over the Pamlico, the sky swirled pink and tangerine. I'm not one to wax poetic over sunsets, but this one is pretty freaking amazing.

"Comfortable is good," I say. Then I wonder if I'm giving away too much ground, opening too much. "My ex-husband is moving home," I say.

Daniel picks up a handful of sand and sifts it through his fingers. "Is that a good or a bad thing?" he asks. He sits there in the sunset, his face a perfect straight-nosed profile.

"Good for Austin," I say. "And Stephen seems to be acting like a grown-up this time." I think about the phone conversations we've had while I found Stephen a rental on the island, how we joked about him living in an RV like I did with my aunt one summer, or camping out in the back room of the hardware store.

Daniel dusts off his hands and reaches into his backpack for a bottle of wine. "Exes are tricky things," he says. I wonder about his exes, but I don't ask yet.

We share some wine. He's forgotten to bring glasses, so we pass the bottle back and forth. "I love how classy we are," I say.

He wipes a little drip from the side of my mouth. Daniel leans over and kisses me then, his lips soft against mine, warm from the wine.

"Classy with a K," Daniel says. He raises the bottle in a miniature toast.

I grab the wine and take a sip. "Klass-tastic."

~

I pull out the scrapbook from my first and only semester at college. The first page is comprised of a picture of Stephen and me, faces pressed together, grins wide. It's pasted on a red heart. Then me and Stephen at an ECU football game, his arm around my shoulder, my hands waving purple pom-poms. Me and Stephen in pajamas, eating waffles in the dining hall during finals. A long shot of me and Stephen sitting under a pine tree with a tall, skinny trunk, his fingers in my hair as I lean against his propped-up knees.

Do you remember the pine on ECU's quad? I text Stephen.

Stephen writes back, *I remember you under the pine. How soft your hair was.*

And how I found a pine needle in my boxers that night. But mostly you.

A warmth courses through me, something soft and familiar, sparkly and new. *I remember you, too,* I write.

And I do.

And I also remember last night, when Daniel brought me a copy of Pablo Neruda's book of sonnets, which I've been wanting to read and don't even remember mentioning to him. I remember the way he stabbed a bite of scallop off of my plate without thinking, then apologized, then looked relieved when I wasn't angry. I remember him shortening his stride so I could keep up as we walked along the beach.

I remember all that, too.

Stephen keeps his word and moves back within the month. He gets onto the island during my lunch hour, so I meet him at a barbecue place in the Food Lion plaza in Avon. Stephen looks good despite the fact that he's resurrected his mustache. He's trim and muscular, and he's still got his sandy blond hair. His face is all angles, with cheekbones so high and sharp you'd think they'd slice your finger if you ran it across them. Attraction was never the issue between us. I still want to jump him.

"How does it feel to be home?" I ask him. I wipe my mouth carefully. I don't want to get sauce on my realtor costume.

Stephen takes a bite out of a rib. "Delicious," he says. He grins, and he looks like he did when we were kids. He's got sauce on the side of his face.

"I bet you missed Hatteras barbecue," I say. I reach over and wipe off his cheek. It feels spontaneous and natural to touch him.

"I missed you," he says. He grabs my sauce-wiping finger and holds my hand. Before I can react, he takes a big, messy bite of rib and kisses my palm with his sauce-lips.

I shriek and wriggle. Stephen places my hand back on my side of the table as if he's presenting me with a gift. "If we eat fast, I can drive with you to the office to get your rental keys," I say. I make a big show of cleaning my hand with a wet wipe.

"I'm excited to see it," Stephen says. "I'm excited to be home."

I'm excited, too.

~

Nate and I deliver the scones our dad makes to the Dancing Turtle, a coffee shop in Hatteras. After we're finished, we sit and eat one as a reward. He carries Lara in a front pack, her fuzzy head the only thing visible.

"Stephen's all settled in," I say. I tell Nate about how Austin and I helped him unpack, how we all took a walk on the beach and built a campfire and roasted hot dogs.

Nate raises his eyebrows. "You seem awfully positive about his return," he says.

I fiddle with my scone, picking out a raspberry. "It makes sense," I say. "He's Austin's father. And we're friends now."

Lara fusses, and Nate pats her back. He shifts her around and leans forward, looking me in the eyes. "He never treated you right," he says.

"We're older now," I say. "He's changed." An old resentment rises in my chest, a feeling that I could never do anything right. "You want Lara to have a family, don't you? If you and Jennie ever split up, wouldn't you consider getting back together for her sake? Just *consider* it?"

Nate sighs. But then he nods. He's not being stoic; it's a nod like he's thinking. "You're a smart woman, Evie," he says.

"I know," I say. I steal the last bite of his scone.

Nate doesn't play along by slapping my hand or yelling at me like when we were kids. "You do what you have to do," he says. "You do what you have to do for your family."

~

Stephen's often at the house when I get home from work. It feels right to pull in and see his car. He's there today, having picked up Austin from school. It smells like they've ordered pizza. "Who the hell is Daniel?" he asks me as I walk in the door.

"I sold his brother a motel," I say. I kick off my shoes and drop my briefcase by the door. Walter thuds his head against a chair leg, and I pick him up and take him outside, barefoot.

Stephen follows us. "Are you dating him?" he asks. He crosses his arms.

"Aren't we too old to date?" I ask.

The door slams, and Austin runs outside. "Dad," he says. "I beat the level." He and Stephen have been engaged in some epic video game on the Xbox that Stephen brought back from Raleigh.

"Good job, buddy," Stephen says, rumpling Austin's hair. Austin hugs him, and for a second I think of him at three years old, hanging on to Stephen's leg as Stephen clumped around the house pretending to be a dinosaur.

"Are you staying for dinner?" I ask Stephen.

"Stay, Dad," Austin says. "Please. Did you tell Mom we got pizza with olives for her?"

Stephen nods. "Sure, I'll stay," he says. He stands with his arm around Austin in the deepening October twilight. I scoop up Walter, and we all go inside for pizza with olives.

It's a strange feeling, me and Stephen and Austin around the dinner table with me not having to wipe SpaghettiOs off Austin's face and Stephen and me talking instead of screaming. It's good. Austin is animated and loud, telling Stephen about school and football and Fiona and building a model volcano. We eat, and then he and Stephen play video games until it's Austin's bedtime. I actually have a chance to clean up the living room and take a bath and read a magazine.

I'm reclined on the big plaid sofa learning about easy chicken recipes when Stephen walks out from Austin's bedroom and sits beside me. "He's so great," he says. "I've missed him."

I put down my magazine. "I can't imagine being away from him," I say. For the first time, I actually consider how hard the divorce was on Stephen. How it must have changed him.

Stephen puts his hand on my leg. "We made an amazing kid," he says. He pats my leg, *pat pat pat, pat pat pat.*

I like this version of Stephen, the one who brings dinner and appreciates my contribution to his gene pool. "I'm glad you moved back," I say.

Walter wanders over and runs into my leg. He paws up at me. He's tired, and he wants to go to bed. "How is that thing still alive?" Stephen asks. He looks at Walter suspiciously.

I lift Walter to the sofa. He circles around and then settles down and licks my arm. His breath smells like rotten tuna, but I let him lick because this is his bedtime routine. "He's a tough old bird," I say. I imagine Walter with feathery wings, flying around the living room smacking into walls, and giggle.

"What?" Stephen asks. He rubs my leg in little circles.

"I was just thinking of Walter as a bird," I say.

Stephen shakes his head. "You make no sense." Then he shifts around so he's facing me. He turns my shoulders toward him. "Listen, Evie," he says. "Forget Daniel. Why don't we give this another try?"

I tug at Walter's grizzled muzzle. I'm not surprised Stephen would ask this. I don't speak for a moment.

Stephen takes my hand and links my fingers through his. We fit together. "We were so young and stupid, and too alike for our own good," Stephen says. "We're smarter now. I want Austin to have a family. I want to have a family. I want you."

I think about coming home to Stephen's car in the driveway. I think about dinners together, talking around the table about volcanoes. I think about Christmases, about getting pictures made in matching garish sweaters.

Walter stands up. He falls off my leg and lands on Stephen's, settling down to lick him. Stephen pushes him back onto my lap. "Gross," he says.

"Don't yell at him," I say. I pick up Walter and snuggle him to my chest.

"Think about how much it would mean to Austin," Stephen says.

I think about Austin's face as he told Stephen about Fiona. I think about Austin's first date, his first prom, his first everything. "I know what it'd mean to Austin," I say. "I'm not sure what it would mean to me." I look at Walter. "Or him."

Stephen nods, but he doesn't respond.

"I just have to think," I say.

~

I invite Daniel over for dinner. I make lasagna and garlic bread, thinking I'll be less likely to kiss him if I smell garlicky. Daniel brings wine for us and a toy rhinoceros for Austin.

"I don't play with toys anymore," Austin says. He sits down with his plate of lasagna and straightens his shoulders. He totally plays with toys. "My dad and I play on the Xbox, but that's it."

Daniel gives Austin a half smile. "Maybe your mom will want it, then," he says.

"I do love a good rhino," I say.

Daniel tells us about the time he went to Africa on a mission trip. Walter stands in the kitchen and barks until I pick him up and put him in front of his water dish. He slurps noisily. I talk about the rich people who stopped by the office today looking to buy property. Austin picks at his food. He doesn't talk, and as soon as he's eaten enough that he knows I won't yell at him, he clumps back to his bedroom. He doesn't slam the door, but he doesn't shut it quietly either.

I lean back and push away my plate. "That was interesting," I say.

Daniel rests his hand on mine, and it feels so right I have to bite my lip. "He's just adjusting to Stephen being back," he says.

I gather up our plates and carry them to the kitchen. Daniel follows with the glasses and napkins. We load the dishwasher in an easy tandem. "What would you like to do tonight?" he asks.

I scrub at a patch of tomato sauce before I load a plate. My dishwasher isn't too powerful. "I think I'd better check on Austin," I say.

Daniel nods. He kisses me on the cheek and takes the plate from my hands. I walk down the hall and knock on Austin's door.

"I'm busy," he says.

I open the door anyway. *Pings* and *bangs* and *zaps* emanate from the video game he's playing. "What's up, kid?" I ask.

Austin bites his lip, focused on the game. I step in front of him so he can't see the screen, and Austin yells at the whooshing electronic sound of doom that follows. He throws down the controller. "Dad should be here for dinner," Austin says. He crosses his arms and refuses to look at me.

"Your dad has his own life, and I have mine," I say.

Austin kicks his heels against the bed frame. "We should have a life together. It's not fair."

He's right, it's not fair. I put my hand on his shoulder, but he jerks away. "I know it makes sense that we should be a family," I say. I think about how right it felt when the three of us ate dinner together. "We can talk about this more later. When you're done with your game, there's ice cream for dessert," I tell him.

I stand out in the hall for a second. Daniel has music playing, something soft and classical. I take a breath. I need to do the right thing. I should be a grown-up. I should think about my family.

When I walk out to the living room, Daniel is squatted down wiping at the floor with a paper towel. Walter lies with his paws stretched out in front of him, methodically licking Daniel's left ankle. Daniel looks up. "Walter had an accident," he says.

"You don't have to do that," I say, bending down to take the towel from him. Our hands brush. "Sorry," I say. I move Walter, midlick, away from Daniel's ankle.

"It's okay. It's good karma," Daniel says. He stands and stretches and then holds out his hand to me. "Hopefully someone will take care of me when I'm an old man peeing on the floor."

I take his hand and stand up. I look at him, his deep eyes and long lashes and crooked smile. I imagine him old and gray. I imagine myself beside him, my hair a wild white bird's nest like my Aunt Fay's. "At least we have laminate floorboards," I say. When Daniel holds me, my head rests on his clavicle, our bodies fitting together like puzzle pieces, curve here, hollow there. Click. Snap. Fit.

Twelve

Into the Neon

— 2016 —

Mike Tyson got into his first fight because someone tore the head off his pet pigeon. The television behind the desk at the Bellagio blares this fact, and everything in my body tenses at Mike Tyson's name. The TV shows him peacefully raising pigeons in Harlem, rows of cooing, head-twitching birds on a brownstone rooftop. Then Iron Mike lifts his hands as if in joyful prayer, setting a pigeon free. Who even has pigeons as pets, anyway? It's eight o'clock in the evening, and I'm waiting to see if I can leave my broken old amoeba-paisley luggage behind the desk for the night at the Bellagio, the prettiest hotel I've seen since I arrived in Vegas three days ago. I have until eight o'clock in the morning to play in Las Vegas, twelve glorious hours alone with no idiot man dragging me down, no responsibilities pulling at me like a 1950s cherub-faced kid tugging at his perfectly coiffed mother's apron strings. My own cherub-faced kid is home with my mom, twenty-five hundred miles away. I'm by myself in this crazy neon Strip that reminds me of an overgrown college campus, the casinos thinly veiled frat house theme parties, the cornhole replaced with high-stakes poker.

Pigeons. He's raising pigeons.

"May I help you?" The woman behind the desk is impeccably styled, narrow-waisted, ruby-lipped. I imagine her gently vacuuming her plush living room carpet in four-inch, peep-toed Manolo Blahniks, her crimson nail polish bright against the sleek handle of her Dyson.

I ask if I can stow my bag for the night. I tell her I've just left a giant jerk of a man across the street at the Flamingo and have nowhere to go, and that I want to play the Bellagio's slot machines and watch the fountains until it's time to leave for my flight. And even though this maven of virtuous femininity must be so good she'd certainly never get herself into such a situation as mine, she softens, the fake smile easing into an expression of pity, and she says she'll see what she can do. She turns to talk with a manager, and I imagine her hair disheveled, the peep-toed Blahniks strewn across the floor, her naked feet propped on a coffee table as she licks her fingers after devouring a bag of chocolate cream bonbons. Or is it *crème*? I never know.

The television comes back from commercial, and Tyson is back again. His tattooed face fills the screen, little-boy lisp voice talking about how he's going to raise pigeons until he dies, talking about Birmingham Rollers and how they spin with such velocity they don't notice they're rotating right into the spattered silver grate of a Mack truck. *Bam.* Feathers everywhere. Iron Mike talks about how pigeons are spiritual, how he comes up on the roof to watch them and drink Kool-Aid.

He probably only raises pigeons so he can teach them how to rape other birds.

The attendant says they'll keep my bag. CLAIRE, her nametag says. Claire has me fill out a form, and I scribble while listening to Mike Tyson talk about pigeons' automatic cooling system and how at peace he is when he's with them. The show cuts to a local newscaster who says that Mike Tyson is in Las Vegas for the week, promoting his new documentary and filming a cameo in a movie.

"Dick."

Claire looks up. "Excuse me?" she says.

I push the form across the shiny desk. "Mike Tyson," I say. I roll my bag around to the opening in the counter, back where people work serving tourists. Back where I usually stand. "I met him once, and it ruined my life."

Claire's eyes widen. "What happened?" she asks.

She takes my bag, and I tell her about being a kid, visiting Ohio, how he watched me do cartwheels, and how, even years later, Mike Tyson's reputation got all tangled up with mine.

Claire tucks my bag under the counter. "That's terrible," she says. She leans in closer. In a whisper, she says, "I heard he's staying at New York New York."

He would be staying at my least favorite hotel. Who wants to stay at a dirty old fake city like New York when there's fake Paris or fake Venice right down the street? An ear-biting rapist, that's who. "Thank you," I say to Claire. And I mean it. In spite of her coiffed perfection, I think Claire and I could be friends. And she's just given me my plan for the night. I'm going to find Mike Tyson, and I'm going to make him pay.

I turn away, digging my cell phone out of my purse as I walk under the blown-glass flowers on the ceiling. I call Charlotte. "Guess who's staying at New York New York?" I ask her before she can say a word.

"Mike Tyson?" Charlotte asks.

I jostle around a group of blond tourists in flowered shirts. "Shut up," I say. "You're supposed to say *who* so I can yell MIKE TYSON."

"He's seriously there? I was just making that up," Charlotte says.

"He's seriously here." I wander past upscale shops and go in to look at a pair of python Prada boots.

"You should get him to beat up Eamon," she says. I'd been updating Charlotte about the Eamon debacle via text message.

"I'm going to make this a double revenge night," I say. "Just call me the Revenging Avenger."

"It's a revenge-o-rama," Charlotte says. "So what's your plan?"

I walk out of the Prada store. The boots cost more than I make in two months. "I don't know," I say, and I head toward the penny slot machines. I was so disappointed when I realized that penny slots didn't actually take pennies. I'd been saving them up and brought a Ziploc-baggie-full with me. Every time I saw a penny on the ground when I took Walter for a walk I'd pick it up in case it was the penny that would make me a gazillionaire.

"Let's think about this," Charlotte says. "The punishment has to fit the crime."

I sit down, hold the phone between my shoulder and chin, and dig out five dollars. "And his crime was twofold," I say. I slide the money into a slot machine and pull the handle; cherries and bells and plums and number sevens roll and whirr. "He made me believe he was good, and then he ruined my reputation."

"So you have to ruin his?" Charlotte asks.

The slot machine stops. A seven, a lemon, and a bar. I pull the handle again. "But how much worse can his rep get?"

"What if you get him to buy you a drink and then slip him a roofie? That sounds like fun."

Cherry, cherry, bell. Dammit. I pull again. "He'd probably just absorb the roofie into his face tattoo," I say.

"That doesn't make any sense," Charlotte says. "Are you drunk?"

Plum, cherry, bar. And my money is gone. That was not entertaining. That was not worth five dollars. "No, but that's brilliant. I'm going to get a giant bong-looking drink and walk down the street with it." I shoulder through the crowd and head to the door.

"I'll be up late on a grading marathon," Charlotte says. "Call me if you find Kid Dynamite."

I put my phone back in my purse. Outside, the dry air rasps over my skin. The absence of water bothers me, the thirstiness of the night sky in this shithole desert. Mike Tyson. How am I supposed to find Mike Tyson? And where do I get a bong-looking drink? I walk up the stairs and go over a crosswalk bridge, resisting the urge to go inside the Flamingo and see if Eamon's discovered that I'm gone yet. I decide to walk to New York New York, and on the way I find a bar that's advertising one-dollar margaritas, so I get in line. It's not a bong-looking drink, but it's cheap, and it'll do to get my courage up. Someone bumps into me, and I turn. It's a short little gray-haired lady who immediately reminds me of Aunt Fay. "Sorry, hon," she says. She pats my arm. I think she's soused.

"No problem," I say. Then I decide to do some recon. "Have you happened to see Mike Tyson around here anywhere?" My mother always says it's best to be direct.

She says no and hiccups. Aunt Fay would never hiccup; she could hold her liquor. She would also never give up. I scribble my phone number on the back of my drugstore receipt for maxi pads and hand it to her. "If you do run into him, could you give me a call?" My margarita tastes like a slushie and doesn't even smell like tequila, so it doesn't feel as illicit as I want it to, to walk around with it, but I go outside and start walking anyway. There's a place past fake Paris that has mojitos for three dollars, so I get one to make up for the lousy margarita. I sip it and tell the businessman next to me that I'm looking for Mike Tyson.

He raises his eyebrows. "Why's a girl like you looking for a man like that?" He swirls his drink, and I imagine him as a 1950s husband who expects his wife to have a steaming green bean casserole on the table for him when he gets home from work.

"I'm going to get revenge on him for ruining my life, but I don't know how to find him."

He sips his scotch. It absolutely has to be scotch. Or maybe whiskey. Whiskey would do. "Easy there, tiger," he says.

"Don't easy there, tiger, me," I say. I finish my mojito—it's good and rummy—and head straight to New York New York. I sit down in an Irish pub inside fake New York and order some French fries. They cost nine dollars, so I don't get a drink to go with them. I talk to two guys with Greek letters on their sweatshirts who love Mike Tyson but haven't seen him. In the bathroom a girl with a pink Mohawk says she'll help me kick him in the balls if I do find him. A motherly looking woman in capri pants and Crocs saw a guy who sort of looked like Mike Tyson going into the Bellagio earlier tonight, but she's not sure it was him. I tell her she's a rock star, then head back down to the Bellagio. It's hot, and I'm tipsy, but I stand with a crowd of people and watch the fountains for a minute. The streams of water waltz and twirl and spin like dancers. I want to go dancing, but I have to find Mike Tyson.

I don't know what else to do, so I go to the bar and take a seat beside a guy who looks like a bodybuilder. I like a man with shoulders, but these things are out of control. I'm about to lean forward and push my arms together to create cleavage and get the bartender's attention, but then I remember two things: one, I'm still dressed in my Eamon-revenge clothes—a short skirt, heels, and a plunging-necked top with a push-up bra—so I don't need to push my arms together to create cleavage; and two, I'm dressed like this in Las Vegas. What was I thinking? There's no way I'm buying my own drink. I cross my legs and turn to the bodybuilder, tossing my hair over my shoulder. "Come here often?" I ask. I actually say that.

The bodybuilder says something in return, but the music has changed to a thumping bass, and I can't hear him. I lean in toward him and cock my head. "I live here," he says. The cadence of his speech reminds me of an old-school gangster. "I'm Vonny," he says. Or maybe he says Donny; I can't really tell, but I decide that Vonny is more interesting. He holds out his thick hand.

"Evie," I say, shaking it. His grip is surprisingly weak. Maybe he sprained something lifting too many barbells. "It's my first time here."

Vonny beckons the bartender. "What'll you have?" he asks me. *Whaddaya have?*

"Anything with tequila in it," I say.

The bartender brings two shots, lime, and salt. I lick the curve between my thumb and forefinger. I can never remember which comes first, the lime or the salt or the tequila, so I wait for Vonny to drink first. He salts, shoots, and limes, and I do the same.

Vonny says something that sounds like *liggaslammasucka*. I lean in closer and he says, "Lick it, slam it, suck it," into my ear. His breath smells like tequila with a hint of vomit. Classy.

"I've got to go find Mike Tyson," I say. I stand up.

"Why do you want to find Mike Tyson for?" Vonny says. He stands, too, and his legs are twig-tiny. I wonder how he doesn't topple over.

"To get revenge," I say. I walk toward the front desk. "He ruined my life. Do you want to come?" I figure it can't hurt to have a little company, and he did buy me that shot.

I spot Claire at the desk and wave, and she beckons me over. She leans over the front desk conspiratorially. "I found out Mike Tyson is doing interviews tonight," she says. "In this hidden back press room in the Venetian. I don't know if you could find it, though."

The hallway tilts slightly; the tequila's kicking in. "I can totally find it. Totally."

Vonny snaps his fingers. "I know the room you mean." I should have known to ask Vonny more questions. Locals are the best resource.

"Will you take me there? Please? I'll buy you a bong-looking drink."

"I'm not in the habit of helping random ladies with revenge."

"I am not a random lady. I am Evie Austin Oden Austin. And I did *not* name my son Austin Austin." I wave goodbye to Claire and walk toward the front door. Vonny, despite his protests, follows me.

"I didn't say you did," he says.

"So you'll take me to Mike Tyson?"

"No."

Dammit. "Please?"

Vonny pats my back, right between my shoulder blades. "I'm awful sorry, Evie Austin Oden Austin."

We walk outside. The fountains spray up to "All That Jazz," and my hips sway in time to the music as I walk, almost of their own accord. "You have to take me to that room."

Vonny's hips don't sway as he walks. His scrawny legs move side to side like a bulldog's. "I can't do that," he says. We merge out into a crowd of people on the sidewalk and move up the Strip.

A half-block down, I pull Vonny through the open doors of a bar and lean over to wave down the bartender. "I'm buying us bong-looking drinks."

Vonny looks confused, but he goes up to the bar with me. I point at a lady wearing a long, plastic, bong-shaped daiquiri around her neck and hold up two fingers, and the bartender brings them. I loop mine over my head, take a sip out of the long straw, hand Vonny his, and we go back out to the Strip.

"Maybe I'm overstating this revenge element," I say. "I already met Mike Tyson once, and I just want to say hello."

I think Vonny realizes I'm lying, but when I look over at him, he's just trundling along on his twig-legs. I take a drink. Strawberry-y.

Vonny shakes his head. It seems like he shakes his head sadly, but I'm also tipsy. "I gotta get home, Evie Austin Oden Austin."

I try to make myself cry, because that always works in movies when a woman wants something, but I've never been an on-demand crier. I look up at him with big eyes. I think about biting my lip to make myself well up, but I'm not into the idea of having a bit-up lip.

Vonny stops walking. We're across the street from fake Paris, and I look up at the fake hot-air balloon. Dang. That's way up in the air. Way up there. And it's strawberry time. I do a little happy shimmy drinking dance. *Strawberry time. Strawberry time.* Wait. Focus. Mike Tyson. I turn to ask Vonny how his drink is, but Vonny's not there. I take the straw out of my mouth, shocked. I turn to a tall man standing beside me taking pictures of the fake hot-air balloon. "Have you seen a giant-shouldered man with tiny, tiny legs?" He smiles but doesn't answer. "No, really. It's like he was two people mashed into one. Big giant dude on top, eleven-year-old boy on bottom." I mimic Vonny's bulldog walk. The man points up the Strip, and there goes Vonny, trundling away as fast as his tiny legs can carry him.

I thank the man and start to run. I feel like those horror movie girls, tottering along in my high heels. "Vonny!" I yell as loud as I can, which might be a little louder than usual since my decibel level tends to hike perceptibly when I've been drinking. Vonny doesn't turn around. He dodges behind a crowd of bachelorette party girls, and then I lose him. I stop running but try yelling again. "Vonny! Get your twig legs back here and take me to Mike Tyson!"

The bachelorette party girls stumble toward me. One of them grabs my arm. "What are you shouting about?" I feel my face reddening. I'm embarrassing myself. If I were home on the Outer Banks and hollered something down the street, at least eight people I know would've heard me. I'd have been related to four of them, and within two minutes, it'd be all over the island that Evie Austin was making a spectacle of herself. Again.

I call Charlotte. "I just made a spectacle of myself," I tell her. "Again."

"I don't think that's possible in Las Vegas, unless you set yourself on fire. You didn't set Mike Tyson on fire, did you?"

I sit down on the sidewalk and drink some more. It doesn't taste like strawberry anymore. It just tastes like rum. "My new friend Claire told me where to go, and I found a guy who knows the right room, but I lost him because I was drinking and making a spectacle of myself."

Charlotte says, "That's a lot of new people. I'm confused."

Rum rum rum. "His name was Vonny Twig-Legs. The guy. Not my new friend."

"Can you find him again? What are you drinking?"

I fiddle with something on the sidewalk. "Gross, a cigarette butt." Before Charlotte can ask me if I'm drinking cigarette butts, I toss it down and tell her that I'm drinking something that was once strawberry goodness but is now mostly rum and maybe more rum. I wipe my fingers on my skirt and stand up. Spinny.

"Just go in the direction you last saw the room guy," Charlotte says.

I start to tear up. Where the hell were those tears when I needed them? "No, I screwed up. I always screw everything up. Or I screw people, and that screws everything up. The bottom line is, I'm a screwup, and I ruined my chance to get revenge on Mike Tyson."

Charlotte sighs. "You're not a screwup, Evie."

I walk over to a drugstore. Its fluorescent-lit familiarity seems comforting, but I wonder if I'll get in trouble for taking in my rum bong. I don't care. I'm a screwup. I might as well get arrested in Las Vegas for rum violations. I swing the door open and browse through the vitamin aisle. "I couldn't even finish pregnant without getting college." That might have been backwards. Whatever.

But Charlotte understands. "You didn't get pregnant all by yourself."

I pick up some hair barrettes. "I wasn't not taking birth control," I say. I've never told anyone this, not even Charlotte. "I just threw up a few times from drinking too much. I must've thrown up the baby-stoppers. I just threw them right on up." I make a barfing sound for Charlotte's benefit.

"It doesn't matter, Evie. Anyone who's going to judge you isn't worth your time."

I try on some fake hair. It's blond, and my hair is dark, but when I look in the wavy mirror on the sunglasses rack, I decide that it looks awesome. I look awesome. The fake hair is within my price range. "I'm buying some fake hair," I tell Charlotte. This drugstore probably has some other things in my price range. I check out the sparkly nail polish. "I was kind of bad, though. But that was Mike Tyson's influence. I blame Mike Tyson."

"You weren't bad. You were human."

I chug the rest of my rum and stash the bong-looking plastic in a corner. I don't want the cashier to hate me and arrest me. I've never even smoked a bong. I've only seen them. "But you agree that Mike Tyson has to pay, right?"

Charlotte sighs again. She's being so sigh-y. I start to tell her that, but she's saying something about a *chain of events that impacted your self-perception and undeniably contributed to your sense of what is and isn't socially acceptable in terms of sexual mores.* I paint each of my fingernails a different sparkly color while she talks. I'm not buying any polish, either. I'm that bad.

I blow on my fingernails to dry them. I'm getting tired of this drugstore, but I don't want to ruin my manicure when I get my wallet to pay for the fake hair. "I'm not so bad that I steal fake hair, though," I say. "I'm not a stealer."

"Evie," Charlotte says. "You have two choices."

I tap my sparkly fingernails together to test their dryness and wait for Charlotte to tell me my choices. Purple fingernail, green fingernail. Tap tap tap. Dry enough. I need more rum.

"You can either forget about Mike Tyson and go have fun in Las Vegas, or you can go try to find that room on your own."

I cradle my phone in my neck and go pay for my fake hair. I really have to pee, but the cashier says there isn't a public bathroom, so I leave. Outside, the Strip sparkles and flashes, a lurid neon night. "Just get on a plane and come here. It's no fun without someone fun."

"Why do you even need revenge, anyway?" Charlotte asks.

"You sound like Vonny." I walk through the jostling crowds. Why do I need revenge?

"Just make the choices you need to make," Charlotte says. I tell her I love her and hang up. I'm going to walk to the Venetian and decide why I need revenge.

I join a pack of girls wearing different kinds of animal ears. One of them, I think she's a cat, claws the air beside me. One of them yells, a high-pitched *wooooo,* and I tell her that yelling *wooooo* is not attractive, but she just *wooooos* again and stumbles into her girlfriends, and they veer off into a casino. "I was just being helpful and polite," I shout after them. Why do I need revenge? Why don't I have animal ears? What animal ears would I pick if I could pick any animal ears?

I go in and out of a bunch more groups of people, an interloper, not belonging with any of them. I get in lines for drinks. Music thumps and everything sparkles and flashes, and a fake volcano explodes. I start to feel like one of those spinning pigeons Mike Tyson was talking about. Like I could smack right into a Mack truck and not even notice. I make sure I'm on the sidewalk. My animal ears would be pigeon ears, only, do pigeons have ears? I don't want to think that it's really sweet that he goes up there and drinks Kool-Aid and talks to the pigeons, but it's really sweet that he goes up there and drinks Kool-Aid and talks to pigeons. Like, that's something Austin would do. Austin would totally talk to a pigeon and drink blue Kool-Aid. I don't want to think about how it would have formed Austin's heart if someone had torn the head off his pet pigeon. It makes me cry. I sit down on a step and cry a little. I really want to call Austin and my mom, but I'm too drunk to figure out what time it is in Buxton.

I get up and I walk and walk some more. My feet hurt. Revenge, revenge, revenge, why? I wish I could call Aunt Fay. She was a total badass, but she also loved her some Jesus. *Turn the other cheek, kid,* she'd say if she was walking with me, and then she'd pinch my butt and laugh. We'd drink some more, and I'd make her go dancing. I take off my heels when I reach the marble terrace of the Venetian. I made it. I half expect a sign that says, MIKE TYSON, THIS WAY, with an arrow, but there's nothing. What am I even going to do to get even? I decide to comb through fake Venice floor by floor while I think. I go through a nightclub with a giant mural of a naked lady getting a massage (or else she's about to get it on with her *lovah*), a champagne bar, a piano lounge with stalactite lights dripping from the ceiling, a sushi restaurant, and all the fancy shops. I go back to the nightclub, grab a drink, and watch the naked lady watching everyone dancing. I walk around a little more. My feet are pretty dirty by now, but I'm not putting those heels back on.

How am I going to find that room? How did I get here in the first place? I know. The front desk. Claire. I go search for the front desk. But how did I get *here* here? I got *here* here by not sleeping with Eamon even though he expected me to, even though everyone I would have known from a long time ago would have expected me to, too. Because I'm not the same. Everything spins and spins and spins and then, suddenly, the spinning stops. I'm Evie Austin Oden Austin, and I'm standing here barefoot in the middle of all this arched opulence, and there's the front desk.

I wave at the guy working. I'm a little sad that he's wearing a navy blazer and not a fake gondolier outfit. He asks if he can help me. "You know Claire at the Bellagio?" I don't wait for him to answer. Of course, he knows Claire. "She was telling me about this press room where Mike Tyson is talking to reporters. Can you show me where that is?"

He cocks his head to the side. He looks a little bit like a pigeon. I can tell he's deciding between being polite and professional and being real and fun. "What is on your head?" he asks.

I reach up and touch my hair. "That's fake hair. It cost three dollars, and it looks awesome."

He tilts his head again. "There's nobody in the press room right now. It's the middle of the night."

Oh. Of course, it's the middle of the night now. I'm suddenly tired, and not really all that drunk. I want to go home. I'm tired of bars, and I'm tired of Las Vegas, and I'm tired of the desert. My home could get obliterated by a hurricane at any moment, it's true, but at least there's real water there. There's water everywhere at home, moving and rushing and sparkling and glimmering, and sometimes, on the sound, standing still in a shimmer of sunset, like a piece of silk I could run my hand over. Like I could wrap it around my shoulders and float up into the sky. And thinking of all that water reminds me that I really, really have to pee.

I ask the front-desk guy where the lobby bathroom is. When I'm all done and washing my hands, I look in the mirror. Oh my God. My hair looks like a long-haired Chihuahua climbed up there and passed out on my head. I rip off the fake hair and toss it in the trash. I slowly leave the Venetian, stopping to stare into the fake canals for a minute before heading back to the Bellagio. People scream and holler and bump and carry on. I snake my way around a cluster watching a fake pirate ship and walk up the Strip. I'm dizzy, but I don't stop until I get to the fountains at the Bellagio. Those fountains are built on a fake lake in the middle of the desert. It should just be sand and rock, but it's not. Instead, it's dancing and swaying and soft pink-and-blue lights and the splish and spray of water shooting up and falling back into itself.

I call Charlotte. "I decided he can have his pigeons and his Kool-Aid. I'm not who I was anymore, either."

"How do you feel?" Charlotte asks. She yawns.

I run my hand along the fountain's fence. I grab on to a rail, lean back, and pretend I'm a showgirl on a stripper pole. "I feel very discombobulated."

"Discombobulated is probably to be expected."

The sky is starting to turn the faintest of pinks, and the fountains dance to something symphonic and classical. I don't know what it is, but it makes me want to stop pretending to be a stripper and start pretending to be a ballerina. The water rushes up and hovers for a moment in midair, a tiny, crystallized instant of antigravity perfection before it falls back down into the lake. "Hatteras changes all the time, doesn't it?" I ask. It's true; it does. Hurricanes blow in new inlets. Houses wash out to sea. "And here, people just build lakes where there used to be sand. If they want Paris or Venice, they put it right up." I start walking over to the veranda. *Veranda* is a lovely word. *Veranda.* "If I ever have a daughter, I'm naming her Veranda," I say to Charlotte.

"When do you have to leave for the airport?"

Shit. I'd forgotten all about the airport. I take the phone away from my face and poke a button to check the time. "Not for another few hours."

"What are you going to do next?"

"I don't know." What am I going to do? I sit down, close my eyes, and lean my head back against the cool marble of the veranda post. I can feel my blood pulsing through my ears, my face, behind my eyes. The music changes. *Luck be a lady tonight.* I don't know what I'm going to do. All I know is that I'm Evie Austin Oden Austin, and I only have a few more hours before I can go home.

Thirteen

How to Stay, How to Go

— 2019 —

You realize now that bake sales are actually good-mom competitions. You didn't realize this seven years ago; back then, when Emma Midgett asked you to donate baked goods to benefit your son's preschool, you bought cheap Pillsbury cutouts and threw them in the oven at the last minute. Okay, you didn't even buy Pillsbury, but the generic store brand, "Our Family." What did you know? You placed them on the table piled with raspberry-filled lemon cupcakes, glazed orange poppy seed muffins, and something called caramel-pecan delights. Your fake-Pillsbury cutouts, not even iced, flatly declared your incompetence. You sat outside Starfish Academy on the side of Highway 12. It was 90 degrees, and the humidity hung like a curtain, the usual Banks breeze still and quiet. Lally Owens's chocolate fudge peppermint brownies melted into their plastic bags. You'd just heard that your husband, Stephen, was having an affair. You wanted to melt, too.

Seven years later, you are wise. You sit in your son's middle school parking lot, which is also the high school parking lot, and look across the street at Starfish Academy. You wonder how you ever could have been so stupid. For this sale, you've stayed up until three in the morning baking two dozen coconut-apricot macaroons. The Cape Hatteras School Festival of Fun writhes around you in a haze of color and heat and noise. You're waiting for your boyfriend, Daniel, to bring you little placards to set up in front of the macaroons. You've been dating for a year now, and his face still astonishes you. A month ago you found out that Daniel was accepted to medical school in Wichita, Kansas, twenty-five hours away from home. He's waitlisted at a school in Athens, Ohio, ten hours from home, and one in San Francisco, too many hours away to count. You went with him to visit the campus in Kansas. Neither of you have family in any of those places.

Two weeks ago, Daniel asked you and your son, Austin, to come with him. You and Daniel had been driving back down the island from Nags Head and had pulled over at Canadian Hole to watch the sunset. The Pamlico was slick calm, the sherbet colors of the setting sun blending from sky to water without a ripple.

"Stephen won't be okay with Austin moving that far away," you said.

"Probably not full-time," Daniel said. Calm and rational, as always. "Would you guys consider splitting custody? Giving Austin summers here? Or maybe he could stay here for school and come to us for breaks and summers?"

When he said it like that, so logically, it sounded, if not easy, at least feasible. Doable. Possible. When he talked, it didn't sound anything at all like how it felt in your body—how it made your stomach tighten and your jaw clench.

You stared at a lone seagull gliding across the sound. "I've never been away from him for that long. I can't understand how you think I can just leave him so easily." This wasn't fair of you to say, but you didn't care.

"Can we please discuss this without the melodrama?" Daniel said. This wasn't fair of him, and you didn't answer.

Daniel said, "I didn't say it would be easy, or that it wouldn't be painful." He shifted in his seat toward you, turning away from the sound. "What I'm saying is that we have to decide if we're all moving toward a future together."

You pictured yourself, Daniel, and Austin stepping onto an airplane together, Daniel lifting your luggage to the overhead bin. You pictured sending Austin onto an airplane, alone. "It's just a lot."

"We could be our own family," he said. "I want that."

You want it, too. You do. But you're not sure how you can live in a flat, landlocked cornfield for eight years. You think you might suffocate. You've thought about it for two weeks. You're supposed to give him your answer today.

Through the festival bustle, you pick out your son's voice, a single thread in a quilt of noise, as he yells to his friends. Austin's happier than you were at ten. When you were ten, you couldn't wait to leave this island; you thought it was a desolate patch of sand that should've been obliterated in a hurricane long ago. You were not the popular kid. If your parents had said you were moving, you'd have been thrilled. But Austin loves it here, loves the wind and sand and waves, loves having his four grandparents and his aunts and uncles and cousins all within a fifteen-mile radius. And his father, your ex, just moved back last year. You watch as Austin navigates the crowd easily, his newly long legs sticking out from a pair of blue plaid shorts like a deer's would, if deer wore blue plaid shorts. He waits in line at the dunking booth, lobbing a ball up and down in his hand, ready to sink his gym teacher. You know that to win the gold cup in a good-mom competition, you'd have to willingly and selflessly sacrifice your relationship with Daniel to stay where Austin is happy.

You close your eyes and absorb the sun, heat radiating into your marrow. You open them and watch the crowd, picking out everyone you know: Dr. Garcia and his daughter, Fiona, eating pink cotton candy; Emma Midgett and Lally Owens dressed up like clowns; your mother painting kids' faces; two of Austin's cousins on your ex's side juggling inflatable bowling pins back and forth; two of your own cousins shouting that there are goldfish to win if you guess how many marbles are in a jar. Your fourth-grade teacher sells hot dogs; your childhood nemesis, Misty Garber, who to this day has puffed-up 1990s bangs, leans out of her makeshift booth to hand children sno-cones. You smile at Misty; she waves in return.

Three months ago, you, Emma, Lally, Misty, and the other members of the Hatteras Island Bridge Moms had joined hands on a frigidly windy day and walked across the new bridge connecting Hatteras to Bodie Island. Together, you'd met and lobbied for the replacement of the rickety old Bonner Bridge, which was thirty years past the age it should have been replaced. Every time you crossed it, you had an escape plan in mind in case it collapsed, had rehearsed how you'd turn to unbuckle Austin as the car plunged, then grab the umbrella with a sharp point you kept in the door pocket to break open a window underwater. You'd all written letters, campaigned, and even traveled to Raleigh to meet with state representatives to get that bridge built so your kids would be safe getting to the mainland. You'd done it together. That day on the new bridge, Emma's cheeks pink from the cold, everyone's hair wild with wind, you'd grinned at each other and chased your kids down the bright yellow center line of the tall, solid, beautiful new bridge. It was a special ceremony just for locals. There were speeches and cheering, and you, Emma, Lally, and Misty had passed a big thermos of hot chocolate spiked with peppermint schnapps back and forth between you, the smooth liquid warming you from the inside out.

Today, you sit there in the sun, cocooned in your community, selling gingersnaps and thumbprint cookies to grocery store owners, librarians, park service rangers, all of whom you know by name. Your brother walks toward the table, his little girl, Lara, holding his hand. Nate grabs a macaroon and tosses five dollars at you, and Lara runs over to hug your legs. "Here's your sunscreen," Nate says, digging a tube out of his pocket. "Mom said you forgot it."

You thank your brother, and he says his wife will be over soon to help with the bake sale table. Nate swings Lara up on his shoulders, and they join the crowd. You're terrified of untwisting yourself from your family and your home. You imagine yourself dangling on the plains of Kansas, wafting in the wind, a lone strand, unconnected, Daniel the only person you know. You're terrified Daniel will outgrow you, will become a doctor and want someone smarter and younger and prettier. You're terrified to spend eight years of your life trapped in Kansas only to have Daniel leave. Only to have to leave him.

Before you left your ex-husband, you stayed. Seven years ago, at the Starfish Academy bake sale, you sat with your stomach roiling, plotting ways to leave that would hurt Stephen the most. Taking Austin in the middle of the night and slipping out, unheard, so Stephen awoke to an empty house. Stealing Stephen's car and skidding out of the driveway, sand and gravel spinning beneath your tires. Or your favorite idea—waiting until Stephen's birthday, then jumping out of a cake to tell him you were leaving. In this fantasy version, Stephen actually died from shock, and you didn't have to deal with a divorce. You were so caught up in picturing Stephen's dead face that you didn't hear Austin, in real life, at the Starfish Academy bake sale, run over to you, crying. You didn't notice him until he was right beside you, bleeding all over your shorts. It was his first nosebleed, and Austin cried and cried, waving his small hands in the air with a franticness you'd never seen. You couldn't make the blood stop. He bled all over you, the stain on your shorts a dark burgundy, spreading into a shape resembling the state of Wisconsin.

You didn't realize dogs could get nosebleeds until Walter stumbled over and bled on your kitchen floor last week. You picked him up, and he bled on your bare arm, ruby rivulets dripping to the linoleum. Daniel got a paper towel, and Walter bled into that. You held Walter on your lap as Daniel drove to the closest after-hours vet in Avon. The vet said Walter's nosebleed was caused by a dental abscess. Walter got injected with antibiotics and prescribed pills for fourteen days, and you felt horribly guilty for not trying harder to brush his teeth. Walter peed on the vet and then, on the way home, peed on you. You and Daniel pulled into the Askins Creek BP station, and you went inside to get paper towels. As you mopped up the mess, Walter sneezed and started bleeding again. You and Daniel sat with Walter on the steps of the little gas station store, holding paper towels to his nose as he jerked his head back and forth trying to avoid you. Tourists stepped around you on their way in to buy gas, lighthouse shot glasses, and posters of the house from *Nights in Rodanthe*. Daniel placed his hand on your thigh, squeezed, and said, gently, "It might be time to think about putting Walter down."

You reeled. "I'm not killing my dog," you said, and held Walter to your chest where he bled on your white shirt, a stain shaped like Rhode Island that you couldn't get out even though you treated it with hydrogen peroxide. You hated euphemisms for death, hated the phrase *put down*. You didn't understand why Daniel wanted you to kill the last remaining link you had to your aunt, the person who helped raise you and understood you best of all. You couldn't just kill Walter; couldn't willingly sever that tie.

"I just think it'd be easier on you if you had some control over it," Daniel said, taking Walter and blotting his grizzled, graying nose.

You thought of how Walter, back in his heyday, would've nipped the paper towel out of Daniel's hand and shook it like he was trying to break its neck. *He's my family*, you tried to explain. But you couldn't get the words out right. All you could do was say again, "I can't kill my dog."

Seven years ago, back when Walter was a feisty biter, you'd sat on the floor of your parents' living room with Austin, halfheartedly stacking brightly colored plastic blocks that Walter would then knock down, causing Austin to shriek with joy. Walter especially liked to bite your father, but he'd never bitten you or Austin, so you shot your dad an annoyed look when he suggested not letting Austin play with the dog. You'd stayed overnight at your parents' inn after the bake sale and nosebleed day, after finding out about your husband's affair. You told your dad you knew what you were doing, but even as you said it, you knew it was a lie. You didn't know what you were doing at all. Your husband had just fucked another woman, and you still didn't want to leave him and move home. You were hurt and angry, yes, but you were in love. You thought you could work it out. Somehow, an affair wasn't a dealbreaker.

"Don't be ridiculous, Evie," your dad had said. He sat on a striped sofa and leaned forward toward you and Austin with his elbows on his knees. "Come home."

You reminded your father that he took your mother back after her affair with Bob the lighthouse-mover. Your father looked at you with sad eyes.

"That was different," was all he said.

"If by different you mean exactly the same."

Your dad moved down to the floor. He stacked a blue plastic

block on top of a yellow one. Austin added a red block, his movements precise. Your dad said, "It was different because we weren't out to hurt one another. It just happened."

You rolled your eyes. It just happened. "But you took her back."

"I checked out first, Evie," he said. "I admit that."

Walter barked twice and ran around the room in a circle, then aimed his pointed Yorkie nose at the stack of blocks, crashing them to the floor in a hurricane of primary colors. Austin clapped and ran after Walter, then sat down and began stacking blocks again. Yellow. Red. Blue.

Your dad said, "You have to think about what kind of example your relationship is going to set for your son." He scooped Austin up off the floor, and that's when Walter bit your dad's ankle, latching on even as your dad waved his leg in the air. He hollered for his sister, your Aunt Fay, to come "restrain this beast!" and carried Austin into the kitchen where your mom was scrambling eggs for breakfast. She'd put Austin's eggs on a plate shaped like a teddy bear's head.

Shortly after you moved in together, Daniel issued a ban on nonstick pans. He scrambled eggs in a stainless steel skillet, which made them fuse in a flaky mess that needed soaking before the pan could go in the dishwasher. Daniel said that Teflon causes cancer. Sweet'N Low causes cancer. Hair dye causes cancer. Daniel was paranoid about cancer, not that you could blame him, since the reason he was there in your kitchen in Buxton, North Carolina, was because, the year before, he'd been biopsied for presumed cancer, which prompted him to make some Life Changes. Daniel stood in your kitchen and leaned against the sink.

"We should really think about getting rid of the microwave," he said. "Irradiated food troubles me."

You looked at him, there in your little kitchen, solid and beautiful and asking you to go back to the Dark Ages of food reheating. "I hear what you're saying," you said. "And I understand. However, I disagree." You were proud of yourself for using "I" statements and arguing in the way your former therapist, Judy, had taught you. You took a bite of Teflon-free scrambled eggs that tasted of rosemary and basil.

Daniel grinned and kissed you on the forehead. This wasn't your first fight; you'd had bad ones before, like when you'd bought Twinkies and nonorganic milk three weeks in a row and Daniel lectured you about *putting healthy things into our bodies.* When he was still living with his brother after four months; when he didn't get you a present for your anniversary. When he'd proposed and you'd said you weren't ready. "I'm still not irradiating my food," he said.

"That's not even scientifically validated," you said, annoyed that in-the-midst-of-med-school-applications Daniel couldn't Google "are microwaves safe" and realize they were.

Austin galumphed into the kitchen, throwing his backpack on the table and dropping a packaged pastry into the toaster, asking what wasn't scientifically validated.

Daniel began explaining electromagnetic radiation, using words like *magnetron* and *thermal effect.* Austin, who'd recently gotten past his Daniel-hating phase, nodded as he poured his orange juice, his brow furrowed in a way that reminded you of Stephen. "We should do a microwave experiment for my science project," Austin said, and your heart jerked at that "we." Austin plucked the Toaster Strudel out of the toaster and dropped it onto a plate, blowing on his fingers. He took a bite, and strawberry goo oozed down his chin.

Now, at the bake sale in the high school/middle school parking lot, amid the Festival of Fun, you rearrange pleasingly lumpy raspberry scones and plump peach tarts, stack fat peanut butter chocolate chip cookies in a pyramid and fan out what's left of the lemon bars. Jennie, your sister-in-law, joins you at the table. She tells you that Nate has their two-year-old and is feeding her cotton candy and winning her goldfish. Jennie's worried the goldfish will die. "How do you explain loss to a two-year-old?" she asks, taking money from a customer for one of your macaroons. You didn't know when Austin was two, and you don't know now.

"Sesame Street never did talk about death," you say. "No Grover Goes to a Funeral episodes."

Jennie thanks the macaroon customer, then turns to you. "How am I supposed to survive with you across the country?"

You say you haven't decided to go yet. You and Jennie discuss the options for what must be the hundredth time—Stephen allowing Austin to go away with you full time, Austin staying with Stephen, or joint custody, and how the idea of losing time with him pulls on your heart like a weight, an anchor. You have full custody, you always have. You don't want it any other way. But you acknowledge that Stephen will probably ask for joint custody if you take his son halfway across the country. Who would you be without Austin? Who would you be for all those months, alone in Wichita or Ohio or San Francisco?

"What about long-distance?" Jennie asks.

But you and Daniel don't want to do a long-distance relationship for eight years. You think if you're going to go, you need to go now. You don't know what to do. It's not like you can just break up. You live together. His life has intertwined with yours, twisting like wires, like tangled hair, like DNA.

Jennie pats your hand. "You'll figure it out," she says.

"How?" you ask. "Tell me how to figure it out." You lean against the metal chair; your back sweats as the sun beats down. The warmth seeps into your skin, becomes part of you. You breathe deeply, and the molecules of heavy, humid beach air settle into your lungs. You love, like always, the way the air moves and feels alive.

Last month, on a balmy, moonless June night, you and Daniel made love underneath the boardwalk, just like in the song. Austin was with Stephen, and you and Daniel had gone to the Captain's Table for dinner and then taken a walk on the beach at the pull-off between Frisco and Hatteras. The island narrows there, and standing on the boardwalk steps leading down to the ocean, you'd looked across Highway 12 to the calm waters of the Pamlico. As you walked on the beach with Daniel, your hand in his like it'd always been there, you realized you'd walked this same spot ten years ago with Stephen, on the icy December afternoon when you'd seen tiny footprints in the sand and decided to keep your baby. You didn't mean to tell Daniel the story, but the words slipped out of your mouth. Daniel squeezed your hand, then led you back beneath the raised deck of the boardwalk. You lay in the sand and kissed, heedless of any possible evening beach-walkers. And just like in a movie, fireworks exploded overhead, bright white, green, and red pops and sprinkles of color over the ocean.

"Did you see that, too?" you asked.

But Daniel's eyes were closed, his face above you, so close to your own.

After, Daniel rested his hand on your cheek and grazed a finger along your jaw—gritty, but you didn't mind. You closed your eyes and listened to the waves shush onto the shore, fireworks exploding behind your eyelids.

Stephen's hands on you were different. Meaner, somehow. Seven years ago, a few days after you'd found out about his affair, you'd gone home to your little white house on Elizabeth Lane, the one

Stephen's family had bought for the two of you. For five years, though, after they tore your little white house down, there was nothing but a gaping hole on Elizabeth Lane where it'd been. The day you went back to Stephen, he'd been watching television in your living room, a baseball game. You'd left Austin at your parents' inn; he'd had another nosebleed that morning.

"Let's talk," you said to Stephen.

He muted the TV and turned to you. "Where's my son? I haven't seen him in three days. Way to put Austin in the middle of our problems."

You said he was at your parents'. You stood in front of the TV. "This isn't about Austin," you said. "This is about you putting your penis into another woman's vagina."

"Look," he said, "it just happened. If I could take it back, I would." Stephen peered around you, then settled back on the sofa.

You asked the question that'd been throbbing around in your brain for the past three days. "Why did you do it?"

But all Stephen said was, "It just happened. It didn't mean anything."

"If it didn't mean anything, then why'd you do it?" you asked. Stephen didn't answer. "Give me one good reason to stay," you said to him.

"Fuck, Evie," he said. He stood up and kissed you then, rough and hard. "If you don't know, then I sure as hell can't tell you." You had sex on the sofa, and at one point, your hip rolled onto the remote control and the baseball game blared.

You stayed. You stayed with Stephen because of blood and bones, yes; because you'd created a person. But also because his mean hands on your breasts, your waist, your ass, excited you and made you feel alive. One day, one year later, after you'd had your own affair, Stephen would place his hands around your throat. He wouldn't squeeze, but his fingers on your pulse, his fingers that could've squeezed, were what finally made you go.

Today, in the bright bake-sale sun, Daniel brings the placards for the macaroons. His hands, as he sets the signs on the table, are slender and long-fingered. You think they'll make good doctor's hands. You look at a card; you squint, but you have no idea what it says.

"What is this?" you ask Daniel, pointing to the scrawl.

"It's a sign that says coconut-apricot macaroons," he says. He shrugs and says hello to Jennie, then sits down on the chair beside you.

"An unreadable sign is not terribly helpful in selling macaroons," you say. You stack the cards facedown and cross your arms. The first thought that pops into your head is that Daniel messed them up on purpose, like Stephen would've done, just to get under your skin. You're about to yell at him and start a fight. You breathe deeply and remember that passive-aggressive placard-making is not how Daniel rolls.

"You said to write on them," Daniel says.

Austin waves and runs over, his stick-legs moving in a fast, pumping blur as he dodges through the crowd. "Fiona wants a chocolate chip cookie," he says. He's not even breathing hard. "Hey," Austin says to Daniel, nodding. They pound fists.

Jennie hands Austin a cookie and pulls some money out of her purse to pay for it. "Take it to her quick, before it melts," she says, and Austin takes off again at a run.

"Is your shift about over?" Daniel asks you.

Jennie says she can handle the bake sale table, that you should go. You sit between them, your family on one side, your love on the other. You know Daniel wants an answer. You feel split in two. You stand up. "Let's go to the beach," you say.

You and Daniel are quiet on the drive to the lighthouse beach. You wind through the National Park in Buxton, past the turtle pond, past the candy-spiral lighthouse, past the pine-smelling maritime forest. You reach one of the lesser-trafficked access ramps and park. The engine clicks as it cools, and you run a hand through your hair. "It's not that I'm stalling on purpose," you say. You kick off your flip-flops and get out of the car, walking over the dune to the beach. You walk fast and try not to pay attention to whether Daniel follows. You just need a minute alone.

You trundle through the thick, hot sand until you reach the shore. You stare at the waves, trying to draw the sound and flow into your body, trying to hold onto the way that staring at the water makes everything else go away. Seven years ago, you told yourself you stayed for Austin. You told yourself Austin needed a mother and a father in the same house. You told yourself that people make mistakes, that nobody is perfect, that you loved Stephen. But really, now, you think you stayed because you were afraid to be alone. Afraid to be alone with that tiny, bloody creature. Now, you're afraid to be alone without him.

You sit in the wet sand, not caring that your shorts get grainy. Waves wash up and back, water flowing over your legs, salty and cool. Daniel's shadow falls over you, and you look up into his face. "We can try long-distance, if you want," he says.

You study his body, his receding hairline and broad shoulders and hairy legs, the freckle on the big toe of his left foot. You think of how life is like a Tetris game, pieces twisting and flipping and turning, just trying to fit. A wave rushes around your legs, over Daniel's feet, splashing his ankles, trailing lace in its wake. Over your heads, a seagull caws.

Daniel sits beside you, and this thing between the two of you, this pact, this connection, this love, just flows and flows.

"If you get in to Ohio, can we go there?"

"That's fair."

"Walter comes, too," you say. Daniel nods. You take his hand. You stay.

You go.

Acknowledgments

Thank you to my wonderful editor, Robin Miura, for all her guidance and support, and to Lynn York and everyone at Blair. Working with you has been a joy. When I was a little girl, I read my favorite book, *Taffy of Torpedo Junction,* over and over and over again. I must have read the name of *Taffy*'s publisher, John F. Blair, hundreds of times. It's a little bit of extra magic for my book to find a home with Blair.

Speaking of home, when I discovered Lee Smith's books, that's what her words felt like—coming home. I'm still in awe that she read something of mine, let alone wrote about it. Thank you.

For my family, thank you for believing in me in so many ways, and for passing along a love of language and learning. My Grandma Frese would drive out in a blizzard to buy a book. My Grandma Gibson, who had to quit school in eighth grade to care for her mother, loved stories and wanted to be a writer. My mom and dad always bought me a book when we traveled to the mall, even though I finished it on the car ride home, and they just laughed when they'd find me reading in the closet when I was supposed to be cleaning up my toys. My brother, Ben, once read one of my stories on a stage in San Francisco when I couldn't get out there for the event, and even moved with me for graduate school when I needed help. And those family vacations, just the four of us, the sides of the tent camper flapping in the salty island breeze of the Frisco National Seashore campground, the golden lighthouse beam sweeping across site C-1 or P-68, were the most foundational and inspirational experiences of my life.

A giant thank you to my husband, José, for all your hard work supporting us and to Jonah, Hannah, and Jordi, my smart, funny, kind, and creative little loves.

I'm so thankful for the deep friendships in my life that inspired the Evie–Charlotte bond. Catherine Matheny Bell, Michelle Buice, Tamara Lockwood, Lesleigh Taylor Berg, and my friends from all my walks of life from Cambridge to Raleigh, thank you. I love you all.

Thank you to the teachers who inspired and believed in me along the way: Peggy Brown, Jane Varley, Diane Rao, Joan Connor, Darrell Spencer, Mark Brazaitis, and Kevin Oderman, and thank you to Janet Peery, whose confidence in Evie carried me through the submissions process.

For everyone in my Ohio and West Virginia writing cohort, thank you for all your thoughtful manuscript comments, especially Rebecca Schwab Cuthbert, Rachel King, Kelly Sundberg, Sarah Einstein, Rebecca Thomas, Connie Pan, Kori Frazier Morgan, and Shane Stricker. Thank you to Sara McKinnon for giving me those cartwheels on the lawn. I miss our hours-long Red Lobster lunches.

And for Jen Colatosti, writing soul mate, your feedback on this project and everything I've written in the past fifteen years has been the most valuable thing in the universe. You've helped me out of countless stuck and heartbroken moments, writing and otherwise, and you know what I'm trying to say when I can't get the words working just right. Our literary codependence is the best thing that ever happened to my writing life, and your friendship is everything. I genuinely could not have written this book without you. Thank you.